The Angel
Whispered
Danger

ALSO BY

Mignon F. Ballard

AUGUSTA GOODNIGHT MYSTERIES

Shadow of an Angel

An Angel to Die For

Angel at Troublesome Creek

❧

The War in Sallie's Station

Minerva Cries Murder

Final Curtain

The Widow's Woods

Deadly Promise

Cry at Dusk

Raven Rock

Aunt Matilda's Ghost

The Angel Whispered Danger

MIGNON F. BALLARD

ST. MARTIN'S MINOTAUR
NEW YORK

www.minotaurbooks.com

Library of Congress Cataloging-in-Publication Data

Ballard, Mignon Franklin
    The angel whispered danger / Mignon F. Ballard.—1st ed.
        p. cm.
    ISBN 0-312-30813-2
        1. Goodnight, Augusta (Fictitious character)—Fiction. 2.
Guardian angels—Fiction. I. Title.

PS3552.A466A865 2003
813'.54—dc21

                                                    2003041401

First Edition: July 2003

10 9 8 7 6 5 4 3 2 1

For Laura, with thanks

The Angel Whispered Danger

CHAPTER ONE

"I saw an angel today," Josie announced.

"Really?" I glanced at the ten-year-old in the passenger seat beside me. My daughter was sometimes given to flights of fancy, but since these were the first words she'd spoken to me in over an hour, I jumped in feetfirst. "And where was that?" I said.

"On the beach this morning. Walked right out of the water—had on a dress."

"She was wearing a *dress* in the ocean? What kind of dress?"

"I don't know . . . a wet one, I guess."

I looked to see if my daughter was teasing, but her expression didn't change. "Looked kinda brownish-green. Jungle-like," she added.

"Did she have wings? How do you know she was an angel?" I asked.

Josie looked out at the green expanse of a cornfield on our right: shoulder high in early July and rinsed tender with last night's rain. The car window was down and wind ruffled her soft butterscotch bangs. "I just know," she told me, adjusting the fluorescent pink-rimmed sunglasses on her sunburned nose. "But I don't think I was supposed to see her."

I smiled. "Why not?"

She shrugged. "Because . . . when I looked back, she was gone."

We could use an angel, I thought. A whole passel of them. How did you count angels? A bevy? A flock? A band? I remembered the stirring refrain from the opera *Hansel and Gretel* I'd learned as a child, something about fourteen angels guarding sleep. Fourteen might get a bit crowded, but we could surely make room for one or two.

I slowed to make a turn and glanced at Josie, who had grown silent again, and now sat stiffly, arms folded. Stubborn to the core, even to her taffy-colored curls that went this way and that and wouldn't stay put if you slicked them with "bear grease," as my mama liked to say. Just like mine, only lighter. But my eyes were blue; Josie's were like her dad's—warm and brown with flecks of light, like the sun on Buttercup Creek, where my sister and I used to wade.

At least she had my imagination. I hoped it was only imagination. Had Ned and I driven our child to hallucinating?

The two of us were on our way to a family reunion at Bramblewood, my great-uncle's sprawling place in the Blue Ridge Mountains of North Carolina, and Josie had made it clear from the first that she didn't want to go. The reunion was an annual event, and the three of us: Ned, Josie and I, usually looked forward to attending, combining it with a visit with my parents, since Bramblewood was just outside Bishop's Bridge, the town where I grew up. This year the festivities were to last several days to mark the fiftieth year Uncle Ernest had hosted the affair. And for the first time, Ned would not be accompanying us.

For the last couple of years, life together had not been all that pleasant for my husband and me, and so at the beginning of the summer, without a whole lot of discussion, we'd decided to try it apart. To appease our daughter, I had just spent what seemed like the longest week of my life in a "borrowed" cottage in Isle of Palms, South Carolina.

"Now, look here, Kate McBride, I'm not taking no for an answer. The time away will do you good," a friend had insisted, pressing the key to her family's beach house into my hand. "Walk on the beach, build sand castles with Josie, relax. You need this time together."

But guilt had led me to invite Josie's friend Paige along for the trip, and the longest conversations the two of us had were over what television shows they certainly were *not* going to watch. I had been more relaxed during the process of a root canal.

"Paige seemed to have a good time," I said to Josie's stony profile. "Did you two have fun together?"

My daughter's lip stuck out far enough to ride to town on. "I don't see why you wouldn't let me stay at Paige's. Her mom said it was okay. Why couldn't you just leave me there until that old reunion's over?"

Josie had been pouting since we had dropped off her friend back in Rock Hill, South Carolina.

"Because, Josie, this is a family reunion, and you happen to be my family."

"Dad's your family, too," she said with a question in her voice.

3

"Yes, of course he is, but he's busy getting ready for that seminar in California. You know that, honey."

"Are you and Daddy getting a divorce?" Josie stared into her lap, and the catch in her voice was barely noticeable. But I noticed it, and it was all I could do to keep from stopping the car, pulling my hurting child into my arms and kissing her doubt away. Lately, however, my daughter had become an untouchable: no good night kisses, no impromptu hugs, and the lack of them was peeling away at my emotions a little at a time. If emotions could bleed, I'd be a big red puddle. A Band-Aid wouldn't help either of us.

"Your dad and I just need to take a little time to work things out," I said, trying to speak in a steady voice. "This training session's important, and he needed extra time to prepare for it. That's why he couldn't go to the beach."

I wished that were the only reason. The truth was that things hadn't been right between my husband and me since we lost our baby during the third month of my pregnancy over two years before. Over a period of time, my once warm and lovable husband had turned into an unapproachable stranger. Ned hadn't been invited to go to the beach, and from all indications, wouldn't have accepted if he had, but I was already in the dump heap as far as Josie was concerned, so why pile on more?

"So, when's he coming home?" she wanted to know.

Please don't ask, because I don't know! "The seminar lasts several weeks," I said, "and your dad's conducting one of the later sessions, but he'll phone, Josie. You know he won't forget you. Your daddy loves you, and so do I."

Something that sounded very much like a snort came from

4

the seat beside me. "Hey, how about some ice cream?" I offered, seeing a fast-food restaurant ahead. "Been a while since lunch."

"I'm not hungry," Josie said.

How could somebody one-third my age who didn't even come to my shoulder aggravate me so? I found myself grinding my teeth. "Come on now, Josie, you have camp to look forward to this summer—why, just think, in a couple of weeks you'll be swimming and canoeing—all that good stuff, and when we get back from Uncle Ernest's, you'll have a brand new bike to ride." Since he would be away for her birthday, Ned had given our daughter her present early.

"I don't want to go to Uncle Ernest's! It's creepy there. Darby says you found a dead man in those woods. And there's an old graveyard back there, too. He says it's haunted."

"Josie, your cousin's just trying to scare you. There used to be a church adjoining Uncle Ernest's property, but it burned years ago. The cemetery behind it has been neglected, I'm afraid, but it certainly isn't haunted. When did Darby tell you that?"

"When we were there at Christmas. He said I wasn't supposed to tell you."

I wondered who had told Darby. My cousin Marge's boy was not much older than Josie, and both were impressionable.

"Well, did you?" she persisted. "Did you really find a dead man? Darby said he'd been murdered!"

"That was a long time ago, honey," I said. "I wasn't much older than you." So why did it seem like yesterday? To this day, I avoided that section of the thicket behind Bramblewood.

"Weren't you scared? Was it somebody you knew?"

Scared wasn't the word. Every time I thought of that day, I

felt again icy flames leap in my belly. The man, a vagrant, had been dead for at least twenty-four hours, we learned later. His blue eyes stared at nothing and dried blood matted his hair. He lay across a fallen log close to the trail that meandered along a tributary of the Yadkin River at the far end of my uncle's property, and the cigarettes that had probably dropped from the pocket of his blue denim shirt were scattered on the ground.

"Of course I was scared. We were all scared, but that's not going to happen again. He was somebody just passing through, and even after we learned his name, nobody knew who he was or why he was killed."

Tobias King. The name still sent a spike of fear right through my middle. My friend Beverly, who had been with me that day, experienced nightmares for years, and my cousin Grady won't talk about it to this day.

"How do you know that whoever killed him won't come back?" Josie asked, glancing over her shoulder as if the murderer were in hot pursuit.

"I don't know why he would. That was almost twenty years ago," I said.

"What if he never left?" Her brown eyes were accusing, as if I were to blame for allowing a murderer to run loose.

"Josie McBride, I'm not going to let anything happen to you! We've gone to Bramblewood every year since you were only a few weeks old. Just remember to stay out of those woods unless an adult is with you and you'll be fine."

"Darby and Jon go back there all the time. They say that place is haunted."

"What place?" I knew my cousin Marge would skin her two boys if she knew they were wandering that close to the river.

"You know—down where that raft washed up a long time ago, but they never found those people who were in it—the ones with the funny names. They drowned, Darby says, and their spirits are still there; he says they're doomed to look forever for their bodies in the river because they did something bad."

"Then their spirits must be shy because I never met them," I said. "And that happened way before I was born."

"Oh, Mom!" Josie rolled her eyes. She didn't think much of anything happened before I was born, except maybe the discovery of fire.

"No, really. And I don't know how bad they were, although people said they did a bad thing. They were supposed to have robbed a grocery store somewhere up near Dobson, but I don't know if it's true."

They were a young couple—hippies, my mother said—and they'd stolen the raft from somebody's vacation cabin several miles upriver. The girl's name had something to do with the moon—Waning Crescent, or something like that. Marge used to laugh and say her father must've been a weatherman. And the boy called himself Shamrock—only it looked as if his luck had run out.

Earlier we had skirted the city of Charlotte and the land began to rise gently as we approached Statesville. Soon we would be in the foothills, and then the mountains themselves, where cold streams boiled and twisted alongside the spiraling road. In another hour or so we would reach Bishop's Bridge and home. I still thought of it as home even though I had lived away for more than ten years. Ned and I had married during our senior year in college, and Josie arrived a few weeks before our first anniversary, just in time for the family reunion. I smiled, remembering how excited we were the first time we brought her home to show her off.

"Uncle Ernest is grouchy," my daughter said, scratching a scab on her knee.

"Uncle Ernest is a bachelor—or as good as one; he's not around children a lot, and you know he doesn't hear so well . . . and don't scratch that, Josie, you'll make it bleed."

My great-uncle had been married briefly when he was in his midthirties, I was told, but Bramblewood had proved too isolated for his young bride. I heard Cousin Violet telling Mama once that she thought Ernest was too set in his ways to have married.

"And that Ella made me eat lumpy oatmeal one time, and she's always burning the toast," Josie continued, referring to Uncle Ernest's longtime housekeeper.

"Ella's old. Give her a break—and she's Miss Stegall to you. Besides, we're not staying with Uncle Ernest. We'll be at Jo-Jo and Papa's," I said, using the names she called my parents.

"But they're not even going to be there! I wish we could go to England with them so we could see Aunt Sara's baby."

My younger sister, Sara, expected her first child within the next few days, and my parents had flown over to greet the arrival and help out with the new baby. Sara's husband was sales manager of a division of a large electronics firm over there, and they lived in a community on the outskirts of London. Mom, who had never been out of the country, was so excited about the baby, she forgot to be afraid of flying all the way across the Atlantic.

"I wish we could be there, too," I said, "but we just can't

afford it right now. Sara's promised to send videos, and they'll be home for Christmas." Also, if I knew my mother, they probably wouldn't be able to get the plane off the ground she'd have so many pictures to bring back. This would be their second grandchild after Josie's birth ten years ago, and it had been a long and frustrating wait, especially after our sad loss.

"I just hope it's not a boy!" Josie said.

"You like Darby and Jon okay, and you've always loved playing with little Hartley." Marge's youngest at three was, according to her, "no bigger than a skeeter bump," but had already managed to climb from the mulberry tree to their garage roof and was a maniac on a tricycle.

"Beats hanging around with that dumb Cynthia," Josie said. "Darby said he bet if she ever had an idea it would bust her head wide open."

"Burst," I said. "And Darby oughta be ashamed talking about his own cousin like that." I hated to admit I had felt the same way about Cynthia's mother, my cousin Deedee, when I was her age.

And she still got under my skin. When we were home just last Christmas, I'd heard Deedee bellowing in the produce department of J & G Groceries, telling Mr. Jim Whitby, who owns the store, that his coconuts didn't slosh. Mr. Whitby's about eighty—deaf in one ear, and can't hear in the other—and the poor thing never did understand what she was saying. I hid behind a pyramid of canned cranberry sauce until she left.

"You don't have to be best friends with somebody in order not to be rude—and she *is* your cousin," I reminded my daughter—as well as myself. And if you could hear eyes roll, Josie's would've sounded like marbles in a can.

"I have to go to the bathroom," she said a few minutes later as we turned onto Highway 16 on the outskirts of Wilkesboro, North Carolina.

I was glad to see a peach stand next to the gas station where we stopped, and took the opportunity to buy a large basket of peaches, some green beans and a few onions. Although I knew Mom would leave her kitchen well-stocked, I wouldn't be able to count on perishables. And since we would be having dinner with Marge and her family that night, I got a basket for them, as well.

Two men in overalls joked with each other as they rearranged produce on long tables, and while Josie waited in the car I took my time admiring shiny jars of strawberry jam, peach pickles and plastic-wrapped loaves of homemade bread. The only other customers were a woman and a young girl. The older one wore a frothy dress in a splash of sunrise colors that looked oddly out of place in a rural produce stand, and she shook her bright head and held up a warning finger as her younger companion reached for a peach. How odd, I thought, since it was a peach stand. Still, it was a comforting place and I wish I could have lingered longer.

I hadn't enjoyed local peaches since the summer before, and the rosy-ripe smell of them almost made me heady. I didn't know if I'd be able to make it all the way to Bishop's Bridge without biting into one—peach fuzz and all. Josie already had, and now she looked around for a place to put the pit, sticky juice running down her arm, and I thought of the young girl back at the stand who had probably meant to do the same. For the first time since we'd left the beach that morning, my daughter looked almost pleasant. "Good as last year's?" I asked, handing her a wipe.

Josie licked her lips. "Mmm . . . maybe even better." She sniffed. "You didn't tell me you bought strawberries, too."

"That's because I didn't. They're out of season now. Don't you remember when I bought some at the farmer's market a few weeks ago, they told me that would be the last of them till next year?" Strawberries were my daughter's favorite fruit, and the ones you bought in the grocery store just didn't taste the same.

"Then why do I smell them?" Josie peered around the back of her seat as if she thought she might find some, like red treasure, hidden there.

"Must be your imagination," I said.

So why did I smell them, too?

CHAPTER TWO

For supper, Marge served chicken pie made with a real crust, baked ham, candied sweet potatoes, green beans and hot biscuits with homemade blackberry jam. I had some of everything. "How do you stay so skinny eating like this?" I asked, pushing myself away from a chocolate cake shaped like a bus, and almost as big. We were celebrating Hartley's third birthday, and he's obsessed with anything with wheels.

"Chase after these three for a while, and you'll see." My cousin served her youngest the first piece, which he plunged into with both fists.

"All of Daddy's side's like that," my cousin Violet said, watching Marge slide wedges of cake onto paper plates with Thomas the Tank Engine on them. "Wouldn't you know I'd take after Mama?" She lifted her fork as if preparing for a relay, and dug into the icing.

"I hadn't noticed that slowing you any," Ma Maggie said.

Ma Maggie is my grandmother on Mama's side and Violet's first cousin, although they act more like sisters since they were born three months apart and raised next door to each other.

Violet didn't answer except to raise a forkful of cake to my grandmother in sort of a salute. I guess by now those two have learned to shove each other's comments in the background, kind of like the sound of the dishwasher running or the babbling of those talk show people on TV.

Now Violet dipped a corner of her napkin into a glass of water to dab at a smear of fudge on her dress. "Will you look what I've gone and done. Oughta wear a bib! Got this dress on sale at Ivey's when I was in Charlotte last year, and I know I'll never find another like it."

My cousin's dress was a shade of purple, as were all her clothes. This one was a crinkley rayon caftan with plum-colored flowers that may or may not have been wisteria blossoms en masse along the hem.

"Ivey's Department Store hasn't been in Charlotte for at least seven years," Ma Maggie mumbled into her coffee.

"Why do you wear purple all the time?" Marge's son Darby asked, ignoring a threatening look from his mother. "Is that the only color you have?"

"Of course not, Darby. But I like to wear this color because of my name, you see—Violet . . . and because my dear friend Hodges always liked it on me. He said it became me."

Cousin Violet's "dear friend" Hodges had courted her for close to twenty years before expiring of rheumatic fever soon after I was born.

"Your *name* isn't Violet, and you know it," Ma Maggie said. "You just made that up."

"How would you like to be named *Ida Clare?*" Cousin Violet washed down her cake with a swig of sweetened iced tea. "Ida' clare, I believe it's going to rain . . . Ida'clare, can you believe it's almost Christmas already? Ida'clare, that boy must've grown a foot . . ." She shrugged. "I could go on and on. It got to where it was enough to make a preacher lose his religion!"

Darby and Jon elbowed each other and giggled.

"You're excused," Marge told her two older sons. "Go directly to the bathroom and wash your hands. Do not pass *go* and do not collect two hundred dollars."

Josie looked from her cousins to me as if she couldn't decide which was worse, being teased by her male relatives or remaining at the table with boring adults.

The boys won out. "You're excused, too," I said, and I heard the screen door slam as she slipped out after them.

"When are Lum and Leona getting here?" Ma Maggie asked of nobody in particular. Lum (short for Columbus) was Ma Maggie's "baby boy." He would be fifty-two on his next birthday.

"Sometime tomorrow," Marge said. "They're staying with Uncle Ernest."

"Then God help 'em," Violet said. "If they want to eat, they'll have to order in. Ella's gotten so blind Ernest says she put salt in the sugar bowl. And careless, too—why, I saw her in town last week in this old black dress so dirty it looked like it had done been wore to four country funerals. Lord only knows how old she is!"

"They're a pair, aren't they?" my grandmother said. "Ernest is getting deaf as a post, and Ella can't see two feet in front of her, but she's been there so long, she's practically a fixture. I expect Ernest will keep her on as long as she wants to stay. Besides," she added, "I don't think it matters to Leona whether she eats or not—always on some kind of diet. Looks undernourished, if you ask me. It's not healthy."

Cousin Violet said she agreed and helped herself to just a *tiny* bit more cake.

"I expect Ernest is lonely up there in that big old house with nobody but poor old Ella for company," Ma Maggie said.

"Might not be that way for long," Violet said with an "I know something" smirk.

My grandmother peered over her bifocals. "What do you mean?"

"Been keeping company, I hear, with that little yellow-haired teacher they hired to take Myrtis Tisdale's place." Miss Tisdale, who had taught Latin at Bishop's Bridge High since Gaul was divided into three parts, had died back in the winter. Rumor was that she died twenty years ago and they just propped her behind a desk.

"Since when?" I could tell Ma Maggie didn't believe her.

"Since soon after she came here, I reckon. She's even got him going to church." Violet hid her magenta lips with a napkin, but I could tell she was smiling.

"Ernest? Our Ernest? I think you're exaggerating. How come I haven't heard about it?"

"Maybe if you'd go to church once in a while, Maggie Brown, you'd know what was going on," Violet told her.

"Surely you don't mean Belinda Donahue? Why, she's young enough to be his daughter!"

"Ernest seems to like them that way," Violet reminded her. "Anyway, the woman's fifty if she's a day."

Sitting between them, I felt the situation might soon call for a referee and, since I wasn't so inclined, signaled desperately to Marge.

"Actually, Uncle Ernest isn't exactly alone up there. There's that fellow who rents the guesthouse," Marge said as she struggled to de-chocolate the hands and face of her squirming birthday child. "Casey . . . whatever his name is, but I doubt if he's much company."

"At least he takes care of the lawn," Violet said. "That big old place is too much for Ernest. I keep telling him he oughta move into town." She shook purple curls. "Of course, we all know that will never happen."

Through the lace curtains of Marge's dining room window I could see her two boys and Josie run to meet Marge's husband, Burdette, as he pulled into the driveway after visiting a sick parishioner. My cousin Marge was the last person in the world I thought would marry a preacher—and a Baptist one at that—but she and Burdette not only accepted the other's customs, but seemed to relish the difference. I only hope the members of the Jumping Branch Baptist never get wind of that St. Patrick's Day back in college when my cousin colored her hair green and went wading in her altogether in the campus fountain. Burdette Cranford, although he wouldn't admit to condoning it, had had a great laugh when Marge finally told him about her wild college prank. He was a giant of a man with ruddy cheeks, calm blue eyes and a laugh you could hear in the next county. Josie, who at two couldn't pronounce his name, still called him "Cudin' Bird" and thought he could do just about anything.

"Ernest is downright lucky to have somebody like Casey

want to live in that old rundown cottage," Violet said. "Of course, he grumbled because he had to patch the roof and put in new plumbing."

"Who's Casey?" I asked as Burdette and the children raced across the lawn. Or at least the children raced; Burdette sort of lumbered, but I couldn't help thinking how refreshing it would be if Ned loosened up that way with Josie. I wouldn't care if he lumbered or not.

"Some kind of writer," Marge said. "Sort of keeps to himself. Supposed to be working on a book, I think. Showed up back in February looking for a place to stay in exchange for keeping the grass cut and whatever upkeep Uncle Ernest needs for the shrubbery and such."

"What shrubbery?" Violet made a face at Hartley, who made one back. "Why, if he doesn't watch out, the woods are going to take over the whole place! Not much yard left, except that pretty little garden Rose planted, and the scrub pine and honeysuckle vines are pushing in on it."

"Maybe Deedee can get the Belle Fleurs Garden Club to take care of it after they get through clearing off that old Remeth Cemetery," Marge said.

My grandmother spoke up. "I'll believe that when I see it! Why, that old church must've burned more than fifty years ago."

Marge shrugged. "Supposed to begin sometime this week. Deedee's even talked Burdette into helping."

"Poor Ernest. I wouldn't think he'd want any reminders of Rose after she left him like she did," Violet said. "Still, it's sweet of him to try to keep up her garden. She did have a way with growing things."

"Pity that marriage didn't work out," Ma Maggie said, trying unsuccessfully to contain a wiggling Hartley on her lap. "All these years alone . . . how long's it been now? Close to forty years."

"Well, Ida'clare," I said, mostly to Violet, as I rose to help Marge clear the table. "Imagine that!"

"Go on, you bad thing!" Violet giggled. "But I do wish Ernest had tried a little harder! If I remember right, Rose was right pretty. I always thought Goat Kidd had a crush on her," she said, referring to our uncle's longtime friend and sparring partner, Judge Barton Kidd. "She was awful young, though; too young for Ernest. I expect the loneliness just got to her, living way up there like that. Couldn't boil water without scorchin' it, and Lord, she had the biggest feet I ever saw—but Ernest sure seemed taken with her; never saw him so smitten. Why, I couldn't believe it when I heard she'd up and left!"

"Didn't like living so far away from town, is all Ernest ever told me," Ma Maggie said. "We never did know where she went from here." She sighed. "Sure knocked the stuffing out of Ernest. I don't reckon he'll ever get over it."

"Then why didn't he go after her?" I asked. "My gosh, they were only married a little over a year, weren't they? Must not have been as dejected as you make him sound."

"Guess he figured a little bit went a long way," Marge hollered from the kitchen doorway.

"*Marge!*" This from Cousin Violet.

"Naturally, I meant *marriage*," Marge said, darting a look at me. Of course, I knew she hadn't. "And I'm glad if Uncle Ernest has found somebody new. He's entitled."

Violet turned up her nose and grunted, and my grandmother waved her hand as if she could scat Marge's opinion away. "Speaking of marriage," she said to me, "what's this ridiculous thing about you and Ned?"

My grandmother spoke in her "I'm so disappointed in you" tone, and reached for my hand as I passed her chair.

"I'm afraid it isn't so ridiculous," I said, resisting an impulse to pull away. "We needed some time apart, that's all. And after that . . . well, we'll just see what happens."

From the look on my grandmother's face, I could tell she thought that was nonsense with a capital N. "Surely it's not something you can't work out between you."

I saw her glance at Marge as if she expected my cousin to back her up, but Marge disappeared into the kitchen so quickly she might have been an apparition. "Let's go see what your brothers are up to out there," she said to Hartley, and I heard the door shut behind them.

Violet, thank goodness, followed suit. "I'm going to see if Marge will let me take home some of her hydrangea blossoms," she said, pushing back her chair so quickly it almost tipped over. "Have you noticed that bush out by the porch? Such a rich color this year—almost violet."

If my grandmother expected me to dump all my domestic problems in her lap, she was going to be disappointed. It just wasn't something I wanted to share just yet, although God knows I needed to talk with somebody, but divorce was frowned upon in our family, and Ma Maggie could frown bigger than anybody. Even Uncle Ernest's long-ago attempt at matrimony was never discussed in his presence.

My grandmother clung to my fingers as I stood beside her. (If I sat, she'd put me through the inquisition!) "Is Ned dissatisfied with his new job? I know he went through a bad time when that company he worked for . . . what do you call it . . . downsized, but I thought things would be easier now."

"No, it's not the job," I said. After months of unemployment and what seemed like endless interviews, my husband had landed a position in the marketing department of a large medical supply company. "He really likes his work." *Why else would he spend more time away than at home?*

"Do you think he might resent yours?" she asked.

"Resent my what?" I freed my hand and began to gather up the tablecloth, concentrating on collecting all the chocolate crumbs. I didn't look at my grandmother.

"Your job, Kate. Some women prefer to stay at home, and I just thought it might be nice if you were there when Ned came home."

"Ned seemed to be perfectly okay with the paycheck I brought home during all those months he didn't have one, and I don't remember him ever complaining about my working at the college." I had taken a job as assistant to the registrar at our local community college when Josie began the first grade, and as far as I knew, none of our family had suffered because of it.

My grandmother rose and went to the window, and she didn't speak for a moment; when she did, all I could see was that beautiful white hair twisted into a coil at the back of her neck. "I was just wondering if things might have been different if you hadn't been working when—"

"I have to go," I said. I knew where she was going with this, and I didn't plan to join her.

"Kate, honey, I'm sorry. I didn't mean . . . please, you don't have to leave."

"We still have sand in our clothes from the beach," I said. "I've loads of wash to do, and I don't want Josie up too late. She's had a busy week." I brushed her cheek with a good-bye kiss.

But Ma Maggie wasn't through. "Have you thought of talking with Burdette?" she said. "He's so good in situations like this. He might be able to—"

"I'll see you tomorrow," I said on my way out.

Don't cry, Kate. Don't you dare cry! I swallowed the boulder in my throat and stood on the back porch for a minute to blink the moisture from my eyes. If I could just get to my parents' house and go to sleep, maybe things would look brighter in the morning.

Marge knelt by the sandbox, patting damp sand around Hartley's bare foot. "Now stand still and I'll show you how to make a frog house," she said to her three-year-old, but her enthusiasm vanished when she turned and saw me standing there.

"Kate, are you all right?"

"Just tired. Dinner was great, Marge, but I think we'll head on out. I'm afraid I got too much sun at the beach this morning, and it was a long drive up here."

"It's Ma Maggie, isn't it? Oh Lordy! What'd she say this time?"

I tried to smile. "I'm afraid I failed the June Cleaver test." I felt in my shorts pocket for my car keys, then remembered I'd left them in the car—along with my purse.

Marge dusted sand from her hands and put a grainy paw on my shoulder. "I'm sorry, Kate. Sometimes she goes too far, but you know I'm here if you ever want to talk."

"Right now all I want to do is sleep," I said, "but thanks."

I found my daughter hanging upside down from a tree limb. "Oh, Mom, do we have to go? Cudin' Bird's built Darby and Jon a two-story tree house, and he's gonna tell us ghost stories out there when it gets dark. Can't I stay?"

Beside me, Marge spoke softly. "Why not let her stay, Kate? The sofa in that little upstairs sitting room makes into a bed, and the boys love having her here."

"Please, Mom! Can't I?" Josie, a smudge of dirt on her cheek, tugged at my shirt. She looked happier than I'd seen her in weeks. "I'll be good, I promise."

"You'll mind Marge and Cudin' Bird and not argue about bedtime?" I said, and my daughter nodded, grinning.

"She'll be fine. Go home and take a long soak in the tub. Come on, I'll help you get Josie's things from the car." Marge lifted long reddish-gold hair from her neck as we walked. It was so fine she couldn't keep it pinned up and moist strands plastered her forehead. Hartley, chasing after us, clung to her long legs. My cousin was the one, I thought, who needed a relaxing soak in the tub, yet she didn't seem nearly as tired as I felt.

Guilt nagged at me as I pulled into my parents' driveway, then dragged my suitcase from the trunk. I was actually *glad* Josie would be staying with her cousins, glad to be away from her obvious resentment. Her dad wasn't around, so I was the one receiving her ten-year-old's version of punishment for the shaky state of our family. And I was tired of it!

The house where I grew up was a yellow Cape Cod that had been built sometime in the 1960s and looked much like a lot of the other houses on the street, except for the wide porch Dad had added in the back and the huge oak out front where our rope swing once hung. I could see that my dad had planted his usual vegetable garden behind the house with tomatoes, bush beans and summer squash, although it would be weeks before they were ready for the table.

The emptiness of the house assailed me from every room. I had expected to experience loneliness, but not to this extent. Maybe it was the dusk-dark, which could sometimes be a melancholy time. I turned on lights as I walked through, wishing with all my heart that I hadn't told Mama I'd represent our family at this reunion. I didn't want to be here. What's more, I didn't even want to be *me*.

My mother had promised to call as soon as my sister's baby arrived, no matter what the hour. Maybe she'd left a message on the voice mail! I hurried to the phone in the small study off the front hall, but the only message was from the dentist's office reminding Mom of an appointment. Apparently everybody else in Bishop's Bridge knew my parents were in England.

Upstairs in the room I had shared with Sara, I sat in the dormer window and watched Miss Julia Arnold across the street take her cocker spaniel out for its evening "squat," as Dad liked to call it, usually in somebody else's yard. Just thinking of Dad made me smile. If only he were here, he would make me feel better. But he wasn't here.

Miss Julia, I knew, would be glad to see me; would probably invite me in for dessert or at least a glass of tea. And of course, she'd ask a hundred questions: "And how is that dear Ned?

What a shame he couldn't come . . . and don't tell me you didn't bring Josie . . ." My husband, Miss Julia claimed, reminded her of a young Jimmy Stewart, except he was better-looking. I couldn't argue with her there. But I wouldn't think of that.

Coming here had been a big mistake. Tomorrow, I thought, I would collect my daughter, give my excuses and head back home. But back home to what?

I kicked off my shoes and had started into the bathroom to fill the tub when I heard something downstairs that turned me into an ice sculpture. It was the sound of breaking glass and it seemed to have come from the room below. Somebody was trying to get into the house! Or, worse still, maybe they already had.

CHAPTER THREE

My parents had never had a telephone installed upstairs. *The one we have is one too many,* Dad had said during my chatty high school years. And naturally I'd left my cell phone in the car. Whoever was downstairs apparently planned to take advantage of my parents' absence and help themselves to the family silver—and anything else they could carry away.

But not if I could help it! Anger surged inside me as I slipped shoeless into the hallway, hugging the wall like a shadow. I was almost sure the sound of broken glass had come from the living room, but there was nothing there of much value. If I waited quietly until they moved to the other part of the house, I could slip out the front door before they suspected my presence. Unless they decided to try their luck upstairs.

I crept to the landing and listened, glad of the huge potted fern my mother kept there. Not only did it partially screen me from view, but if anyone approached, I could shove it down the stairs like a great bowling ball with fronds. And for the second time that day, I was relieved that Josie had chosen to stay at Marge's.

Unless the burglar was in the habit of talking to himself, I was almost certain there were two of them, as I could hear muted fragments of conversation, but I couldn't make out what they were saying. Probably just as well. I would risk being seen if I tried to make it to my car, but if I could dash across the street to Miss Julia's and call the police, they might be able to nab them before they got away.

Now I heard soft footsteps in the kitchen, a lightweight by the sound of it, but even a lightweight can fire a gun. My former bravado immediately turned to mush. Maybe I would crawl back upstairs—hide in the closet, under the bed. But what if they found me? And what if they made off with the pocket watch that had been my great-grandfather's, the fragile sapphire pendant Dad had given Mama on their last anniversary. Treasured things.

I stiffened and strained to hear: nothing, then drew in my breath and bolted downstairs.

A centipede in wooden shoes couldn't have made more noise.

A girl who looked to be about thirteen greeted me in the front hall. "Oh, goodness!" she said. Her large gray eyes were fringed by the longest lashes I'd ever seen, and even as terrified and outraged as I was, I couldn't help thinking there were people who would give up chocolate for eyes like that.

"Goodness has nothing to do with it," I told her. The girl wore her dark brown hair in a shaggy elfin cut that accentuated her huge eyes and dainty features, and a gray feathered creature that looked like a small bird—dear God, it *was* a bird—perched on her shoulder. She wore no makeup and no jewelry and looked so innocent standing there I almost began to feel sorry for her. But not quite.

"Oh . . . I'm sorry! I didn't mean . . ." The dustpan she held clattered to the floor, and the girl leaned over to pick it up, the jagged hem of her skirt brushing bare feet. The bird—a sparrow, I think—fluttered its wings but hung on. There was something vaguely familiar about the girl, I thought, then I knew I'd seen her before—that same afternoon at the peach stand. But there was something else about her, like a fragment of a dream that wouldn't go away, but I couldn't bring it into focus. That was when I noticed the broom in her other hand.

"I was trying . . . was going to . . ." she continued, backing away from me, and I'll be darned if she wasn't crying!

"Penelope didn't mean to break the dish. It was an accident, and one we sincerely regret. This kind of thing doesn't usually happen." The woman who spoke stood behind me, and I suppose I must've jumped because she smiled and touched my arm with slender, shell-pink fingers. "Please don't be afraid. We aren't here to harm you."

Well, that's a relief! You're only here to take anything that isn't nailed down. "Then what are you here for?" I asked. I was sure she was the same person I'd seen shopping for produce.

The woman wore her silken gold hair like a crown and her face reminded me of something you might see on the front of a Christmas card. She didn't *look* like a criminal. What she did look was slightly annoyed, although I could see she was trying to hide it. The nerve!

"Why, to help you, of course," she said, with just the hint of a sigh. "Although I do believe you might be one of my tougher assignments—except maybe for that Roosevelt fellow."

"Roosevelt? You mean FDR?" This woman was a babbling psychopath. Humor her.

"No, no! That other one . . . Teddy. Always charging around on horses, putting himself in danger. Kept me on my toes, as they say. I'll have to admit I was relieved to pass him along to somebody else. It was one of those times I was truly grateful it was only a temporary assignment."

The whole time she spoke the stranger was scooping up shards of glass with the broom and dustpan Penelope had dropped, and tossing them into a trash can as if she had every right to be there. She wore a crinkly, free-flowing dress she might have lifted from Cousin Violet's closet. The skirt cascaded in tiers of green, blue and purple, scattered with tiny pink flowers, and it seemed to float when she walked. A long strand of dazzling crystal-like stones the colors of a sunset swung from her long, graceful neck. They looked expensive. I wondered where she'd stolen them.

She didn't seem to have a weapon, or at least I didn't see one, and the young girl, who had obviously broken the dish, had withdrawn, solemn-faced, to stand nearby. She had stopped crying now but looked as if she might begin anew at any moment. The little bird had now ventured to her wrist and she stroked it with one finger.

"You've yet to explain what you're doing in this house," I told the broom wielder who seemed to be making one final sweep. "Did you think you could just help yourselves to whatever took your fancy? The police here take a dim view of breaking and entering."

The broom stopped in midarc. "As I explained, the broken dish was an accident, but entering . . . ? Entering what?"

"Entering this house, of course! This is a private residence in case you haven't noticed, and just because my parents are out of town doesn't mean it's an invitation to open house. And that bird—well, we just can't have a bird flying about in here. It might—"

"The fledgling was lonely," the woman explained in a matter-of-fact voice. "Recently left its nest, you see, and isn't yet accustomed to being alone. Penelope's only helping it along a bit. It should soon be ready to leave."

"And speaking of leaving," I began. "I think it's time—" I broke off in exasperation.

"I can see you're upset. You'll feel much better after a cup of tea, and maybe some of my cranberry scones."

In one smooth movement, the intruder picked up the trash can and presented the cleaning accessories to her young accomplice. "Penelope dear, would you like to put the kettle on?"

"Oh, yes!" The girl nodded and smiled as if she'd been given a rare gift, and waltzed nimbly toward the kitchen.

"Do watch out for the—" her friend called out.

The fragile hurricane lamp on the hall table tottered as Penelope swept past—literally—when the broom caught one of the table legs. Oh, no! Not again! Was this a demolition crew? I closed my eyes and braced myself for the crash.

None came. When I opened them, the golden-haired woman stood with the lamp in her hands. "That was a bit of a close call," she said, setting it back on the table.

"How did you do that?" I asked.

"Do what?" She preceded me into the kitchen.

"Move like that. You were all the way across the room. How did you manage to catch that lamp before it hit the floor?"

The woman removed a dainty embroidered tea towel from a plate of something on the kitchen counter. It smelled like heaven. I was sure it hadn't been there when I came in. "You've heard perhaps of Connie Mack?" she said.

"Had something to do with baseball, didn't he?" *Forget the phone*, I thought, edging for the back door. *Just run for it, Kate old girl.*

She smiled and whisked plates and cups from my mother's cabinet . . . *and she seemed to know just where they were kept!*

"The greatest baseball manager of all times, and a catcher, as well. Led the Philadelphia Athletics in nine World Series."

I had never heard of the Philadelphia Athletics. "And?" I said, hoping I hadn't locked the back door when I came in. I estimated the number of steps it would take to reach it. Six maybe; five if I sprinted.

"He was kind enough to teach me some of the stunts of the craft." She stood between me and the door with a kettle of boiling water. "Do sit," she said, pulling out a chair.

I sat. "Stunts?" I repeated numbly.

"Yes, tricks, I believe they call it."

She must mean tricks of the trade, I thought, watching her pour steaming water into a pot. The essence of something sweet and summery wafted past.

"Strawberry mint," the woman said. "My own blend. Penelope, would you please pass the scones?"

I didn't know much about baseball, but I knew Connie

Mack was dead. Long dead. And Teddy Roosevelt hadn't been around for a while, either. Why was I allowing this strange woman to play hostess in my own mother's kitchen? It was dark out now and most of the neighbors had probably gone to bed. I could yell my head off and none of them would hear me, yet for some reason I wasn't afraid. In fact, I felt just the opposite, as if I'd been wrapped in that bedraggled old blanket I used to carry around as a child. Nubbins. I'd called my security blanket Nubbins. Now, what made me think of that?

It was almost as if this odd person had cast a spell over me. But it was a nice spell. A scone was placed in front of me along with butter molded in the shape of a strawberry and a small pot of orange marmalade with an enticing ginger smell. The scone was warm to the touch and steamed when I broke it open. Penelope, I noticed, had already eaten one and started on another. She ate in dainty little cat bites, but quickly, as if she were in a great hurry.

Probably because the law was on their trail.

How long had these two been staying in my parents' house? They hadn't been gone quite a week, so it couldn't have been longer than that. I shoved my scone aside. "You don't seem to understand." I spoke calmly to the one with the twinkling necklace. She seemed to be in charge. "It's illegal to stay in someone's home without permission. You could get in a lot of trouble. If you need help, a place to stay until you get back on your feet, there are agencies, churches . . ." I thought of Burdette, who would carry the troubles of the world if he could. "My cousin is a minister; he knows about these things. I'm sure he'd be glad to find a place for you, might even know of a job."

"She already has a job," Penelope said, reaching for another scone. The bird hopped to the back of her chair and twittered at me.

"You mustn't talk with your mouth full, Penelope, and I believe you've eaten enough. Remember what I taught you about greed."

The woman brought her cup and sat beside me, then dribbled marmalade on a scone. "Penelope's an apprentice," she said with a smile—as if that explained everything.

"Oh," I said. If she said she was a sorcerer, I wouldn't have been surprised.

"And she's right about my job. I do have one. It's you."

"Me?"

"I believe you did wish for an angel. Actually, though, I'd already been assigned to you—on a temporary basis, of course. Lucretia thought I might be better qualified in your particular situation." She smiled at me over her teacup.

"What situation? And who's Lucretia?"

Her necklace winked in amethyst and indigo as she refilled my cup. I had drunk the tea and found it soothing, as well as delicious. Now I nibbled on the scone—or I meant to nibble, but it was still hot and tasted of nutmeg, so I added a dollop of marmalade and scarfed down the whole thing.

"Lucretia wasn't quite sure about that; it was just a feeling she had. Nothing to worry about." She smiled, but something in her ocean-depth eyes told me there was. "Lucretia's your guardian angel." The woman spoke as casually as if she were telling me the time of day. "She asked me to step in for a while."

"Lucretia? I thought she went around poisoning people," I

said, glancing at Penelope to see how she reacted to that bit about the angel, but she seemed unconcerned. In fact, she looked downright bored, with a yawn as large as it was loud.

"That was another Lucretia. I'm afraid I've never made her acquaintance; she's assigned to that other neighborhood—if you know what I mean."

"No, I don't know what you mean," I told her, "but I do know it's time for you to leave." I didn't think the pair was dangerous, but all this talk about angels was making me leery. "If there's somebody you'd like me to call, just say the word. Otherwise, you and your friend Penelope are going to have to find another place to light—that is if you can get her to stay awake that long. This has gone on far too long."

"I'm afraid I didn't make myself clear. How remiss of me! I hope you'll forgive the oversight. I'm Augusta Goodnight, Kathryn, your guardian angel."

She took my hands in both of hers, and the tenseness and doubt, the anger I'd felt toward my husband and grandmother, even my daughter, sort of oozed away. I sensed a warm spot in the middle of my stomach not unlike the feeling you get from drinking hot mulled wine. "Kate," I said. "You can call me Kate."

The small bird flew to the top of my mother's kitchen curtains—the ones with the stenciled flowers that took her hours to finish—and twitched its tail feathers in an alarming way.

"Oh, no!" I sighed aloud, and was relieved when Augusta opened the back door and waved it outside. "Time to make your way in the world," she said, watching it fly away.

"Penelope, do go and curl up somewhere, dear," Augusta said to the girl, who now dozed with her chin on her chest.

33

"It's her first day, you see," she told me, "and there's so very much to learn."

"She was on the beach this morning, wasn't she?" I asked. That was another reason why the girl had seemed familiar. Josie had described her to me earlier. "My daughter said she saw an angel in the ocean."

"A little slipup on Penelope's part, I'm afraid," Augusta whispered after her young charge had disappeared into the living room. I didn't hear any crashes so I assumed she was asleep.

"You mean she wasn't supposed to see her?"

"Most people don't. It shouldn't happen again."

I stood and went to the window. Could this really be happening? If this strange woman wasn't crazy, then I must be! "Then why do I see you?" I said.

Augusta came to stand beside me. "Because I think you need someone you can talk to."

Was it that obvious? Could she *see* how much I hurt? "Then I guess you know about Ned." I waited for her answer, and when it didn't come right away, I thought my doubts were justified.

Augusta spoke softly. "Of course I do, Kate. And the baby, as well."

How could she know? Just then I didn't care how. What mattered was, she was *there*. "I lost the baby," I said, feeling the familiar wetness seeping into my eyes. "We waited so long, and I lost the baby. I don't even know if it was a boy or a girl . . . Augusta, it wasn't my fault."

She put her arms around me and the smell of strawberries was like a faint perfume. "Of course, it wasn't your fault. I don't believe your husband blamed you, did he? That wasn't in my notes . . ."

I wiped away tears with the dainty, lace-edged hankie she pressed into my hand. "No, he didn't blame me, but he grieved alone. For years after having Josie we tried to have another child, and when we found I was expecting, Ned was ecstatic. He had lost his job and hadn't yet found another, but this was such a happy thing, it made the other seem unimportant. Then, when I was less than three months along, I had a miscarriage."

A defective sperm or egg, my doctor had said. It was nature's way of cleaning house. Nobody's fault. We could try again.

"He shut me out," I told Augusta. "I felt empty to the bone, but he had no room in his heart for me—only his own grief." I blew my nose as I paced the kitchen. "Self-pity, that's all it was. He lost his job, he lost his baby. Well, I was hurting, too!" I didn't have the nerve to tell her Ned and I hadn't been intimate in months.

The handkerchief was soggy and Augusta passed me another. "Have you tried talking about this?" she said.

"When? He's never home, and when he is, he's tired or he doesn't want to discuss it. Frankly, I'm tired of trying. I begged him to see a counselor with me, but it was like talking to a wall." I shrugged. "Finally, I just went by myself."

"And did that help?" she asked.

"I think it helped me to become stronger, to learn to face things by myself. But Ned resented it, you know. Said he didn't like our problems being flaunted in front of perfect strangers." I blew my nose. "*He's* the one who's a stranger!"

Augusta Goodnight stood by the window and the moonlight caught her hair so that we needed no other light. "Just try and be patient, Kate," she said, "it's not over . . ."

I waited for the angelic announcement that would bring purpose to my life.

"It's not over," the angel continued, "until the plump lady performs."

At the risk of offending my otherworldly guest, I laughed all the way upstairs, then giggled in my sleep. If she had done nothing else, Augusta had brought a respite of amusement into my bleak existence. But I didn't think that was the main reason for her being here. Even though she hadn't said so, I had a strong feeling the angel was sent to warn me. But warn me of what?

CHAPTER FOUR

ust why are you here?" I asked my angel again the next morning. If I'd had any doubts about her heavenly connections, they vanished when I tasted Augusta's coffee. And pancakes, so crisp and light they almost floated, seemed to multiply as fast as we could eat them, although Penelope did her best to keep up until Augusta gave her a warning lift of the brow.

"As I said, I'm filling in." She smiled. "More coffee?"

I held out my cup. "But why?"

"As to that, we'll have to wait and see." She began to fill the sink with rainbow bubbles. "We can start by getting these dishes cleared away so you can join the others in your family. Penelope, you may help dry."

Oh, no! Not with Mama's good china! "Oh, please, let me," I said, grabbing a dishtowel from the drawer.

"Very well, but she has to learn. What good is it if we do everything for her?" Augusta tossed the girl a sponge. "I suppose you can start by wiping crumbs from the table and sweeping underneath . . . on second thought, forget the sweeping. We'll work on that tomorrow.

"This is the first occasion I've had to help train an apprentice," Augusta explained as an aside to me, "and I want to be thorough . . . although sometimes I do find it a test of my patience. Perhaps that was why I was given this opportunity."

"And what do you usually do when you're not filling in for someone else?" I asked.

Augusta whisked off her large pink polka-dotted apron and hung it on the back of the pantry door. "Tend strawberries," she said. "Acres and acres of them. And sometimes I help with the flowers. Oh, you should see our flower fields, Kate! We've every blossom known to man, and many that aren't."

I told her I'd like to see them, but hoped it wouldn't be any time soon.

"Tell me about your family," Augusta said when we finished putting away the dishes. Penelope had gone outside to water my mother's petunias—a fairly uncomplicated task, I hoped, and the two of us watched from the window seat in the family room adjoining the kitchen. "My notes are rather sketchy, I'm afraid, as this was a bit of a last-minute assignment, and I'd really like to know more."

I watched as she dug a small notebook from what must have been the very bottom of a large tapestry bag, then groped again for a pencil.

"Uncle Ernest is my grandmother's older brother," I explained. "His home is where we always have our reunions— I guess because it was where most of them grew up. We call his place Bramblewood, and that's pretty much what it is—a lot of woods and brambles. A trail that follows the Yadkin River winds along about a mile or so behind it and has always been popular with hikers."

Augusta nodded but didn't write anything down. "Your uncle Ernest," she said, "does he have a large family?"

"No children, if that's what you mean. Married once, but it didn't work out. He has some peculiar habits, I guess. Likes his napkin folded in a certain way, eats a soft-boiled egg every morning for breakfast and has a fit if you mess up his newspaper—things like that. Sort of keeps to himself, although I hear he's been seeing somebody lately. He's retired now, but Uncle Ernest taught science for years at a small college over in Boone, and wrote a bunch of textbooks nobody read unless they had to, but I've always gotten along with him fine." I smiled. "When I was little, he made me a tiny water wheel to spin in the creek, and he knows all about trees and plants."

Now and then Augusta made brief notes as I told her about Marge and her family, then Cousin Violet and Ma Maggie. "And then there's Uncle Lum, my mother's younger brother, and his wife, Leona. They have a son, Grady, who's a little older than I am." I couldn't bring myself to admit I was related to Deedee, but I was sure she'd find out in time.

Marge called a few minutes later to tell me Josie was fine and if it was all right with me, she'd like to take her swimming at the local pool with the boys. "Ma Maggie says they're ordering barbecue for everybody tonight, so why don't I just meet you there later this afternoon?"

I said that would be okay and went to find something cool and comfortable to wear. Our main dinner, a covered-dish affair usually eaten picnic style under the big white oaks in my uncle's yard, would be later in the week, so it seemed Uncle Ernest was taking the easy way out tonight. Remembering Ella's attempts at cooking, I was grateful. The last time we were here she made a pound cake and forgot the eggs. It weighed a lot more than a pound!

"Cuz! Thank God you got here before Deedee! Let's you and me cut outta here and give the Serpent Lady the slip." Grady Roundtree jumped up from his seat on Uncle Ernest's front steps and hurried to open the door of my car.

I returned his hug, as glad to see him as he was me. "I'd almost forgotten we called her that," I said, referring to our nickname for Deedee, who frequently "spoke with forked tongue." "I'd love to escape, but first let me speak to Uncle Ernest and your parents. Have you been here long?"

"Mom and Dad got here in time for lunch, poor chumps. You'd think they'd know by now! I drove from Chattanooga; been here less than an hour," he said.

I glanced at my cousin as we started inside together. Still youthfully handsome at thirty, he had been engaged three times, but somehow always managed to wiggle out before the invitations were mailed. His mother, my aunt Leona, seemed to think it was because he never got over Beverly.

Beverly Briscoe and I had been best friends growing up, and

she was sixteen when she started dating Grady, then in his sophomore year at Appalachian State. The relationship lasted until Bev went off to college and decided she wanted to see other people. I remembered when she broke the news to Grady during Christmas break. He was so despondent, it just about ruined the holidays for the rest of us, and as far as I know, my cousin didn't date anyone for over a year after that.

Then, this past winter, the two had renewed their interest in each other when Beverly, currently working on her doctorate at a university in Pennsylvania, telephoned Grady out of the blue. She planned to come back to North Carolina after completing the requirements for her degree, she said, and just wanted to touch base. After that, the two kept in touch almost daily by e-mail and telephone, and everyone thought they might resume their romance until Beverly was suddenly killed in an accident in February. The roads had been slick from a recent rain, and Beverly's brakes were said to have failed as she tried to maneuver a treacherous curve near her home.

Beverly had seemed more sure of herself when I'd seen her at a party the Christmas before while we were both home for the holidays. We'd chatted briefly, but people were milling around a crowded room, drifting from group to group, and she had left before we had a chance to say more than a few words. I wished now that we'd spent more time together.

"I'm so sorry about Beverly," I said, touching his arm. "I wanted to come for the funeral, but Josie had the flu and Ned was out of town. "I wish—well, I wish things could've worked out differently."

My cousin squeezed my hand but didn't answer.

"So, where is old Ned?" Grady said finally. "Hiding out on the golf course?"

"Big conference in California," I told him. Enough for now; he'd find out soon enough. "Said to tell you hi." A lie. Although he never admitted it, I knew my husband resented Grady Roundtree, the closeness of our relationship. He needn't have, but I didn't tell him that.

A huge porch lined with rocking chairs stretched across the front of the house, and my uncle's old collie, Amos, slept on the flagstones in front of the door so that we had to step over him to get inside. Ivy clung to the six stone columns, cooling the porch, as well as the interior of the house, so that it felt almost chilly even on a hot July day. The living room was large and shabby with threadbare rugs, overstuffed furniture with fat, shiny arms and hardwood floors I'm told were once beautiful. It smelled of old ashes from the huge stone fireplace. Uncle Ernest, who sat in his favorite brown club chair by the empty grate, smelled of Old Spice and bourbon. He reached for my hand, and his smile turned to a frown. "Kathryn. You look thin. Are you taking care of yourself?"

I kissed his cheek, taut and tan as an army tent. "Had to get ready for the swimsuit season," I said, speaking louder than usual, and he nodded, although I don't think he heard me. My uncle's hair had always reminded me of a wire brush, but today I noticed it didn't look as bristly as usual, and he'd finally replaced those awful black rims on his glasses. If I didn't know better, I'd never guess he would soon be seventy-six.

"This good old mountain air will build up your appetite," he said, moving his feet to make room for me on the lopsided hassock.

Fine. As long as I don't have to eat Ella's cooking, I thought, looking around for the housekeeper.

"Leona's out in the kitchen looking for some kind of rabbit food," Uncle Ernest said, following my gaze. "I think Lum went out back to see if he could find any ripe tomatoes."

"But I thought we were having barbecue tonight." My stomach wanted to turn around and go home. I thought of Augusta's light-as-clouds pancakes.

My uncle laid aside a book heavy enough to give you a hernia, and I could tell by the dog-eared pages he probably knew most of it by heart. "Barbecue? Oh, we are! You'll have to thank your uncle Lum for that. Leona was planning to feed us something with frozen vegetables and imitation cheese." He made a face. "Thank God he put a stop to that! Leona's in a snit, I reckon—can't be helped. Why don't you go see if you can't mellow her up a bit?"

I said I'd try, although I thought that was more in Grady's line. He'd been wrapping his mama around his finger so long, she oughta have a shape like a corkscrew, but he had disappeared upstairs.

I got a whiff of Aunt Leona's Misty Glade perfume and followed my nose to the kitchen where I found her standing on a stool with her head inside a cabinet. She turned when she heard me enter and almost toppled off her perch.

"Whoa!" I rushed to steady her. "You taking inventory?"

"No, but somebody should. I don't know when's the last time Ella's cleaned these cabinets. I was looking for some pickles to go in my egg salad, but all I could find was a jar of olives, and no telling how long that's been in there." My aunt accepted my hand as she stepped down. In spite of her explo-

43

ration into Ella's dusty realm, Leona's crisp, white blouse remained spotless, and her blue Barbie-size slacks had creases sharp enough to slice you in two.

"Olives should still be okay," I said, turning my head to avoid the cloying Misty Glade.

Aunt Leona's expression told me she'd sooner eat river mud and she muttered something about fat and calories.

"Saw Grady out front," I said. "Looks great. The big city must agree with him." My cousin had moved up a couple of rungs in his company when he accepted a position in Chattanooga the year before.

She nodded, pride beaming from every pore. She and Uncle Lum had adopted Grady when he was eight and slathered so much attention on him, it's a wonder he hadn't turned out rotten through and through. But he hadn't, and I'd been grateful during our growing-up years for an ally against the obnoxious Deedee.

"I just wish he'd settle down now. It's time." Aunt Leona got eggs from the refrigerator and set them to boil.

"Is he seeing anybody special?" I asked.

"Not that I know of. Especially after what happened to Beverly. Grady thought—well, we all thought something might come of that."

"A shame he didn't go up there to see her," I said. My mother had told me the two only communicated from a distance.

"Maybe he was afraid of being hurt again. I know he must regret it now, but I think Grady wanted to give things a little more time—didn't want to rush things."

"Aunt Leona, that was . . . what . . . eleven years ago, and

Beverly was only eighteen when they stopped seeing each other!"

"Shh! Keep your voice down," my aunt warned. "Wouldn't want him to hear us. Grady doesn't like to talk about it."

My aunt had put eggs on to boil and the sulfur smell was now competing with Misty Glade. I stepped back as far as I could, trying not to be obvious.

"Well, I found a couple, but I'm afraid the worms got to them first." The screen door slammed as Uncle Lum wandered in from the back porch and set two tomatoes on the counter. He squinted at me from under the brim of his canvas hat. "Kate! It's good to see you, sugar. I'd hug you, but it's a mite sticky out there, and the mosquitoes about chewed me up. If Uncle Ernest doesn't start using some kind of insect control, they're gonna carry him off." He nodded toward the living room. "You seen him yet?"

I grinned. "In there buried in a book."

"One of those tomes about the War Between the States, I guess," my uncle said. "Bet he's read just about everything written on the subject." He peered into the pot of eggs and rolled his eyes at me behind Aunt Leona's back. "Maybe he's trying to find out where Great-great-great-granddaddy Templeton hid that Confederate gold."

"Columbus Roundtree, you big silly! Your great . . . whatever-granddaddy never hid any gold around here." Leona tied a faded apron about her twenty-two-inch waist and set vinegar and mustard on the counter with a double thunk.

"Makes a darn good story, though. Besides, how do you know he didn't?" Uncle Lum winked at me.

"Grady and I dug holes all over the place looking for that gold when we were little," I said. "Uncle Ernest told us it was buried out behind the house. I think he just wanted us to dig a place for him to plant tomatoes!"

"Which reminds me, if we're going to have tomatoes with that barbecue tonight, I'd better run down to the J and G and see if Jim has any local produce." Uncle Lum made it a point not to glance at his wife, who shuddered slightly as the mention of barbecue.

My aunt decided to clean out the cabinets, and since I wanted no part of that, I slipped quietly out of the kitchen. Uncle Ernest was engrossed in his book, so I wandered out to the porch where Grady lay back in a rocker, hands across his stomach, with the dog at his feet.

"It's a shame you can't relax," I said, pulling up a chair beside him.

He immediately jumped to his feet. "Hey, don't sit down! Uncle Ernest tells me Deedee and family are on their way. Let's go down by Webster's wall and see if the blackberries are ripe."

Webster Templeton was our ancestor who was supposed to have buried the gold—or so Cousin Violet claims, and the crumbling stone walls of what was left of his house was a favorite berry-picking spot.

I grabbed a pail from the back porch and scooted myself with insect repellent, glad I had worn long pants that day. "Maybe Ella will make us one of her famous blackberry cobblers," I said, referring to the time the housekeeper forgot the sugar, as we made our way along the familiar path.

Grady made a gagging noise. "I hope you've learned to cook. Mom's gotten to where she doesn't even buy sugar anymore."

"You furnish the blackberries; I'll take care of the cobbler," I assured him. "And where is Ella anyway? Did you know your mother is in there cleaning out her cabinets?"

My cousin groaned. "I doubt if she'll even notice. You'll have to admit they probably need it, and Ella's getting too old to stand on ladders and scrub those high shelves. Hadn't seen her lately, but she was looking for her cat right after I got here. Said it got out somehow."

The housekeeper always kept her cat, Dagwood, in her own part of the house. The animal was afraid, she claimed, of Amos the collie, but frankly, I think it was the other way around.

I was relieved to find the path wasn't as overgrown with weeds as I had expected. Someone—probably Casey, the writer-caretaker—had mown it recently and the air smelled of freshly cut grass. I took a deep breath, glad to be relaxing in the company of an old friend in a dear, familiar place.

We found a treasure of ripe berries tumbling over the ruined foundations of the old house and soon had the pail almost full.

"So, who else is coming?" Grady asked, popping a couple of blackberries into his mouth.

I was sure he must have guessed there was a problem between Ned and me, and was waiting for me to explain, but I wasn't ready. Not yet, anyway.

"Ma Maggie, of course, then Marge and Burdette and their bunch. Josie's with them at the pool . . . Deedee and Cyn-thia . . . and I guess Parker will be here, too." Deedee was married to a perfectly nice man who seemed to think she was normal, or if he didn't, he accepted her the way she was. Lucky Deedee!

"And Cousin Violet," I added, smiling. It was hard not to smile at the mention of our eccentric relative.

Grady untangled himself from a briar. "She still painting everything that doesn't move?"

"As far as I know. Mama says she's painted her porch furniture three times this year." It had always been a family joke that if you stood still long enough, Violet would have a go at you with her paintbrush.

"Let's go home the other way," I suggested after the pail was full. "Maybe we'll find some early apples in the old orchard." The pathway looped from the ruins of the earlier house, past Remeth churchyard, then meandered above the river for a while before circling what once had been an apple orchard within sight of our uncle's place. It was farther that way, but the trees would give more shade, and my shirt was already sticking to me.

"Have you met the new girlfriend?" I asked as we started back.

"Whose new girlfriend?"

"Uncle Ernest's. Belinda somebody. Marge says they seem to have a thing going."

"First a horse, and now a romance! What's up with Uncle Ernest lately?"

"What horse?" I asked.

"Why, Shortcake! Haven't you seen her? Strawberry roan and wild as a mountain lion. Won't let anybody near her.

"Now, tell me about this Belinda," Grady said. "Do you think she'll show up for the reunion?"

But I didn't have a chance to answer because we heard somebody moaning just then, and it seemed to be coming from a nearby ravine.

CHAPTER FIVE

The sounds were coming from a wooded area to our left. Dense with hardwoods and strewn with boulders, the terrain dropped in giant stair steps to the twisting stream below. Ferns and rhododendrons created a dark curtain of green. I couldn't see a thing.

The noises were almost animal-like in their timbre. A wildcat could be waiting to pounce, or a protective mother bear. I could hear myself breathing, and whatever was out there probably could, too. "What *is* it?" I set the pail of berries beside the path and grabbed Grady's arm. *Bears like berries, so you're welcome to them*, I thought. Just leave us alone!

I felt him stiffen as the groaning came again, this time ending in a thin wail.

"Sounds like somebody's hurt!" Grady said. "Must be down there somewhere. Wait here."

"Oh, no you don't! You're not leaving me here for bear bait! I'm coming, too." After a fleeting moment's consideration, I decided to let my cousin take the lead, and padded along behind him while he battled the almost-impenetrable under-brush. Branches whacked me in the face, and vines grabbed at my ankles. Crouching sideways, I slid down a mossy bank, feel-ing stones roll under my feet. And since the tail of Grady's shirt was handy, I snatched it for support.

With an arm out to signal silence, Grady stopped to listen. I glimpsed the river far below, but we were too high above it to hear the rush of water.

"Are you sure it's a person?" I whispered, and he pointed to something I couldn't see.

"Down there," he said. "Thought I saw something move."

Was he thinking, as I was, of that awful day almost twenty years before when he and Beverly and I had discovered the body of a murdered vagrant not far from where we now stood? It was all I could do to keep from turning and clawing my way back up the hill.

All I could see below was a network of vines in a jungle of rhododendrons. Poplar and sourwood, oak and hickory com-peted for the sun and shut out the light, briars tore at my hair. "You'd better know what you're talking about," I said.

Grady reached for my hand. "Watch your step, there's kind of a drop-off here."

Only when we inched our way down and could get a better look did I see what looked like a bundle of old clothes at the bottom of an overhang.

The bundle moved. It wore green plaid pants and a pink flowered blouse. Glasses, miraculously unbroken, hung from a chain around her neck. Ella!

"She's still alive." Crouching beside her, Grady held her

fragile old wrist. "We've got to get help—now!"

Ella's eyes were closed, and dirt and abrasions stood out against the pale background of her face. I touched her hair, whispered her name. She whimpered.

"I'll go," I said, scrambling to my knees. "The guesthouse is closer. I'll get the caretaker to call."

"No!" Grady put a hand on my shoulder. "Mom said Casey left this morning. Some kind of family emergency. It'll be faster if I go, Kate. I'll be back as soon as I can."

He was already halfway up the hillside before I could answer.

I didn't like staying behind, but Grady was right, I thought, as I knelt beside the injured woman. He could run faster, yell louder and Ella needed help sooner rather than later. She lay curled with one arm pinned beneath her, her leg at an unnatural angle. Small twigs and leaves were caught in her thinning gray hair. I dared not move her, but I attempted to make her as comfortable as possible. Gently I wiped her face with a tissue, then took off my blouse and folded it as a buffer between Ella's face and the scratchy bush that probably stopped her fall. No time for modesty now. Surely, whoever answered Grady's summons had seen a bra before.

"I'm right here," I told her, covering her hand with my own. "Help is on the way, Ella. We're going to get you out of here." I hoped I sounded more confident than I felt.

Her eyes opened briefly, and there was pain there—and something else. She struggled to speak. "Dag—"

"Dagwood? Is that what you were doing when you fell? Looking for your cat?" I stroked her cheek, hoping Ella would open her eyes again. "I'm sure he's all right. Why, I'll bet he's already back home by—"

"Not fell," she whispered. "Pushed."

"What?" I leaned closer.

Again Ella opened her eyes, and this time she looked up at the ledge where she must have been standing when she fell. "Pushed," she said, her fingers clutching mine.

I could tell she wanted me to look there, too, so I did, but of course, there was no one there. If anyone had pushed the housekeeper off the ledge, they would be long gone by now. But why in the world would anybody want to hurt Ella Stegall?

"Ella, are you sure?" I asked. "Maybe you lost your footing? If you were standing on moss, it can be slippery, and it's easy for rocks to become dislodged . . ."

I didn't know which of us I was trying to convince, but it didn't matter anyway, for Ella had lapsed again into unconsciousness.

Please don't die! The ground was deep in leaves from years before, and I made a little sitting nest for myself beside her and watched her chest go up and down. But what if it stopped? I had taken a course in CPR when Josie was small, and I went over the steps in my mind: Call for help . . . we'd done that . . . check pulse . . . listen for breathing . . .

Something snapped in the woods below me and I know I must have jumped, but Ella didn't notice. Was somebody watching? If Ella had been pushed from the ledge, was the person who did it waiting to come back and finish the job—and me?

A bird chirped from a limb above me, and a squirrel scurried through the underbrush. I scratched a bite on my ankle, wiped the sweat from my eyes and tried to see the sky. I couldn't. Ella made sort of a grunting noise and grimaced in pain. "It won't be long now," I told her, carefully removing leaves from her hair. "Stay with me, Ella. Help should be here any minute." *God, please don't make a liar of me!*

An outcropping of rock, partially covered in moss and underbrush, jutted from beneath the place where Ella had been standing. If she had landed there on her way down, it was a wonder she was still alive.

I shifted my position and listened for the sound of approaching rescuers. Nothing. What was taking so long?

Earlier that day, Augusta had tried to warn me, only not in so many words. But warn me of what? Was my life in danger here? I felt suddenly cool, vulnerable without my blouse, as if someone were watching. The woods seemed quieter than before; not even a breeze ruffled the leaves. I tried not to think of the ghost stories we used to tell about the spooks in Remeth graveyard: the Yankee soldier who went around with a lantern looking for his lost unit; the woman who swore to haunt her young widower if he ever married again. When he did, they say his hair turned white overnight.

And not a word of them is true, I told myself. *You are not ten years old, Kate McBride! Grow up and act your age. Think of something pleasant, positive.*

Augusta.

Surely I hadn't dreamed that unconventional duo! No! Those scones were real, and the pancakes. . . . But had I really met my guardian angel? If so, I wished she were here.

"It won't be long now," a voice said behind me, and I turned to find Augusta sitting there.

"Well, it's about time!" I said. "I'm afraid Ella's badly hurt, and I don't know what else to do for her." I broke off a frond of leaves and fanned the pesky gnats from Ella's still face.

Augusta looked at the woman who lay beside me. "What you've done is fine, and the others should be here soon." She slipped off her silvery sandals and tossed them aside. Her toenails, I noticed, were painted a metallic pink.

"Maybe you didn't hear me," I said, lowering my voice just in case Ella might hear. "She fell from all the way up there, probably hit those rocks on the way down. Don't just sit there, *do* something!"

"Kathryn . . ." Her voice was patient, although I could tell it was an effort. "I think we need to come to an understanding. Just what is it you expect me to do?"

"Whatever it takes to save her life. Don't you have some kind of heavenly magic? You are an angel, aren't you?"

"It doesn't work quite that way." She slipped from her tree stump seat and came to stand beside me, her long dress swirling about her. Today she wore a broomstick skirt of what looked like crinkle cotton that fell from the bodice in tiers of pastel colors. A halo of daisies sat atop a pouf of coppery sunlight hair. "We can't undo what's already done," she said.

"Then can't you make her better?" I moved aside so that Augusta could sit in my place and watched while the angel touched Ella's bruised and bleeding forehead with her long, beautiful fingers. Ella slept on.

"I don't believe she's in pain now," Augusta said, observing Ella's quiet face. "Now all we can do is wait for help."

"That's *all*? Then what good are you? What good are any of you? And where, might I ask, is Ella's guardian angel?"

She adjusted her daisy crown and gathered up her skirt to make room for me beside her. "We aren't magicians, Kate, and except in very rare cases do angels perform miracles. However, we do watch over you, do our best to direct you in the right path and try to protect you as best we can."

"Yeah, right!" I said. "Somebody sure fouled up today."

One glimpse into her troubled angel eyes made me want to take back my hateful accusations. My heart literally hurt, and it wasn't from something I ate.

A lock of her hair came loose and tumbled over her forehead, and Augusta tried to tuck it back without much success. "Haven't you ever sensed a warning, Kate, when you were close to danger?" she asked.

"Of course I have. We all have, but—"

"And don't you sometimes, without knowing why, choose to do one thing instead of another?" Augusta held out her palm for a butterfly, who seemed quite at home there.

"You mean like today?" Ordinarily I would have chosen to return to my uncle's the way we had come, but this afternoon, Grady and I had elected to take the longer route.

Augusta nodded. "Life is all about decisions, choices. Sometimes we make the wrong ones, as it seems Ella did today."

I shrugged. "So, what happened? Did her angel give her a shove in the wrong direction?"

"Certainly not!" If Augusta had wings, she would have flapped them. "I imagine that in Ella's search for her missing pet, she chose to ignore the warning, or perhaps she didn't hear it. At any rate, you and your cousin came along to find her." Augusta touched my arm. "And that was no accident, Kate."

"You mean her angel sort of directed us here?"

"No doubt about it. We're meant to look after each other, you know—humans and angels alike," Augusta said.

"Wait a minute! How did you know about Dagwood?" I asked, and seeing her puzzled expression, realized she didn't know what I meant.

"Ella's cat. You said she was looking for her missing pet," I explained.

She smiled. "I heard her tell you, of course. I've been keeping an eye on you, Kate."

"Then you might've seen Ella fall! She says she was pushed. Is that true?"

Augusta's smiled vanished and her sea-green eyes turned to gray. "I wouldn't know about that. I've only been here since you and your friend left the path when you heard her cry out."

"But how—"

"I've been teaching Penelope to make daisy chains, and we were just over in the meadow. I left her there playing with a huge yellow cat—your friend's missing Dagwood, I suppose." Augusta stood and brushed off her skirt. "Shh! I think I hear someone coming."

I stood and listened, too, but I couldn't hear a thing. Ella still lay where we had found her, her cheek nestled against my wadded-up blouse. She was breathing, but I didn't know for how long. "I hope they get here in time," I said, trying not to cry.

Augusta stepped into her sandals. "It should be any minute now." She took both my hands in hers, and if eyes could talk, hers would say *trouble*. "I want you to promise you'll be careful," she said.

"Careful about what? What's going on here, Augusta? Am I in some kind of danger? Is that why you're here?"

"That I don't know—at least not yet. Just don't take

chances, *please*. Because of my duties with Penelope, you understand, I can't be with you every minute." Augusta glanced at the broken figure at our feet. "And as you can see, it takes less time than that for—"

"There they are! I see them—right down there!"

I looked up to see my loudmouth cousin Deedee practically rolling down the bank in her name-brand, have-to-be-dry-cleaned linen shorts set that would never be white again. Grady and two men with a stretcher were right behind her, while Uncle Lum straggled along in the rear.

"My God, Kate!" Deedee stopped so short she almost tumbled headfirst into what looked suspiciously like poison ivy. "At least have the decency to put on a shirt or something!"

I was so glad to see professional help arrive, I didn't even lose my cool, but I could swear I heard someone laughing behind me.

Of course, when I turned around, Augusta was gone.

CHAPTER SIX

Poor Ella! Can't see two feet in front of her," Ma Maggie said as we gathered in Uncle Ernest's living room. Uncle Ernest himself had ridden to the hospital in the ambulance with Ella. "She probably didn't even realize she was standing on a ledge." She looked about for a tissue, then fumbled in her purse until she found a handkerchief and turned away to dab at her eyes.

"I'm not so sure about that." Violet fanned herself with a dog-eared bulletin from Bishop's Bridge Presbyterian Church, then frowned as she read an item on the back. "I'll be doggoned, I didn't know Sally Rae Johnson had had her baby! A boy this time, named for—"

"Never mind Sally Rae Johnson!" Ma Maggie's face was red and she puffed out her cheeks like she might blow any minute. "What makes you say that?"

"Say what?" Our cousin started fanning again.

"That you aren't sure Ella stumbled off that ledge." My

grandmother walked across the room to stand over Violet. She cast a long shadow. "Are you saying it wasn't an accident?"

Violet sat straighter. "I'm saying it *might* not have been, that's all. After all, Ella *told* Kate she was pushed, and I heard somebody down in those woods today—sounded like two people talking. Could've been one of them."

Uncle Lum frowned. "I can't imagine why. When was this?"

"Just a little while ago . . . an hour or so, I guess. I was helping Ella look for her cat." Violet's lip trembled. "You know how she dotes on that animal." She frowned. "And Ella said something else, something about a voice—or voices. Maybe she heard them, too."

Deedee sat across from her, absently rubbing a spot on her shorts. It didn't go away. "You probably heard the Belle Fleurs cleaning off the cemetery," she said.

"The what?" Uncle Lum started to smile, then apparently thought better of it.

"The Belle Fleurs Garden Club. They were to start clearing that old graveyard today, the one that adjoins this property."

"Remeth. Yes, I know. Lived down the road from it all my life," Violet reminded her. "But the voices weren't coming from there. They were more in the direction of the river; and I thought I saw somebody moving about down there."

"People hike through there all the time," Grady reminded her. "I wouldn't take what Ella said about being pushed too seriously; after all, she got a pretty bad lick on the head."

Ma Maggie moved to the window and pushed aside draperies that used to be green, but now were more of a coppery tan. Dust motes swirled in the sun. "It doesn't look good," she said. "Especially at her age. I think we . . . why, there's that cat!"

I hurried to stand beside her. "What cat? You mean Dagwood?"

"See for yourself," my grandmother said, stepping aside so I could get a better look. And sure enough, there was Ella's big orange cat curled up on one of the stone banisters fast asleep. Our uncle's collie, Amos, dozed nearby.

"Well, what do you know about that?" Aunt Leona came in from the kitchen just then with a tray of lemonade (sugar-free, of course). "Probably been here all along."

Violet peered over my shoulder. "Unless those men frightened him away—poor baby."

"What men?" Lum wanted to know.

"Why, the men I heard earlier in the woods. I expect they were looking for the gold." Violet nodded in agreement with herself.

"What gold?" Grady winked at me behind her back.

"The Confederate gold, silly! Everybody knows Webster Templeton was one of the party that accompanied what was left of the Confederate gold out of Richmond—and then it just disappeared. It could be here as well as anywhere." She frowned at all of us in turn. "Well, couldn't it?"

Nobody spoke. Leona chugalugged a lemonade. Ma Maggie closed her eyes for so long I thought she'd fallen asleep.

"Poor Ella might've come upon them just as they found it," Violet added, looking about. "Yes, and they would have had to make sure she didn't tell."

"How convenient for them that she wandered to the edge of

a drop-off looking for a lost cat," Grady muttered. But Violet didn't hear him.

My grandmother looked at Violet and shook her head. "Whatever the reason, I think some of us should get over to the hospital and keep Ernest company. That's a lonely vigil, and who knows what might happen with Ella. Violet, why don't you and I—"

Uncle Lum put a hand on her shoulder. "No, Mama. Let me go. Grady can come with me—give us a chance to catch up on things, won't it, son? We'll call if there are any changes."

Marge and family arrived with Josie soon after Lum and Grady left, and of course, we had to explain what had happened.

"Good heavens, Kate!" Marge whispered when I told her about waiting with Ella for help to come. "What if somebody really did push her? Why, they might've still been around somewhere! Did you hear anything—out of the ordinary, I mean."

I shook my head. "I was too busy worrying about Ella. To tell the truth, it was almost too quiet. Gave me the creeps."

My eavesdropping daughter spoke up. "It was probably a ghost. I told you that old cemetery's haunted—the Yankee soldier, I'll bet. He must not've liked old Ella hanging around so close to where he was trying to rest."

"Or one of those hippie people," Darby suggested. "Didn't they drown somewhere around there?"

"This is not something to joke about," I told the two. "Ella was seriously hurt, and if Grady and I hadn't come along when we did, I don't know when we would've found her."

I had the sensation that somebody was staring at me and

turned to find Cousin Deedee giving me the once-over. "Why, Kate," she said, drawing each word out slowly. "I haven't seen hide nor hair of Ned. Don't tell me he's not coming?"

Then don't ask! I wanted to say. Instead I managed to reply as calmly as possible that my husband was attending a seminar on the other side of the country and sent his regrets. Josie stuck out her lip at me, but I don't think Deedee noticed it.

"And where is Parker?" Marge wanted to know. "And Cynthia. They'll be here, won't they?"

Deedee sipped lemonade and nodded. "Parker's collecting Cynthia from pageant rehearsal. She's in the running for Miss Junior Mountain Sunshine at the summer festival this year. Anyway, I phoned him to pick up the barbecue from the Friendly Pig since Uncle Lum probably won't be back in time."

For the time being, my cousin Deedee had redeemed herself.

"We want to see the new horse," Darby said. "Can we ride her, Mom, please?"

"Not this horse!" Ma Maggie spoke up. "That Shortcake's wild as a hant. Won't even let you get near her. You stay away from that animal."

"Then just let us pet her. Please, *please!*" Josie used her "I'll die if you don't give into me" voice, but my grandmother wasn't swayed.

"Not now," she said. "Maybe your uncle Ernest can coax her up to the fence for you tomorrow."

"Ha!" Violet said.

Defeated, Josie and Darby deserted us to play Monopoly in

the large upstairs hallway that had become over the years a sort of catchall sitting room where dark-stained shelves were crammed with books so old the pages were falling out. As a child I had read one of what must've been an original *Bobbsey Twins* adventure, and I remembered playing with that same Monopoly game I'm sure had belonged to my grandmother.

Burdette gave the two younger boys a wheelbarrow ride on the lawn while Marge, Deedee and I set up card tables on the porch for our soon-to-arrive supper. Leona had unearthed a supply of paper plates, probably from a past reunion, and was distributing them on the tables when we saw an unfamiliar car approaching.

"Does Parker have a new Saturn?" Marge asked Deedee as the small white car came to a stop under a pecan tree in the side yard.

Deedee shook her head and frowned. "Still drives that old beat-up Dodge; I'm embarrassed to be seen in it, but I'm not expecting him for at least half an hour. Had to get Cynthia before he stopped by the Friendly Pig."

Leona muttered something about making more lemonade and dashed back inside. The rest of us watched as a trim blonde woman in a pale blue blouse and darker denim skirt stepped out from behind the wheel, glanced up at the house and waved.

We waved back. "Who's that?" I asked, trying not to be obvious.

Marge grinned. "Looks like Belinda Donahue, Uncle Ernest's new lady friend," she whispered. "Bet he invited her to join us tonight and never thought to call and cancel after what happened to Ella." Extending a hand, she started to meet her, and the two stood talking quietly together at the foot of the steps until Hartley abandoned the game with his dad and ran toward the house clutching a delicate part of his anatomy.

"Mama, I gotta pee!" he shouted, pushing past the two woman and charging up the steps with his red-faced father in pursuit.

"Oh, my goodness, you'll have to excuse him! I'm sorry." Marge laughed in spite of herself, and so did the rest of us.

"Please don't be! I was feeling rather like an intruder after learning of your family's sudden tragedy, but I must admit, I feel a bit more at ease now." The newcomer composed herself and followed Marge to the shady end of the porch where I introduced myself and offered her a seat in one of the rocking chairs.

"Thank you, but I won't stay long." Belinda perched on the edge of the seat as if she might take off in flight at any second. "Didn't realize about poor Ella . . . oh, I do hope she'll be all right!" She looked at each of us in turn. "Is there anything I can do? Anything at all?"

"You can stay and have supper with us," Marge said. "With three of us at the hospital with Ella we'll have more barbecue than we need."

"Oh dear, no. I couldn't." Belinda inched even closer to the edge of the chair. "I told Ernest this reunion was a time for family, but he insisted I come."

"I expect he'd welcome your company at the hospital then," I said. "There's really no need for him to wear himself out over there. Maybe you can talk him into coming home."

She smiled and placed her hands on the arms of the chair, preparing to leave. "I'll see what I can do."

"But first won't you stay just a minute and say hello to Ma Maggie and Violet? They're upstairs in Ella's rooms getting together some things she might need, and I know they'd be disappointed not to see you." Marge sneaked a glance at me and I knew what she was up to. Our grandmother would be royally pissed if she missed a chance to size up Uncle Ernest's new girlfriend.

Deedee excused herself to find more folding chairs and I was left alone with our visitor while Marge went to look for Violet and Ma Maggie. Belinda Donahue was a dainty, small-boned woman blessed with that rare complexion that seems to age well. I guessed she must be at least fifty or more, but I could see no signs of wrinkles, and I suspected that her hair, so fair it was almost silver, had been professionally tinted its original color. She wore tiny silver earrings in the likeness of owls and a plain gold band swung from a chain around her neck.

"My grandmother's," she explained when she saw me looking at it. "She had such small hands, I can't wear it." Her own fingers, I noticed, were bare, but I could see indications that she once wore a ring on the third finger of her left hand.

Belinda seemed eager to leave and a bit uncomfortable exchanging small talk while we waited, so I was glad when Ma Maggie and Violet joined us.

"I'm so glad you came," my grandmother told her. "Ernest was in such a dither when he left, I'm not surprised he didn't think to call you, but if you're going by the hospital, I'd appreciate it if you'd take some of poor Ella's things—her hairbrush and nighties, and whatever that is she soaks her teeth in."

From the way poor Ella looked when I last saw her, I doubted if she would be needing anything like that for a while, but at least it gave Ma Maggie and Violet something to do, and Belinda said she'd be glad to oblige.

"So, what did you think of Uncle Ernest's new love interest?" Marge asked our grandmother after Belinda left.

"I've seen her from a distance, but she's just as pretty up close," Ma Maggie answered. "I can see why Ernest is taken with her, but she seems a little shy. I guess all of us being here at once must've overwhelmed her."

"Poor Ella's accident unnerved all of us," I said.

"I doubt if she'll lose any sleep over what happened to Ella," Violet said. "No love lost between those two."

Marge took a folding chair from Deedee and opened it. "What do you mean?"

"Couldn't stand being in the same room together. Atmosphere as thick as cold oatmeal, and about as pleasant." Violet picked up the cat and stroked it. "Maybe it's my imagination, but I couldn't help but feel it. Ella sometimes sat with me when she came to church, but since Ernest started coming with Belinda, she sits on the other side of the sanctuary. It's obvious there's something going on."

Deedee snorted. "Surely she's not jealous! Bless her heart, Ella Stegall's eighty if she's a day."

"Uncle Ernest isn't far behind," Marge reminded her. "Maybe the two women met somewhere before, had some kind of run-in. I hate to say it, but poor Ella's kind of like a bottle of wine missing its cork. Gets more vinegary every day."

"I expect she just resents another woman's presence," my

grandmother said. "Ella's been running the show now for over forty years—ever since Rose left."

"Before Rose left," Violet said. "She lived in the guesthouse then, but did most of the cleaning and cooking."

I laughed. "Then that explains why Rose left!"

Parker and Cynthia arrived soon after that and we ate a rather subdued supper on the porch—or as subdued as it could be with three active boys and two little girls who didn't get along. Cynthia, seated next to Josie, monopolized the conversation with details of the "simply super" party she'd been to, and how her mother had said *she* could have a real dinner party when she turned eleven—with boys and everything.

"Why?" my daughter asked, stuffing potato chips into her mouth.

I could see relations were only going to go downhill from there, so I was pleased when after supper Burdette suggested the children catch lightning bugs on the lawn. The girls weren't too receptive to the idea at first, but when twilight deepened into dusk and the first winking glows flickered in the trees, even Cynthia decided it might be fun to try. And as we sat on the porch watching the children play, and listening to their laughter, I almost forgot for a little while what had happened earlier.

"Look at them," Deedee observed. "I haven't seen Cynthia act like that since she was little."

"She's still little," I said. "She's a child. What's your hurry?"

Deedee didn't answer, and I couldn't see her face in the dark. I knew I shouldn't have said it, but she's rushed that little girl from babyhood like a bear was behind her. *Two, going on twenty-two*, my cousin would say when somebody asked Cynthia's age. Or, *three, going on thirty.*

How different we were! Sometimes I longed to stop the clock on Josie and keep her a little girl for a while longer—although not lately, I'll admit!

The lightning bug game soon turned to tag, then hide-and-seek, and we were getting ready to call the children in from their play when Darby came running to tell us there was somebody moving around in the orchard with a light.

"You're probably just seeing lightning bugs," his mother said, leading a protesting Hartley inside.

"No. No! It's a flashlight," Darby said. "Josie saw it, too. So did Cynthia." The two girls confirmed that this was true.

Burdette waded into the middle of them. "You all wouldn't be pulling my leg, now, would you? That was a bad thing that happened to poor Ella today. I don't like you making light of it."

"But we're not, Daddy, honest! Come and see for yourself." Darby took his father's hand. "Hurry, before he gets away!"

Ma Maggie and Violet had left a few minutes earlier, and Leona had disappeared upstairs for a long soak in the tub, she said, so only Marge, Deedee and their families remained. Deedee was telling us about the dress she was thinking of buying Cynthia for the Miss Junior Mountain Sunshine competition when Burdette came back with a peculiar look on his face.

"I'm not sure what's going on over there, but it really does look like somebody's wandering around with a flashlight." He waited until we herded the children inside. "I don't think it's anything to worry about, but it bears checking out."

69

"I'll go with you," Parker said. "Could be somebody came up from the river trail and decided to camp there for the night."

I couldn't remember that happening before, but I hoped what he said proved to be true.

It wasn't. The two men had been gone close to half an hour when we saw their lights approaching from the orchard—at least we hoped it was their lights!

Marge had bathed Hartley, dressed him in pajamas and was reading him a bedtime story when Burdette and Parker returned, red-faced and out of breath.

"It was a man, all right," Parker said, collapsing in the nearest chair. "But I don't think he'll be back. We chased him all the way past Webster's wall and into Remeth churchyard. I'll bet he's halfway to town by now."

"Good. I hope he keeps on going," Marge said. "Could you tell what he looked like?"

Burdette shook his head. "Medium height, I'd say, and he had on a cap of some kind. It was too dark to see his face, but I turned my light on him as he was climbing that cemetery wall, and it looked like he was wearing jeans and some kind of blue shirt."

"Blue! I told you," Darby said. "I told you it's the ghost of that Yankee soldier!"

Chapter Seven

Who in the world would be prowling around out there this time of night?" I asked Marge. Deedee and family had already left and Burdette was rounding up his boys and Josie in preparation to drive back to town. "What do you suppose he was doing?"

"Might've been teenagers romancing over in that old cemetery." She grinned. "Remember what the poet said? 'None, I think, do there embrace?' Of course, Marvell didn't know the kids around here."

"I hope you're right," I said. "Frankly, I'd rather it be a case of good old-fashioned lust. After what happened to Ella, I'm not thrilled with the idea of having somebody wandering about out there."

Marge yawned as she gathered up her boys' discarded shoes. "Burdette says the sheriff's sending somebody out here to look around. If it's a vagrant or somebody like that, they might even pass him on the road." She lowered her voice.

"Kate, you don't really think poor Ella was pushed, do you?"

"I don't know what to believe," I told her. "I didn't think so at first, but now I'm not so sure."

"But why would anybody want to hurt Ella, of all people? The poor old soul is harmless . . . unless you take into account that casserole she made when she mistook canned cherries for tomatoes."

I didn't have an answer for that.

I didn't have an answer as to why my daughter made a point of ignoring me, either. "I hope you don't mind Josie staying with you for a few more days," I began. "I'm hanging out here with Leona until the others get back from the hospital and I'll probably end up spending the night. If anything weird *is* going on out there, I'd rather Josie not be around."

My expression must have given me away because Marge tossed the shoes aside and wrapped her long arms around me. "Kate, this too shall pass—I promise. That young'un's just showing her skinny little fanny—making you dance to her tune, but I honestly don't think she's enjoying it."

My cousin pulled away, her hands still on my shoulders. "We love having Josie with us, don't worry about that. You're the one who concerns me." Marge frowned, ignoring Jon, who tugged at her sleeve. "It's Ned, isn't it? Something's wrong. You can't fool me, Kate McBride."

I didn't answer, which I knew was as good as an admission. "Not my best summer vacation," I mumbled.

Burdette appeared behind us carrying a sleeping Hartley as he shepherded Josie and the two older boys before him. "You kids get in the car and be quick about it . . . or I might be forced to sing."

72

"Mi-mi-mi!" he rasped off-key, then made a face. "We wouldn't want that now, would we?"

The three scampered out the door shrieking, with my daughter in the lead. She didn't look back.

Marge again gathered up the shoes and followed, pausing in the doorway. "Look, you don't have to stay here, you know. Uncle Ernest and the others should be back at any minute. Why don't you come along with us—for tonight at least? It'll give us a chance to talk." She lowered her voice to a whisper. "There's leftover peach cobbler, and I hid some ice cream behind the frozen broccoli."

I laughed. "Hey, don't tempt me, but Leona would freak out if she came downstairs and found everybody gone, and frankly I wouldn't feel so good about leaving her." I followed her out to the porch. "I would like to talk, though. Maybe we can sneak away tomorrow and snatch a few minutes alone."

"Fat chance," my cousin said, "but we'll work on it."

I tested locks on all the doors as soon as Marge and the others left, then called my parents' answering machine to see if they'd left a message informing me of my "aunthood," although I felt certain they would telephone us at Bramblewood if Sara's baby had come. My mother would never settle on leaving such an important announcement on a machine, and I knew she wouldn't be satisfied until she described in great detail my new little niece or nephew.

And my parents weren't the only ones who hadn't phoned. I knew I shouldn't hope, but it seemed that whenever I was at my most vulnerable, an annoying little smiley face would spring out from deep inside of me and sing sunshiny lyrics like "He'll be comin' 'round the mountain when he comes." I quickly squashed the saccharine intruder. My husband wouldn't be coming around this mountain any time soon—if ever—and he wasn't going to telephone, either.

Uncle Lum had called earlier to tell us that he and Grady had finally convinced Uncle Ernest to go home and get some sleep and that the three of them were stopping for a bite of supper on the way.

Amos settled himself on the rug in front of the door and promptly went to sleep, and I wandered around the empty house picking up paper cups and napkins that had been overlooked when we collected our after-supper litter. My aunt Leona would be sacked out by now in the bedroom at the end of the upstairs hall—too far away to hear me yell if the flashlight-bearing prowler in blue decided to return. And I knew she slept with earplugs because we'd all heard her complain of Uncle Lum's snoring. The old house creaked for no good reason except that it was night, and that's what old houses usually do then. At least, that's what I told myself. I looked at the clock on the mantel. Marge and company had been gone over half an hour. Surely Grady and my uncles would be home soon.

There was nothing of interest on Uncle Ernest's bookshelves. (No surprise there!) And if I turned on the television, I might not be able to hear if anyone *was* trying to force his way inside. It occurred to me that maybe this wasn't such a bad idea, and I was checking the newspaper for the schedule when I heard the cat meowing from the kitchen.

Poor Dagwood! In the frenzy of the day, I doubted if any-one had thought to feed him. I was on my way to remedy that and had one hand on the swinging door when I heard the whir of the can opener and realized somebody had gotten there before me!

Uncle Ernest had a key, of course, but Amos hadn't barked and I hadn't heard anyone drive up. I stopped where I was and tried to ease the door shut before whoever was in there saw me. It squeaked, of course. Too late now.

"Aren't you coming in? I thought I'd put on a pot of cof-fee—or tea, if you prefer." Augusta stood at the sink; the wreath of daisies, still fresh, in her hair, and it made me sad to see them. My bridesmaids had carried Shasta daisies, and Ned used to remember anniversaries with an arrangement of the sunshiny flowers.

"Such an efficient little machine," Augusta said, nodding toward the electric can opener. "Zips open a tin in no time."

The open "tin" she referred to sat on the countertop and so did the cat. Penelope perched beside it dangling long legs while she stroked Dagwood's gingery back.

"You nearly scared me to death!" I said. "I don't suppose you've ever considered letting a person know when to expect you?"

"We thought you might be lonely, and perhaps even a bit apprehensive after the afternoon's shocking misfortune." Augusta filled my uncle's dented metal pot with water and measured in coffee. She seemed to know where everything was kept.

"Ella! She's not—"

"Still unconscious, and that's probably for the best." Her

eyes grew sad. "Ella's been terribly injured, Kate, but I don't believe she's suffering."

"Do you think she was pushed?" I watched her face as she answered.

"I'm afraid I do." Augusta took mugs from the cabinet and set them on the kitchen table, then pulled out two chairs, indicating that I was to sit. Her face grew troubled and I noticed that the necklace she wore, although it still sparkled, had turned from a dazzling purple to kind of a grayish blue.

"There's something you're not telling me," I said, and Augusta didn't deny it.

"I wanted to be certain first. Kathryn, I think your friend Ella was led to believe her cat was down in that ravine."

Dagwood, as if realizing he was being discussed, finished his food, and settled in Penelope's lap to wash his paws. Penelope laughed, sounding faintly like distant wind chimes.

"How do you know he wasn't?" I asked.

"Oh, the cat was down there all right, but he was inside a box." Augusta rose to turn down the flame under the pot. Then she spoke softly to her charge. "Penelope, do wash out that tin please. It has a most dreadful odor."

"A box? What kind of box?" I asked.

"A corrugated box, such as the kind you use for storing or shipping." Augusta poured steaming coffee into mugs. It had a rich chocolate smell, although I hadn't noticed her adding other flavoring. "Just think about it, Kathryn. If someone wanted to use a cat's crying to lure Ella to the edge of a dangerous precipice, there is no way they could get the animal to stay in one place." She smiled. "Cats have minds of their own, you know."

I nodded, remembering how Josie used to try and dress her kitten in doll's clothing and wheel it around in a tiny carriage.

"But how do you know it was in a box?" I asked, taking a swallow of the chocolate-laced brew.

Augusta sipped before speaking. "When Penelope and I found the cat in the meadow just before you heard Ella crying, the poor animal was frightened to death. Something had upset it, and later when you told me Ella had been looking for her pet, I started to think about it. I know enough about cats to realize it wouldn't have stayed in one place long—unless it was being held against its will . . . but how?"

"So you think somebody deliberately took Ella's cat from her rooms? But how can you be sure about the box?" I asked, refreshing my cup and Augusta's.

"Because we went back and found it there—or at least Penelope did. It was concealed in a small hollow beneath the ledge and hidden by dense vines. It was obvious that the flaps had been sealed with some kind of heavy tape, and one end was shredded where the cat had clawed its way out," Augusta said.

Penelope eyed longingly some leftover chocolate chip cookies Marge had left behind, and Augusta lifted an elegant brow at me. "Do you mind if she—"

"Oh, please help yourself," I said. "And there's cold milk in the refrigerator."

"No more than two, Penelope . . . oh, all right, three. But wash your hands first." Augusta gave me the kind of "weary mother" glance I've often exchanged with other parents. I guess being responsible for another person can be wearing—even on an angel.

"Is the box still there? What did you do with it?" I asked.

Dagwood curled around Augusta's feet as she sipped her coffee and she leaned down now and then to stroke him. "Don't worry, it's in a safe place."

"In the attic," Penelope said, seeming rather proud of herself. "We put some old papers and notebooks in there and hid it in the back."

"Good thinking!" I told her, and Penelope smiled so big she almost forgot to finish her last cookie.

"That must have been what the blue ghost with the flashlight was looking for!" I said.

"Blue ghost?" Augusta looked puzzled.

"A man dressed in blue. The children think it's a ghost."

"I'm afraid he was real enough," Augusta said. "Probably waited until dark to go back and retrieve the box—only it wasn't there."

"I'm surprised somebody didn't see it earlier when they came to take Ella to the hospital," I said. "I guess we were so worried about getting her there, we didn't do much looking around."

Augusta whisked our empty mugs to the sink to wash. "And why would you?" she asked over her shoulder. "At the time, no one took what Ella said to heart. After all, why would anyone want to cause her harm?"

I shook my head. "And what's worse, it had to have been somebody here. Surely even Uncle Ernest would've noticed a stranger making off with poor Ella's cat."

Augusta didn't answer right away. I suppose she must have been thinking the same thing.

"Just who *was* here today?" she asked finally.

"Well . . . you've heard me mention Marge and her family; Josie's staying with them. Marge's mother is my aunt Jane, but they live in Alabama and couldn't be here because her dad just had hernia surgery. And then there's Deedee, who's married to Parker Driscoll, and their daughter, Cynthia."

Augusta reached in her bag for a hankie, which she presented to Penelope, who was licking chocolate from her fingers, then nodded in my direction, apparently impatient for me to get on with it. "And?" she said.

"Uncle Lum, Aunt Leona and their son, Grady . . ." I counted on my fingers. "Then Uncle Ernest, of course, and Ma Maggie and Violet . . . I think that's all . . . no, wait! I forgot Belinda, only she didn't show up until this afternoon."

And then I had to explain to Augusta about Belinda Donahue and her connection to the family. "Violet says she and Ella didn't get along," I said, "but that doesn't mean she shoved her over a ledge, and Uncle Ernest didn't mention her being here earlier." *Which didn't mean a thing,* I thought. My uncle isn't the chatty type.

"Burdette phoned the sheriff's department after he and Parker chased the trespasser all the way to Remeth Cemetery," I told her, "and they promised to come out and look around, but I doubt if they'll find anything now."

Augusta peered at her reflection in the kitchen window and tweaked a strand of straying hair, then flushed when she saw me watching. I don't know why. If I had hair like Augusta's, I'd carry a mirror in front of me.

She turned quickly from the window and came to stand

beside my chair. "I think it would be a good idea tomorrow," she said, "if you told these policemen about the box."

But I almost forgot about that the next morning when members of the Belle Fleurs Garden Club turned up a skeleton in old Remeth churchyard. One that wasn't supposed to be there.

CHAPTER EIGHT

We heard it first from Burdette. Leona and Lum hadn't come downstairs yet, and Uncle Ernest had already left for the hospital. Grady and I had finished our cereal and were on our second cup of coffee when we heard somebody hollering outside. I jumped up, recognizing the voice at once. My cousin Burdette's accustomed to projecting into the far corners of the sanctuary—with or without a microphone. *Something had happened to Josie, or to Marge or one of the boys!*

By the time I reached the door, Burdette was already halfway up the front steps and his round face was as colorless as a slice of white bread. "Cell phone's dead," he said, charging past me. "Gotta use the phone."

I stepped aside, too terrified to do anything but stammer, "W-what's wrong?" Following him, I tugged at his elbow. "Burdette, is somebody hurt? Is Josie all right? Tell me! What's going on?"

Burdette mopped his brow with a crumpled red bandanna

and shook his head. "No, Josie's fine, Kate. Everybody's okay . . ." He stopped to catch his breath. "It's just that we found—Well, we were trying to dig up this old wisteria vine in the churchyard over there, and we pulled up a skeleton with it!"

"Dear God!" I said, wishing I had skipped that second cup of coffee. "Can't you just shove it back in and cover it up?"

"You found a *what*?" I turned to find Grady standing in the kitchen doorway.

"A skeleton." Burdette punched in the emergency numbers and told the dispatcher what he'd just shared with Grady and me.

"Yes, ma'am, I know we can expect to find skeletons in a cemetery," he said, "but this one was buried in a shallow grave with no marker, and it appears to have been wrapped in some sort of tarp . . . *tarp*, yes . . . one of those plastic covers you use to keep out the rain."

I could see that Burdette, although usually calm, was beginning to lose his cool because his face was getting flushed. "No, ma'am, I don't know how long it's been there, but I suggest you get in touch with the people from forensics who might be able to find out . . . the police. Right. Whoever this person was didn't wrap up in that tarp and climb in by himself. Or maybe it was herself. That's another thing they'll have to find out."

I glanced at Grady and the two of us couldn't help but smile at our cousin, who was usually the model of composure. Burdette's shirt and face were wet from perspiration, so I went to the kitchen for ice water while he gave the woman directions on how to reach Remeth churchyard.

"Good Lord, what a shock! I couldn't believe what I was seeing," Burdette said. "I guess I'd better get back over there before the police come. I left Parker and three or four others who had volunteered to help clear the old place off, and they're as curious as I am to find out what this is all about."

"Sounds like it's all about murder to me," I said. "Why else would somebody dump a body in an abandoned graveyard?"

"Where did you find it?" Grady asked.

Burdette drained his second glass of water. "Over by that far corner, sort of away from the rest. There aren't any graves around there, so you can imagine what a jolt it was to dig up a skull!"

"You can send the police over here when they're finished with you," I told him as he started to leave. "I have something to show them, too."

I told them about the box that had held Ella's cat, only I had to lie and say I'd picked it up in the woods the day before but hadn't noticed the claw marks until last night when I went to throw it out.

"Why didn't you say something sooner?" Grady wanted to know. "I can't believe you didn't tell me this morning."

"It might not mean a thing," I said. "I didn't want to cause a panic."

Burdette stuffed the bandanna into his pocket. "You'll have to admit it makes sense, though. If somebody wanted to draw Ella to the edge of that ravine, that would've been the way to do it."

"Well, this is turning out to be one fine reunion, isn't it?" Uncle Ernest said over our lunch of bacon, lettuce and tomato sandwiches—or lettuce and tomato sandwiches in Aunt Leona's case. My uncle had returned from the hospital about an hour before to tell us that Ella's condition was unchanged. The housekeeper remained in intensive care and the nurse had assured him they would call if Ella's condition worsened. No one, including Uncle Ernest, seemed to think it would improve. "They only let me in to see her for a few minutes," he told us, "and she didn't even know I was there."

"Can you think of anybody who would want Ella out of the way?" Lum asked him, and Uncle Ernest shook his head. "Strangest thing I ever heard," he said. "I just can't believe anybody would do such a thing."

Uncle Ernest turned to me, "Kate, are you sure a cat was in that box?"

"You saw it," I said. "How else could it have been shredded from the inside?" Only a few minutes before, the police had left with the cardboard box after questioning all of us about the activities at Bramblewood during the past few days. They seemed especially interested in Ella Stegall's background.

"I never really knew much about poor Ella," Grady admitted. "She was just always here."

My uncle raised a bristly brow. "Beg pardon?"

"I said, Ella was just always *here*," Grady told him.

"Be forty-one years come October," Uncle Ernest said. "Came from somewhere in Virginia, she said. Had a brother there. As far as I know, he was her only kin." He paced the living room, pulling out the contents of drawers, turning vases upside down, and I knew he was looking for his pipe. Uncle Ernest never smoked his pipe unless he was upset about something.

"It's on the mantel," I told him, pointing the way. "Behind that picture of Nana." (Nana was the name we used for our Great-grandmother Templeton.)

"She hides it, you know—Ella does. Says she can't stand the smell." My uncle tapped his pipe to empty the bowl, and frankly, I wasn't too keen on the odor, either.

"What on earth made you hire her?" Aunt Leona went straight to the point. "I mean, the woman couldn't cook—even when she could see—and her housekeeping was hit and miss, to put it graciously. It couldn't have been for her sparkling personality, and I certainly don't remember Ella being any great beauty."

"Leona!" Uncle Lum looked as if he wanted to smother his wife. "That's an awful thing to say, and with poor Ella lying—"

"That's just it," Uncle Ernest said. "Poor Ella. She's always been such a sad creature, even when she was young—or younger. I don't think Ella was ever young. Must've been somewhere in her midthirties when she came here. Worked for a while at Horace Warren's insurance agency, but Horace never was much of a businessman, and the firm went under. Horace felt kind of responsible for Ella, I guess . . . the woman had nowhere to go, and he asked me if I could use some help."

"But forty-one years! That's going over and aboveboard, isn't it?" Aunt Leona said, ignoring her husband's scowl.

"Who else do you know who would be content to live way up here so far from town?" Uncle Ernest came close to growling. "The guesthouse was empty and Ella seemed glad to get it. Then, as she got older, I fixed up some rooms for her here. She never got in my way, and I never got in hers. Seemed to work out just fine."

That was all well and good, I thought, but it still didn't answer the question of who might have had it in for Ella Stegall. "By the way," I said, giving my scheming side full rein, "did Belinda Donahue find you yesterday? Said she planned to go by the hospital."

Uncle Ernest frowned. "Did who *what*?"

"Belinda Donahue. Did she find you at the hospital?"

He nodded, drawing on his pipe, then leaned back in his chair. "Stayed for almost an hour. It really bothered Belinda, I think, this happening to Ella that way." Uncle Ernest blinked at us over the smoke. "Didn't get along, you know."

I started to say I'd heard, but my uncle didn't give me a chance. "Guess you might as well hear this before everybody else does—bound to come out sooner or later . . . Belinda was married to Ella's younger brother back in Virginia. It wasn't a happy arrangement, but she stuck it out far longer than she should've. They had a daughter—married now and lives in Atlanta. After the daughter left home, Belinda filed for divorce and took a teaching position somewhere in North Carolina using her maiden name. Her husband never did reconcile himself to it, it seems, and according to Ella, the man grieved himself to death. Died a couple of years after that—of cancer, Belinda says, but Ella never forgave her for leaving him."

Uncle Ernest chuckled almost to himself. "You should've seen Ella's face when Belinda Donahue showed up here in Bishop's Bridge!"

"What was the matter with her husband?" Grady asked. "Was he abusive or something?"

"Abusive? No, not physically," our uncle said, "but I think

he must've been a negative sort; put her down a lot, and wouldn't let go of a dime. Belinda doesn't talk about it much, but I think she just got to where she'd had enough."

"I'll bet you thought I wouldn't remember you promised me a blackberry pie," Grady said after lunch.

He was right. I had completely forgotten the pail of berries we'd dropped on the path when we heard Ella's cry the day before, only it seemed much longer ago than that. "I doubt if they'll be any good," I said. "Most of them spilled on the ground."

But my cousin insisted we make certain, and sure enough, we discovered over half the pail still filled with blackberries. It didn't take long with both of us picking to get enough for a cobbler for supper.

"Mom says Uncle Ernest wants to go ahead with the reunion picnic tomorrow," Grady told me, untangling himself from a thorny branch. "The doctor said Ella's vital signs are stable; she might linger like this for days."

"Maybe in time she'll even recover," I said. "I wish she could at least regain consciousness long enough to tell us what happened."

Grady stuck a bleeding finger in his mouth. "She did tell you what happened. She said she was pushed, and that box you found had been shredded from the inside. Had to have been Dagwood in there."

"But what if she remembers more? Ella was in a lot of pain

when we found her—good Lord, look how far she fell! There's a chance she might have seen who pushed her."

"Even if she lives, Uncle Ernest won't be able to take care of her here," Grady said as we walked back to the house. "Spooky as she was, Uncle's going to miss her. Heck, I guess we all will! I remember when I was little, she used to make me hot chocolate." Grady laughed. "It was awful, but if you put enough marshmallows in it, you could get it down.

"Have you ever wondered what will happen to this place when Uncle Ernest goes?" he asked.

I honestly hadn't. I couldn't imagine Bramblewood without Uncle Ernest. "I don't think any of us would love it the way he does," I said, and as I spoke, I saw our uncle walking alone in the meadow. He wore an old beat-up canvas hat that was probably as old as he was, and swung his arms as he walked. Now and then he would pause and gesture at something and I could hear his laughter all the way to the orchard.

"Did you hear that, Kate?" Grady shook his head. "Looks like the old man's goin' 'round the bend. What do you suppose he's laughing about?"

"Probably just clearing his head. Sitting in a hospital waiting room all those hours has to take its toll," I said. We stood quietly until our uncle strolled out of sight, knowing he wouldn't want witnesses to such a private moment. I knew Uncle Ernest was accustomed to taking long walks and that his beloved fields and woods were like personal friends to him, but I'd never seen him talk to them before.

Back at the house we took our berries to the kitchen, where Grady put them in a colander to wash while I started on the pastry. My cousin went upstairs to change, and I was up to my elbows in flour when Uncle Ernest returned and poured two fingers of bourbon over a small glass of ice.

"Thanks, but I really don't care for any," I said, reminding him he hadn't offered.

My uncle smiled. "Sorry, Kathryn. Sometimes I forget you're all grown up now."

I noticed that he still didn't offer me anything to drink, but that was okay. Grady had the makings for margaritas in the refrigerator, and after picking berries and baking them into a cobbler, I was about ready for one.

Uncle Ernest tasted the drink and swished it around in his glass. "And where's Miss Josie?" he asked.

"Oh, she'll be here tomorrow for the reunion," I said, speaking slowly so he could hear. "She's staying with Marge for now."

"Sorry I missed her this afternoon—saw her little friend out there. Funny little thing—do you know, a fawn came right out of the woods and nuzzled her hand? I wouldn't have believed it if I hadn't seen it with my own eyes!" He took another swallow and looked pleased with himself.

"Out where?" I asked, wondering just how many drinks my uncle had tossed down. "Uncle Ernest, Josie hasn't been here since last night. She and Darby went fishing today with the youth group from Burdette's church."

He frowned. "Why, out in the meadow just now—I saw a girl. Thought she must've been a friend of Josie's since she seemed about her age—maybe a little older." My uncle laughed. "I reckon she must've been a woods sprite. Looked a lot like one of those old illustrations from a fairy-tale book. Did my heart good to hear her laugh!"

89

I turned away to put the cobbler in the oven, glad Uncle Ernest couldn't see my face. It looked like Penelope was being careless again.

"Have they found out anything about those bones they dug up this morning?" Uncle Lum asked of no one in particular as we sat on the porch after supper.

"Uncle Ernest said they don't know much of anything except they've been there for a while." Aunt Leona fanned herself with one of those old cardboard fans with Jesus blessing the children on the front that probably came from the local funeral home.

"How long is a while?" her husband wanted to know.

"Well, my goodness, Lum, how should I know? Thirty or forty years, I think he said. Maybe even longer." Leona fanned faster.

Uncle Ernest had left earlier for the hospital and the four of us had just blimped out on warm blackberry cobbler with ice cream on it—except for Aunt Leona, who only had a little doll-size helping with about a teaspoon of ice cream on top.

"I just wish they'd hurry and find out who it is," she said. "Makes me sad thinking about that poor soul lying there all those years without even a proper marker."

Grady stretched his long legs in front of him. "I'd kinda like to know who put him there," he said, "and why."

Because of the two margaritas I'd drunk earlier, I decided to stay again at Bramblewood instead of risking the steep curving road back to town. My uncle and aunt retired fairly early and Grady had some work he needed to do, so I waited downstairs reading one of Carolyn Hart's classic mysteries until Uncle Ernest came home from the hospital. I could tell even before asking that Ella was the same.

The telephone rang just as I was getting ready for bed, and I answered it quickly before it could wake my aunt and uncle. What time was it in California? Maybe Ned had taken a break from his busy agenda to check on his family on the other side of the States.

It wasn't my husband calling, but it was the next best thing.

"Mama . . ." Josie's little voice sounded lost and far away.

"Josie? Are you all right, honey? Is anything wrong?"

"No, I'm okay. It's just that everybody's asleep but me, and well . . . I just wanted to tell you good night."

I went to bed smiling. In spite of Ella's "fall" into the ravine and the Belle Fleurs Garden Club digging up old bones next door, I should sleep soundly tonight.

That was why it was hard to force myself awake a few hours later when somebody sat at the foot of my bed and jerked the covers from me.

CHAPTER NINE

For a minute I thought I was back in my own home and Josie was waking me with a nightmare. But my daughter's hair—even as light as it is—doesn't shimmer with an aura of coppery gold.

"Wake up!" Augusta said, bouncing lightly as she leaned over me. "Somebody's out there digging. Sounds like it's coming from behind the house."

I rubbed my eyes and blinked. "Maybe they're looking for fishing worms . . . I'm really tired, Augusta." I yawned and tried to roll over but she had a most unangelic grip on my arm.

"Hurry now, and try to be as quiet as you can. It wouldn't do for them to hear you." She grabbed a robe from the chair and tossed it in my direction. "Where are your shoes?"

I fumbled for them under my bed. "They just dug up bones from where there shouldn't have been any, somebody shoved poor Ella off a bluff and now you want me to *go out there in the dark*? What kind of guardian angel are you?"

Her glittering necklace winked turquoise and violet in the dusk and Augusta gave me an impatient little smile. "I'm here, aren't I?" she said. "We might never know who it is if we don't get closer. You *do* want to know, don't you?"

I grunted a yes.

It must have been just before dawn because there was barely enough light to see, and I sensed, more than felt, her small hand on my shoulder, urging me from the room. "Do jiggle a limb now, Kate, we don't have time to dawdle!" But I noticed she took time to glance at herself in the mirror as we hurried out the door.

The floor creaked as we crept down the dim hallway past rooms where my relatives slept, and from the far end of the passage, I could hear Uncle Lum's staccato snoring. Feeling my way in the dark, my hand trailed past the place where the wallpaper was beginning to peel . . . and dear God, what was that brushing against my leg? Something soft and tickly that sent shivers up my spine! I almost bit my lip to keep from yelling before I realized it was Ella's cat, Dagwood.

I kept close to Augusta as we made our way downstairs, hoping we wouldn't wake Amos, who slept on a mat by the door. If suddenly roused, the dog would go into a frenzy of barking loud enough to wake the entire household. Augusta held up a hand in warning as Amos groaned in his sleep. The angel smelled of lavender that reminded me of the dried sachets Ma Maggie kept in her linen closet, and her chiffonlike dress swirled behind her as she walked. By the light of the table lamp in the window it looked creamy white with a spray of dainty pink flowers trailing about the hem.

We slipped silently past the sleeping dog and into the

kitchen where the sound of digging seemed even louder. Crouched behind Augusta, I hesitated at the door that led to the back porch. "What on earth could anybody be looking for out there?" I whispered as Augusta edged slowly outside.

"That's what we want to find out," she said, beckoning me to follow.

The wind ruffled the leaves in the fig bush by the back steps and there was a hint of rain in the air. Augusta and I stood on the brick walk that led to the garage and listened. The noise was coming from that area of the yard Ma Maggie referred to as Rose's flower garden. My grandmother said there had once been a fence around the garden, but that was long gone. Now a straggly tangle of pines, honeysuckle and knee-high weeds surrounded a tiny, well-kept garden plot. With Augusta's prompting, I crossed the yard and hid behind the large sycamore that halfway screened the small garden from the house. I couldn't see who was digging, but now and then I did glimpse the pale beam of a flashlight. Was this the same person who ran from Parker and Burdette the night before?

A family of mosquitoes enjoyed a midnight snack on my neck and a tendril of some kind of vine whipped my ankle—at least, I hoped it was a vine. The thought of snakes crawling about my feet in the dark scared me more than being discovered by the mysterious digger.

While I quietly battled insects, the treasure hunter, or whoever he was, moved his search to another part of the overgrown garden and I saw the light flicker on and off twice as he renewed his digging. How long was the blasted man (if it *was* a man) going to pursue this ridiculous quest? And how was I ever going to get close enough to see his face? My foot was asleep and I'd made the mistake of drinking a large glass of tea with supper so I really needed to go to the bathroom! I looked for Augusta to try and signal her of my distress, but she had stationed herself under the scuppernong arbor and couldn't see my face. I don't suppose angels ever have to go to the bathroom, so naturally my discomfort would mean nothing to her. I had decided to go inside without her when a loud clap of thunder came out of nowhere and seconds later lightning sizzled in the sky. It gave me just enough light to see the silhouette of a dark figure through the trees. I flattened myself against the sycamore as the person tramped through the junglelike border of weeds and saplings and passed almost close enough to touch as he made his way to the toolshed. He wore a slouchy old hat pulled low over his forehead, and I couldn't see his face, but he smelled of bourbon and pipe tobacco. *Uncle Ernest!*

We waited until my uncle had time to put away his shovel and watched him go inside. The kitchen light came on and I knew he was making his ritual nighttime drink of something called Chocolate Comfort before retiring. It seemed to take forever before he finally turned off the light! I mentally timed Uncle Ernest getting out of his dirty clothes and washing up before going back to bed. He probably wouldn't have heard us if we'd tramped in right behind him, but we huddled under the scuppernong arbor at least fifteen minutes as raindrops as big as cherries started to fall. "Enough of this!" I whispered, shivering. They began to pelt us even faster as we finally bolted for the kitchen door. It was locked.

"Well, this is another fine mess you've gotten us into!" I said, not expecting Augusta to understand the reference.

But she did. "Laurel and Hardy!" She clapped her hands. "Oh, what fun they were! Not still around, I suppose?"

I shook my head. "What do we do now, Augusta? I really have to *go!*"

"I don't like to do this as a rule, mind you . . . but in this case . . ." Augusta disappeared from beside me, and seconds later opened the door from the inside.

Besides being rain-soaked and miserable, I was now wide awake, and while I went upstairs to change, Augusta made hot chocolate and produced from somewhere dainty jam-filled pastries dusted with powdered sugar and crisp triangles of toast that tasted of oranges.

Penelope, who had rendezvoused with raccoons and a fox or two, she said, in the orchard beyond the house, stood by the open oven drying herself from the rain. I offered a towel and a change of clothes, but she smiled and shook her head, and soon I knew why. In only seconds her bronze and gold sleeveless shift looked as if it had just come from the cleaners. She draped herself in a fringed shawl of dappled green and pulled out a chair for herself at the table, and it was a good thing I was standing beside her because, almost in slow motion, the chair began to topple.

I was able to catch it before it hit the floor, but I didn't have as much luck with the mug of chocolate that spilled in a spreading pool across the table and made a brown puddle on the faded green linoleum.

"Oh, dear! Now look what I've done!" Penelope's eyes filled with tears and her lap with hot chocolate.

I grabbed a couple of dishtowels and began to sponge her dress. "It's okay, Penelope. I expect you're just chilled from the rain. It's nothing that can't be cleaned up. It didn't burn you, did it?"

"No, but I made such a mess . . ." She looked at Augusta, whose mouth looked kind of pinched at the corners.

"It's all right, Penelope, dear, but you must try to move more slowly." Augusta's shoulders heaved as she wet a sponge at the sink. "Why don't you take care of the spilled drink on the floor and we'll see what we can do with your dress. There's more chocolate where that came from."

Later, as Penelope, soothed and dried, nursed her cup of chocolate by the stove, Augusta sat across from me at the table and sipped silently from her cup. The chocolate was dark and rich with a hint of peppermint, and the pastries tasted of raspberries.

"I don't know what to think," I said, wiping what I knew must be a milky brown mustache from my lip. "What was Uncle Ernest looking for out there? It must be something he didn't want us to know about or he wouldn't have been digging in the middle of the night. I wonder if it has something to do with the skeleton they found in the churchyard."

"Whatever it was, I'd like to know if he found it," Augusta said. "And why does your uncle keep that little garden the way he does? Surrounded by such a tangle of undergrowth, you can hardly see it from the house. Seems a shame to hide it that way—rather a sad place, don't you think?"

"My grandmother said that for the longest time he couldn't bring himself to come near it," I told her. "But it's been like it is now for as long as I can remember. Uncle Ernest takes care of it himself—won't let anyone else in there. A lot of his wife's roses are still there. Ma Maggie says it's the only part of his marriage that's still alive . . . I wonder if it's because he still loves her or just feels guilty that he couldn't make things work."

"There's one way you might shed some light on this," Augusta said, dipping her toast in chocolate. "You might just come right out and ask him."

But did I really want to know?

"I thought I heard somebody digging out back last night," I said the next morning at breakfast.

Uncle Ernest shook the salt shaker over his egg three distinct times, and the pepper twice. He didn't look up. "Did somebody make brownies or something in here?" he asked. "The whole house smelled of chocolate this morning . . . and who do I thank for those little pastries I found on the table?"

"Oh, I picked those up at a bakery," I said, pouring orange juice all around—and spilling about half of it.

"Maybe it was Casey you heard," Grady offered. "Must've come back last night: I saw him trimming the shrubbery when I went out to get the paper this morning."

"Why would Casey be digging in the middle of the night?" his mother wanted to know.

Grady shrugged. "To get an early start? Told me he was planning to mow that field behind the orchard so the children could play games this afternoon."

Every year at the reunion all the children competed in sack races and relay games in the big field where I'd seen my uncle walking the day before, and later, some of the adults joined in for a family softball game. Parker and Burdette were due over soon to help Grady set up long tables, made of boards laid across sawhorses, under the large oaks at the edge of the yard, and family members who lived out of town would be arriving all during the day with potato salad, baked ham, fried chicken and just about every kind of cake and pie I'd ever heard of— and some I hadn't.

Uncle Lum peered over his coffee cup. "Did anybody else hear that thunder last night? Sounded like a gully washer there for a while. Sure glad it moved on in time for the picnic."

Grady and I both said we'd heard it, too, but Uncle Ernest, jamming on his familiar hat, excused himself to go to the hospital.

"Mosquitoes just about chewed me alive out on the porch yesterday," Aunt Leona said as he was leaving. "Might be a good idea to ask Casey to get rid of some of those weeds around where Rose—Around the flowerbed back there. I believe they must be breeding in there."

I could have told her that.

Since my uncle was in a hurry to see about Ella, I told him I'd talk to Casey about the weeds. Frankly, I was curious about the man, plus I wanted to see where Uncle Ernest had been digging in the garden.

I found the caretaker on the riding mower behind the orchard, and even after I chased him down, the tractor made such a racket I almost had to risk being run over to get his attention. Casey Grindle was large and red-cheeked. A green-checkered shirt, open at the neck, strained over his bulging stomach, and he wore jeans and a straw hat about as big as a bushel basket. Wild gray hair stuck out from beneath it, making him look kind of like a rotund scarecrow.

While I introduced myself and explained my errand, he took the opportunity to wipe his face with a soiled hand towel. I noticed that he wore thick gardening gloves, which really didn't surprise me since Violet had said he was a writer and I supposed he would need to take care of his hands to use a computer or whatever he wrote on. He didn't look much like a writer, though—or at least my idea of one.

"You're talking about that little garden behind the house that's surrounded with all those trees?" he said. His voice was sort of scratchy like an old phonograph record. "I asked about that earlier, but he didn't seem to want anything done about it. Lot of underbrush around there."

"I know. I don't think he expects you to clean it out in one day, but maybe you can get some of the worst of it. I'll show you, if you like."

Even with Casey riding, I managed to get there first as he had to go the long way around and I cut across the yard.

It was obvious that somebody had been digging around the roses, and the dirt had been put back loosely in several places, but an excavation in a far corner of the garden was still uncovered, with a mound of dirt and grass piled beside a hole that looked to be over a foot deep and two or three times as wide.

"Your uncle intending to plant something here?" Casey asked, wading through knee-deep weeds to stand beside me.

"He hasn't mentioned it," I said. "Probably some of the children playing at digging for buried treasure."

"Or somebody meaning to bury something," he said.

I hadn't thought of that. But why dig all those holes to bury something—unless it was in several pieces? But I didn't even want to go there.

"My cousin tells me you're a writer," I said. "Do you think I might've read any of your titles?"

"Not yet, but maybe someday." He started back to the tractor. "Still trying to get published. Took a year off to see what I could do."

"Any particular genre?"

"Something in the category of historical romance, more or less," he said, swinging into the seat.

"Oh," I said. It was all I could think to say since that wasn't at all what I expected. Suspense, maybe, or even science fiction, but not romance! "Well, do join us for our picnic tonight," I said. "There'll be plenty of good food and you're welcome to come. Uncle Ernest probably hasn't had a chance to invite you after what happened to Ella."

"Yeah, that was a pretty bad thing . . . just learned about it yesterday." Casey Grindle jammed his grimy towel in a back pocket and clattered away. He never did answer about the picnic.

"We have a problem," I said to Grady when I found him practicing his putting on the shady side of the house.

He frowned. I had made him miss putting his golf ball into a circle of string. "Whatdaya mean?"

I told him about Uncle Ernest and the midnight digging.

"You think it might have something to do with that skeleton they found?" he asked.

I didn't know, but I felt as if a chunk of iron was wedged inside my chest. Neither of us wanted to mention who we thought the skeleton might be.

CHAPTER TEN

Grady tried to flip up golf balls with his wedge the way Tiger Woods does, but it didn't work too well. With one hand on my shoulder, he steered me away from the house. "Kate, surely you don't think that skeleton could be hers . . ."

"You mean Rose's? Yes, I do. I hate to say it, Grady, but do *you* know what happened to her? Does anybody? As far as I know, nobody's laid eyes on the woman since she left here—and it was about the same time somebody dumped that body in the Remeth burying ground."

My cousin thought about that for a minute. "You're right," he said finally, "but that doesn't mean *Uncle Ernest* did it! Could've been somebody else, and it might not be Rose at all. Didn't those two rafters disappear about the same time?"

"Dear God, I hope you're right! This is Uncle Ernest we're talking about! I can't imagine him doing a thing like that, but this was long before we were even born, and who knows what a person might do in a fit of jealousy—or rage. And everybody says she was beautiful. Maybe she played around. Violet thinks Judge Kidd had a crush on her."

Grady's face grew almost stormy. He ran a hand through his dark hair and bent to collect his golf balls. "We can stand here and make suppositions all day, but it doesn't prove a thing. Whatever happened to those hippie rafters? Were their bodies ever found? How come everybody's so certain they drowned?"

"They found their overturned raft and some of their belongings snagged on debris downriver," I said, "and both of them dropped out of sight—never came back."

Grady smiled that familiar "older cousin know-it-all" smile that made me want to smack him. "Would you wave your arms and yell, 'Look at me!' if you were wanted for robbing a store?"

"But from what I've heard, they never went back to their families. Even if they stayed in hiding for however long it takes for the statute of limitations to run out, you'd think they would eventually surface, wouldn't you? Or maybe you haven't heard about the statue of limitations." I slung my words hard enough to knock him cold.

He laughed instead. "Touché. Okay, so maybe they did drown. But there must've been something about it in the paper when it happened. Even a name would help. All I've ever heard were those kooky monikers."

"Great, then why don't we go down to *The Bulletin* and see what we can dig up, if you'll excuse the expression? We ought to have just enough time before all the kin start pouring in."

Grady glanced at his watch. "You forget I have to help set up grazing tables. It's almost ten now. Burdette and Parker should be getting here any minute."

And I had promised Josie I'd make homemade peach ice cream if Ma Maggie could round up her churn—which also meant I needed to stop by the store for ingredients. "I'll be back by noon," I told him, dashing into the house for my keys. "Get ready to help turn the crank!"

The Bulletin was located in a mustard-colored brick building, built around the turn of the last century, that had housed the Bank of Bishop's Bridge until they moved into an upscale stone-and-glass monstrosity a few blocks down the street. The receptionist didn't look much older than Josie, and I must have interrupted her in an especially intriguing passage of the romance novel she was reading because she seemed reluctant to put it aside.

"I wanted to look up some old issues," I said. "Do you have a morgue here?"

"A *what?*" She shifted her gum to the other side of her mouth. "Ma'am, this is a *newspaper* office. I think you must be looking for the funeral home or something."

"No, I mean a newspaper morgue—a place where they keep old issues." I tried to keep a straight face.

"Oh. Well, that's all on microfilm now. You'll have to go to the library for that." She picked up the book again.

Fine. But I hadn't the faintest idea of the year the rafters had disappeared.

"Is Mr. Hollingsworth still here?" I asked, referring to the editor who had been there when I was in high school.

"He's semiretired now. Only comes in twice a week."

"Then do you know when he'll be in?" I asked, resisting the urge to look at my watch. The morning was already half-gone.

She looked at me as if I had my head on backwards. "Oh, he's in—or I reckon he is; saw him getting coffee 'bout an hour ago."

I followed the woman's pointing finger to a small office in the back where I found Charles Hollingsworth reared back in his chair, eyes closed, with his hands across his chest. He looked a bit thinner, and a lot grayer than I remembered. The door was open, but I knocked anyway and he leapt to his feet and invited me in, seeming glad of the company.

"I know who you are," he said when I started to introduce myself. "Look just like your old man . . . and how's England? Any baby news yet?"

I smiled and shook my head. Sometimes I forget just how small Bishop's Bridge is! "I'm hoping you can help me," I said, and told him about Burdette unearthing the skeleton in Remeth churchyard. "My cousin and I were wondering if it might be one of the rafters who disappeared on the river some-time back in the sixties, but we aren't sure of the year."

The old editor smiled. "Front-page news, that skeleton! Bishop's Bridge hasn't had a story like that since . . . well, probably since those two young rafters disappeared. Bo Crane was all over it yesterday—you probably don't know our reporter, Bo; came here after you left." He leaned back in his chair and laughed. "The man made enough pictures to paper a house! 'Course the police wouldn't tell him much—probably because they don't know much."

"They didn't tell us anything, either," I said, "but Burdette said they think it must've been there close to forty years and

106

that would've been about when the two rafters were supposed to have drowned."

"By golly, you're right! You just might have something there." The man who had been dozing a few minutes before came to life as if somebody had plugged him in. "And I'm fairly sure of the date, too, because it was the year after I came here; happened around the time Christine and I married because I remember everybody talking about it at all the parties." He frowned. "Never did find 'em, but we kept gnawing on the subject until the story—and the interest—finally fizzled. Can't be sure of the exact date, but it was toward the end of July."

The editor's lean face took on a look that can only be described as cunning, and he lowered his voice a notch. "Mind if an old man comes along? I'd like to get a look at those back issues, too."

I had a feeling young Bo Crane was about to be scooped.

A walk around the block and a few minutes later, we found the news item we were looking for.

> Local authorities are puzzled by the discovery of an overturned, partially deflated raft on a branch of the Yakdin River this week. The raft matches the description of one reported stolen several days ago from a vacation cottage belonging to Stanley Hardin of Elkin.
>
> A spokesperson for the Bishop's Bridge Police, near where the raft was found, said it might have been taken by a young couple suspected of robbing a store near Dobson earlier this month.
>
> Quincy Puckett, 19, calling himself Shamrock, and a young woman known by the aliases Vanessa Doyle, Valerie Dutton and Waning Crescent, are feared drowned while fleeing police.

We scrolled carefully through successive issues reading follow-up stories, many written by Charles Hollingsworth himself, but learned nothing further about the two except that they were believed to have come from somewhere in Ohio.

"So, do you think one or both of them might still be alive?" I said. *Please let it be just one!*

He nodded, watching the film rewind. "It's possible. I hounded the police about that case for a couple of years after they found that raft. They dredged up some shoes they thought might've belonged to the boy, and several items of women's clothing."

"Anything else turn up?" I asked.

My companion held the door for me as we stepped out onto the sidewalk and I could feel the heat from the pavement through the flimsy soles of my sandals. "Not to my knowledge," he answered. "Seemed to me as if they more or less abandoned the case. After all, these people were hippies—folks here didn't think much of that sort then—and they were suspected of breaking the law. I got the feeling the police just figured it was good riddance!"

He waved to Roselyn Davis, who was arranging a sales rack in front of her dress shop across the street, and stopped to admire a display of fishing gear in the window of Woods 'n Water Sporting Goods, but I could tell something was on his mind.

"Those two were somebody's children," he went on. "Somebody's brother, sister, niece, nephew. I can't believe their families didn't pursue it."

"Maybe they did," I said. We walked to where I had left my

car in the semishade of a crape myrtle in front of the old yellow building. "How can we find out?"

Charles Hollingsworth shook my hand as we said good-bye. "Tell you what—give me an hour or so and let me see what I can come up with. Friend of mine has a son on the police force here—nice kid. Maybe he'll help us out."

It was close to noon when I looked at the clock on my dashboard, so I drove straight to Marge's, hoping to catch them before they left for Bramblewood.

I was in luck.

I found my cousin loading the family van with containers of marinated slaw, pimento cheese sandwiches and her wonderful blueberry pound cake.

"Hi!" she yelled, juggling a stack of shifting boxes. "You just missed her."

"Missed who?" I rescued a relish tray and what looked like a week's supply of peanut butter cookies.

"Ma Maggie. Said she was tired of waiting for you to come and get the ice-cream churn, so she's taking it to Bramblewood with her."

"Which means I'd better get my act together—and I haven't even been to the store," I said. "Josie can help me shop; actually, she's better at it than I am."

"I'll holler for her," Marge said. "She and the boys have made up some kind of silly game where you have to talk backward. Even Hartley has gotten into the act. Listen . . ."

Even from where I stood, I could hear the four of them laughing upstairs.

My cousin put a hand on my shoulder and practically shoved me inside. "But first, let's grab a few minutes to talk while we can. You've got a cloud hanging over you as dark as the inside of a chimney. What's going on, Kate McBride?"

What I had to say would take longer than a few minutes, but I explained as quickly as I could that the distance between Ned and me amounted to more than miles. "He won't admit it, but I think he blames me for losing the baby, Marge."

My cousin stood across the kitchen table from me and brushed the hair from her face the way she usually does when she's thinking. Finally she shook her head. "Ned has more sense than that. Have you two seen a counselor?"

"I talked to someone, but he wasn't interested. I tried to get him to go with me, but Ned said he didn't need it. Frankly, I don't think he wanted me to go, either. He doesn't even seem to care." I felt hot, tattletale tears getting ready to start their run. "And so why should *I*?" I said.

"Don't give up on him, Kate." Marge reached out and took my hand. "What you have is too good to throw away, but it sounds like you might need somebody to help you through this. Burdette can probably recommend a—"

Just then Hartley came in crying that the others wouldn't let him play, so I didn't get a chance to tell her about Uncle Ernest's midnight digging. That would have to wait.

On our way to Bramblewood, Josie and I stopped at J & G Groceries for whipping cream, peaches and ice cream salt and, on impulse, I also grabbed a couple of cartons of eggs. I haven't been to a family picnic yet where they didn't serve deviled eggs, and Josie even agreed to help me boil them.

"Are you having a good time with Darby and Jon?" I asked as we wound back up the mountain.

"Yeah! They have this old board game where you have to figure out the murderer and the weapon and everything, 'cept Cudin' Bird always wins. I wish we did stuff like that at our house."

Clue . . . I wished it would be that easy to find out who was responsible for the skeleton next door. "But we play games," I reminded her, naming a few. My husband's favorite was crazy eights.

"When?" She looked up at me.

"Why, almost every night at the beach. Don't you remember? We played—"

"But Dad wasn't there."

I didn't have an answer for that.

A police car was leaving as we turned into the drive at Bramblewood and I wondered if they had learned any more about the skeleton. Uncle Ernest stood on the front steps with an unlit pipe in his teeth and I could tell by the look of him he wasn't in the mood for questions. Josie and I went in the back way.

We found Ma Maggie, Cousin Violet and Aunt Leona congregated in the kitchen, and from the pitch of their voices, it sounded as if all three wanted to be in charge.

"I'm telling you, we don't need any more sugar in that tea!" Cousin Violet was saying. "Why do you have to be so dad-blasted stubborn?" This was directed at my grandmother.

Ma Maggie turned her back and checked something in the oven. It smelled like baked beans. "I'm just telling you what I think . . . and what you should think, too!" she said.

"Some people prefer unsweetened tea." Aunt Leona didn't look up as she sliced cantaloupe into a large blue bowl. "In fact, I think we have entirely—"

"Has anybody heard about Ella?" I asked, finding space for my purchases on the counter.

"Some better, I believe," Leona said, "but still in intensive care. Uncle Ernest says she seems to be coming out of it, but she's still not coherent."

"We passed a police car when we turned in the driveway," I said, looking for a pot for the eggs. "Any news about . . ." I glanced at Josie. ". . . about what they found yesterday?"

"Oh, I know all about the skeleton, Mom." My daughter filled the pan with water at the sink and carefully put the eggs in one by one.

"They just wanted to talk to Ernest," my grandmother said. "Don't know what they expected him to tell them."

"Must've told them something because they spoke for a good while." Violet searched for just the right cookie on the platter she'd brought and ate a chocolate one. "I saw them talking with that man Casey, too, although I don't know why they'd bother with him. Been here less than a year."

Ma Maggie frowned. "What on earth's he doing around Rose's old garden? Looks like he's been digging out there."

"Kate asked him to get rid of some of the weeds—thank

112

goodness!" Leona said. "Looks like a jungle out there! Breeding place for chiggers, and probably snakes, too. He said a lot of those old roses needed fertilizer, too, and a couple of them had black spot real bad, but he thought he might be able to save them."

My grandmother's face went stiff. "And what did you say?"

Leona shrugged. "I said, 'Go to it,' of course. I know he tries, but Uncle Ernest is getting too old to take care of that plot like he used to, and besides, why hire a caretaker if you're not going to let him take care of things?"

"Ernest won't like it," Ma Maggie said. And she was right. Later, when I took my turn with the ice-cream churn out on the back porch, I heard Uncle Ernest telling Casey he wasn't to bother with that part of the yard anymore. He didn't yell or sound mean or anything, but my uncle spoke with a tightness in his voice that signaled red.

I wondered what was out there in that old garden he didn't want anybody to find.

CHAPTER ELEVEN

*B*elinda Donahue noticed the difference right away when she showed up later that afternoon with a huge pot of something so heavy it took both Uncle Lum and Grady to carry it from the car.

"Why, I've never even noticed this pretty little garden back here before," she said, pausing to sniff a yellow-pink blossom. "Was there a fence or something around it?"

"Just straggly old trees and waist-high weeds," Aunt Leona said, following her into the kitchen. "What's in the pot?"

"Chicken bog. It's an old South Carolina recipe. My mother came from there, you know."

"Ours, too," Cousin Violet said, lifting the lid. "Or at least our grandmother did. Charleston, wasn't it, Maggie?"

My grandmother was on her hands and knees rattling things in the kitchen cabinets. "Now, where in the world do you suppose Ella put that big green glass fruit bowl?" She frowned at Violet over her shoulder. "What was that about Charleston?"

"Our grandmother, Nannie Jane! Wasn't she from South Carolina? Remember how Nannie used to make chicken bog?"

Violet glared at what she saw in the pot. "Why, this has *tomatoes* in it! I never in my life heard of putting tomatoes in chicken bog. Chicken and rice—maybe a little onion—cooked in seasoned chicken stock. Now *that's* chicken bog!"

"Smells fine to me." Uncle Lum inhaled deeply and winked at Belinda, who looked as though she might be counting under her breath. "Don't believe I've ever met a chicken bog I didn't like."

"And what do you know about it, Columbus Roundtree?" Violet clanged the lid on the pot and poked him with a magenta-nailed finger.

"Oh, I reckon I know a little bit—for an old fart."

Aunt Leona almost dropped a bowl of slaw. "For heaven's sakes, Lum, do you really have to be so crude?"

But Grady laughed. "If Dad's an old fart, what does that make you, Mom?"

"Guess it makes her an old fartress," his father said, ducking out the door.

Ma Maggie gave both of them a withering look as she sighed and rose to her feet. "Belinda, if you don't mind, would you give me a hand with the cloths for the picnic tables? I think Ella keeps them in that wicker chest in the laundry room."

"I know where they are, Maggie. I'll get them," Violet offered, distancing herself from the offending chicken bog. But my grandmother, obviously upset by Violet's rudeness, ignored her.

Belinda, clearly distressed by the turn of events, didn't seem to know which way to go. "Why don't I gather some of those gorgeous roses?" she said with a forced brightness in her voice. "We can use them on the tables."

My cousin Violet crossed her arms. "Those are Rose's flowers. Ernest never lets anyone cut them."

"Then it's time he did," Leona said, with a hand on Belinda's arm. "Come on; I'll help you round up some vases."

The telephone rang just then and I was relieved when Grady, who had rushed to answer it, said it was for me.

"I'm afraid we've run into a blank wall," a man's voice said.

"What?" I was so distressed by Violet's scene in the kitchen, the person might as well have been speaking Greek.

"Charles Hollingsworth. About those two who were supposed to have drowned here back in the sixties . . . Ron Vickers at the police department tracked down the brother of the young man. Took some doing, but with computers it's a whole lot easier than it used to be."

"So, what did you find out?"

"Not much," he said. "Quincy Puckett's brother still lives in Ohio; says his parents died several years ago, still hoping the guy would turn up, but he never did."

"What about the girl?" I asked.

"The Puckett fellow didn't know much about her. Said she was somebody his brother took up with after he left home. Her real name, though, was Valerie Dutton, and she came from some little town outside of Baltimore."

"Would anybody there know what happened to her?" I *wanted* that skeleton to belong to one of those people. And I wanted to let Uncle Ernest off the hook.

"I doubt it," Charles Hollingsworth said. "Not after all this time. Her family left there a year or so after that happened. She had two or three sisters, I think, but they're all scattered now. Don't even know if any of them are still alive—much less where to find them."

"So I guess that's that." I gripped the receiver as if I could squeeze some hope from it. "Do you think it could've been one of them they unearthed over at Remeth?"

"Could've been," he said. "I asked if the skeleton belonged to a man or a woman, but didn't get to first base. Police are being closemouthed about that." He paused. "Curious. And then there's that peculiar thing about the Briscoe girl. She was about your age, wasn't she?"

"Beverly? We were close friends all through school, but sort've grew apart when we went away to college." I didn't mention that Grady's anguish over their breaking up was partially responsible for that. "What do you mean *peculiar*? You're talking about her accident, I suppose?" I asked, curious as to why he used that particular adjective.

"That's what we all assumed it was, but the police seem to think differently now. Looks like somebody might've tampered with the brakes."

"Not Beverly . . . but this happened way back in—when was it? February? Why are they just now suspecting she might have been . . ." I couldn't bring myself to say the word.

"Kate." I could hear him breathe. "Beverly's car missed the curve at a—well, an extremely steep precipice. The car fell—"

"Oh." I leaned against the wall in the small alcove where the telephone sat on a recessed shelf. I didn't want to hear any more. "Does anyone else know this?" *Does Grady?* If not, I didn't want to be the one to tell him.

"I doubt it. They just got the report from the police up there. Naturally they're investigating anyone she might've been in touch with, family, close friends . . ."

"Do they have any idea who might be responsible?" I couldn't imagine why anyone would want to kill Beverly. She had always been a little on the shy side, and during our school days was a serious student, active in the Latin Club, Junior Science Society—things like that. In fact, my mother had encouraged our friendship because she thought Beverly would be a steadying influence on me.

"I hate to be the bearer of bad news," he was saying, and I nodded, as if he could see me over the phone. I felt as if we were losing Beverly twice.

"You look like a rabbit ran over your grave. What's wrong?" Marge came in from outside with a squirming Hartley under one arm and what looked like a change of clothing in the other. "Been here less than an hour and he's already found every mud puddle on the place!"

"It's Beverly," I whispered, following her into the bathroom where she began to strip and scrub her youngest. "They're saying it might not have been an accident." I told her what I had just heard from Charles Hollingsworth.

"Dear God! Why would anybody do a thing like that? Does Grady know?" Ignoring his protests, Marge ran a washcloth over Hartley's dirt-smeared face.

"I don't think so. I'm pretty sure he doesn't. He and his dad were ganging up on Aunt Leona in the kitchen a while ago."

"About what?"

"Not much of anything," I said. "I think they were just trying to lighten things up a little." And I told her of Violet's irrational behavior.

"What you reckon's gotten into her? She scatted outside a while ago looking like she'd just laid a square egg!"

"Maybe she's jealous," I said.

Marge frowned. "Of Belinda?"

"More like she just out and out resents her. Uncle Ernest has been without anybody all these years—just like Violet. No spouse, no children—only I never thought it bothered Uncle Ernest that much, once you got past the 'Rose Memorial Garden.'"

"I never thought it mattered to Violet, either. At least, not until now." My cousin toweled her son dry, stuffed him into clean clothes and gave him a pat on the rear. "Try to stay out of the mud until after we eat!" she called as he ran outside, slamming the screen door behind him.

Now she gathered Hartley's soiled clothing into a bundle. "I'm still in shock about Beverly. Do they have any idea who did it?"

"You know what I know," I told her. "But, now that I think of it, when I saw Bev at Ellie Holcomb's drop-in last Christmas, she did mention something about a weird neighbor."

"What do you mean, weird? What'd she say?"

"Just that she'd be glad to be finished with the requirements for her degree and come back to North Carolina. I got the idea she didn't like the place where she was living."

"How so?" Marge paused in the hallway and looked around, probably to be sure Grady wasn't nearby.

"It was a dinky little apartment stuck in the middle of nowhere, but Bev said it was all she could afford. She said she hardly saw any of the other tenants except for this one weird guy who kept asking her out."

Hearing Aunt Leona and Belinda Donahue talking as they clattered about in the kitchen, I lowered my voice. "You know how nice Beverly was—didn't want to just come right out and tell the guy she wasn't interested. She said she was running out of excuses."

"Kate, you should mention that to the police," Marge said. "The man was probably harmless, but it could be important."

"You're right. Maybe I should—"

"What's with all this whispering going on? Maybe you should what?" Grady came in from outside with an empty tray in his hands. "Ma Majesty is ready for the condiments now," he said, heading for the kitchen.

"Kate and I were just saying we should've thought of the croquet set," Marge said. "Remember how we all used to play? I'll bet that old thing is still in the attic." She turned to me. "Do you have time to—"

"I'll look," I said, eager to escape to somewhere peaceful and boring—even if it was 110 degrees up there.

Marge gave me a look that meant, *Call now!* "Then I'll give Grady a hand," she said. "Where's another tray?"

As soon as they were gone, I hurried to leave a message with the dispatcher at the police station who promised to have Ron Vickers return my call. Frankly, I hoped Grady wouldn't learn of it until after the picnic. Having a skeleton turn up next door, not to mention what happened to Ella, had made everyone jumpy. But I still had trouble believing somebody had deliberately sabotaged Beverly's car.

Only a dim bulb illuminated the enclosed stairs to the attic, and I didn't even want to know the last time they had been swept. As children, Beverly and I had sometimes played dress-up here while Ma Maggie visited downstairs with her brother. Now I pictured my friend at eight or nine prancing about in a trailing dress with flounces, a floppy hat trimmed in faded pink flowers, and something caught in my throat. It wasn't dust.

During college, Beverly had spent summers away as a counselor at science camp, or interning with special programs in her field, and we rarely saw each other. Other than our brief conversation last Christmas, we hadn't seen each other in years. Now, I wished I had made more of an effort to keep in touch. I hesitated at the top of the stairs, glad of an opportunity to compose myself before all the relatives descended on us. My hand was reaching for the doorknob when I heard a muffled thump, and it was coming from the attic!

I did an abrupt about-face and started down, trying to creep as quietly as possible. If the person who had pushed Ella was hiding in the attic, I didn't want to meet him. Or her?

As luck would have it, I picked that particular time to sneeze.

CHAPTER TWELVE

*K*ate, is that you?"

I had made it about halfway down the stairs on wobbly legs when the attic door opened above me and I turned to see Augusta standing there. "Penelope had a bit of an accident with a rocking chair," she said. "Wasn't as sturdy as it seemed, I'm afraid."

I was so relieved to see her there, I didn't care if Penelope had broken every chair in the attic. "It's okay," I said, and sneezed again. "What are you doing up there?"

Augusta stepped back to allow me to enter. "With all your relatives descending, it seemed as good a place to dangle as any." She made room for me on a straight-backed bench I remembered seeing in my uncle's upstairs hall.

"Dangle?" I lifted a brow.

"Dangle, yes. To be suspended, such as when you're only destroying time."

I smiled. "You're *hanging*, you mean; or *hanging out*." I decided to pass on her version of killing time.

Augusta let that go by with a nod. "I see another carload has arrived," she said, moving to the open window. "And by the way, what are you doing up here? Hiding from kin?"

"In a way," I said. "Actually, I'm supposed to be looking for a croquet set." I went over to stand beside her, surprised at how comfortable it was up here with a cross breeze between the two open windows. This part of the attic was shaded by a large white oak whose branches brushed the rooftop. Looking down I recognized bossy Great-aunt Geraldine and her two meek daughters, who had driven all the way from Surrey County and a slew of South Carolina cousins from my great-grandmother's side.

"I believe I saw a croquet set over there behind that old wardrobe," Augusta said, making her way across the room. "I always loved that game. Did you know that if your ball hits someone else's, you can put your foot on your ball and whack the other one into the next county!" She laughed as she gave her purple pleated skirt a twitch; the loose tunic, printed in a pastel floral pattern, floated about her when she walked.

"That's not a very angelic way to behave," I told her as I dragged out the old wooden set and wiped it off with a piece of torn blanket.

"So, why did you really come up here, Kate?" Augusta seemed to be studying me as I looked about for the rusty wickets.

I glanced at Penelope, happily rummaging through the contents of an old trunk set back under the eaves, and lowered my voice. "I feel like I'm sinking over my head in muddy water," I said, and told her what I'd learned about Beverly's death.

"We don't know if that had anything to do with what's taking place here." Augusta's words were calming, but I wasn't calmed. Her eyes, I noticed, held a not-so-sure expression.

"And Uncle Ernest isn't himself at all—why was he digging in the garden last night? He doesn't like anyone to go in there, either. Jumped all over poor Casey this morning. Frankly, I'm beginning to wonder if there's something buried there."

"Do you think your uncle is hiding something?" Augusta trailed her finger along the surface of a streaky mirror.

"What else are we to think? And I'm not so sure I want to know what it is."

"What do you think it is?" Augusta asked.

"Something of Rose's . . . or Rose herself—unless that was Rose they uncovered in the churchyard." I shuddered. "What an awful thought! I can't believe I'm saying it—and of Uncle Ernest, too, who's never been anything but . . . well, Uncle Ernest. And the police were here this morning questioning him for the longest time.

"Augusta, I don't like this one bit. I'm worried. I'll admit, he's a bit peculiar, but I can't imagine him being party to something grisly."

I gathered the wickets, most of which were made from bent coat hangers, and counted the croquet balls. It was amazing all eight of them were still there after fifty years or more. I knew I should go downstairs and set up the game, but I wasn't in any hurry to join my family now congregating on the lawn.

"I wish I'd never come to this reunion," I said. "My parents are in England, my husband's on the other side of the country and now everything here seems to be falling apart. Even Violet, usually the best-natured one of the lot, has taken a nasty turn." I told Augusta about my cousin's recent hostility toward Belinda Donahue.

"But you *are* here." Augusta looked at me with her steady, turquoise gaze and ran the bright stones of her necklace through her fingers. "You can't choose your family, but you can choose how you interact with them, and just now I think they could use your support."

I was going to tell her I had trouble enough trying to be strong for my daughter and myself without bearing somebody else's burdens. Besides, hadn't she, herself, warned me to be careful? What did she expect of me?

Penelope chose that moment to twirl our way in a rust-streaked rose taffeta cape and green fringed scarf she had dragged from the trunk. Her simple calico dress in a patchwork of brown and gold made an odd contrast to the once-elegant garments.

Augusta and I both dived to rescue a ceramic umbrella stand that tottered as Penelope whirled by.

"Look what I found! I wonder who it belonged to." The piece of jewelry Penelope held was tarnished almost black and appeared to be a bracelet of some kind.

"Where did you find it?" Augusta steadied the stand, now layered with dust, and held out a hand for the trinket.

"In the trunk. It must have been wrapped in this scarf because it fell out when I put it around me. The scarf was all wadded up in the bottom." Penelope's eyes grew even wider. "I didn't do anything wrong, did I?"

"Not as long as you put everything back the way you found it," Augusta said, holding the bracelet to the light.

"It doesn't look like anything valuable," I said. "It's an ID bracelet—silver, I think."

"ID?" Augusta passed it along to me.

"Identification—only this looks a little small for that." I looked at it closer, trying to make out the name engraved on the front. "Must be an anklet. You still see them once in a while, but I think they used to be popular years ago. Mom has one in her jewelry box." I rubbed a finger over the tarnish. "Can you make out the name?"

Together we studied it closely while Penelope dug for more treasure. "Starts with a V," Augusta said finally. "V-a-l-e-r . . . something."

"Valerie." We had removed enough tarnish to see the lettering now. "That was the name of the girl who was supposed to have drowned in the river before I was even born," I said. "What is her anklet doing in Uncle Ernest's attic?"

Augusta weighed the anklet in her hand and studied it for a minute. "I'm not sure," she said, "but I think the best thing to do right now is to see what else might be in that trunk, then put this back where Penelope found it."

Shaking each garment carefully, we searched through the trunk's contents of dresses spotted with age, crumpled shoes that looked as though they might have been worn in the 1930s and even a dance program that had belonged to my great-grandmother dated April 18, 1922. I coughed as I tried to fan away the suffocating musty smell. "I don't see a thing in here that might be related to that jewelry," I said. "It doesn't fit with the rest of this stuff. Looks like somebody put it in here at a later time."

"And wrapped it in that scarf so it wouldn't be easily found." Augusta had a question in her eyes, but I didn't have the answer.

She tucked the anklet back inside the folds of the shawl and we replaced all the contents as neatly as we could—including the taffeta cape, which Penelope reluctantly surrendered.

I was trying to find room for the last item, a smushed cloche hat with a drooping feather, when we heard screaming from the lawn below.

From the attic window I could see in the distance a figure running toward the house but the heavy leaves of the oak were partially blocking my view, and I shifted to get a better position. It was a woman, small and blonde, and she seemed to be batting at the air as she ran. Belinda Donahue. Soon others were hurrying toward her from every direction. Burdette raced from the front of the house, then Marge and Grady, carrying a huge picnic hamper between them, dropped it and ran to meet her, trailed by Aunt Leona clutching what looked like a pitcher of tea. Uncle Ernest followed, skinny legs tottering at this unaccustomed pace. But it was Casey who reached her first.

Snatching a cloth from one of the tables, the caretaker first flapped it at Belinda, then wrapped her in it, squirming and kicking, and picked her up in his arms.

By the time I raced downstairs he had carried her to the porch where, still partially shrouded, she struggled to raise herself to a sitting position on the wicker settee. I saw three or four red welts on her face and at least two on her arm as she reached out to Uncle Ernest.

"My purse . . . oh, hurry, please!" Belinda's voice was thin and raspy and she seemed to be pointing to the living room. "The kit—it's in my purse . . ."

Uncle Ernest slid in behind her and propped her against his chest. "Her kit—she's highly allergic to bee stings! She needs her kit *now*!"

Ma Maggie leaned over her. "Where is it, Belinda? Where did you leave it?"

"In there—table by door. Please hurry." Belinda's face was pale and she seemed to be having trouble breathing while Marge rushed inside to look for the kit.

Great-aunt Gertrude, red-faced and puffing, pushed her way through the crowd. "Somebody *do* something!" she shouted. "Call an ambulance! Call nine-one-one! Does anybody know CPR?"

Three or four people tried to crowd in the door after Marge, while Leona, who I suppose was trying to be helpful, wormed her way through them to bring Belinda a glass of water.

"She can't swallow," Uncle Ernest told her. "Her throat's closing up!"

"I think I might have some Benadryl out in the car," Burdette said, taking the steps two at a time.

Marge came back outside just then, looking as if she might be having trouble breathing herself. "It's not there," she told Belinda. "Are you sure that's where you put it?"

Belinda answered with a definite nod of her head. The fear in her eyes was contagious. I felt like a chicken running in a circle. Something terrible was happening, and I didn't know what to do about it.

"We've looked everywhere," Grady told her, and Uncle Lum nodded. "I checked the kitchen, dining room—even the downstairs bedroom. What color is her handbag?"

"Blue," Ma Maggie said. "Straw with yellow flowers. I saw it when she came in."

The children, attracted by all the excitement, gathered on the steps.

"Have any of you seen a blue straw purse with yellow flowers?" I asked them. "*Think!* This is an emergency."

Josie spoke up. "I think I saw something like that a while ago. Hartley was playing with it."

"Where is Hartley?" Marge said. "I left him playing with Amos under the pecan tree not five minutes ago."

Except for Uncle Ernest and Ma Maggie, who remained to try to calm Belinda, everybody—including me—scattered, calling Hartley's name.

"He couldn't have gone far!" Marge raced past me, panting. "Said he was going to make Amos look pretty."

"Hartley!" I yelled again, then pointed as a little face emerged from the bushes by the side of the house. "There he is!"

"Where is the blue pocketbook, Hartley?" Marge said, stooping beside him, and I could tell she was struggling to stay calm. "The one you were playing with. We need it now. What have you done with it?"

Hartley, who had started to cry, pointed to the shrubbery behind him. "It's in there—in the cave—just where I found it."

Burdette, who had had some emergency medical training, quickly injected the antidote of epinephrine, and when Belinda felt a little stronger, Ma Maggie took her inside to tend to her stings. Uncle Ernest had tried to persuade her to go to the hospital, but Belinda waved him away, saying they wouldn't do anything that hadn't already been done. The rest of us gathered on and around the porch, looking as if we'd raced ten miles in the hot sun. Casey, whom I had noticed standing at a distance during the frantic moments before, turned and started to walk away.

Uncle Ernest, seeing him, braced himself against the stone porch column and called out, "Hey! Just a minute there!"

He meant to thank Casey, I thought, for his quick actions in helping Belinda. I was wrong.

"Just a damn minute!" my uncle bellowed. "I told you Belinda was allergic to bee stings. You were supposed to get rid of those yellow jacket nests."

"I didn't know it was there," Casey mumbled, shaking his head. "Thought I got them all. I really feel terrible about this."

"You damn well should," Uncle Ernest said. "The woman could've died—almost did."

"He was just trying to help," Grady told him. "Belinda asked him where she could find some wildflowers. There's Queen Anne's lace and daisies all over the place in that field down there."

"And a nest full of yellow jackets." Still glaring, my uncle shook his head.

"I'm sorry. It's a big place and I haven't had time to get to that area yet. I thought the flowers down there would look sort of pretty for the picnic and all." Casey looked as though he might cry. I felt sorry for him.

"Hell, man, I didn't hire you to think," Uncle Ernest said.

I had heard about enough. "Maybe you didn't notice it, Uncle Ernest, but if Casey hadn't wrapped Belinda in that tablecloth and rushed her to the house, it might've been worse than it was."

His only answer was a grunt, but at least he turned and went into the house, slamming the screen door behind him. Casey shook his head and walked away.

"I'm sorry!" I called after him, and Burdette, who with the rest of us had witnessed the scene, hurried after him to apologize, I hoped, for our uncle's behavior.

Marge jumped to her feet. "I'm going to have a word or two with Hartley Cranford," she muttered.

Hartley, playing in the yard with the others, saw her coming and started to run away, but his mother, who had longer legs than he did, soon caught up with him and marched him to the porch.

"I thought you knew better than to take something that doesn't belong to you," she began in a voice that scared even me. "Can you tell me why you took Ms. Donahue's purse off the table?"

"I didn't." Tears spilled down Hartley's cheeks and I wanted to comfort him but didn't dare.

"Then how did you come by it?" his mother persisted. "Tell me the truth now, Hartley. It didn't get behind those bushes by itself."

"But it *was* there! I found it back in the cave under some leaves. I was just going to make Amos look pretty, Mama."

Burdette, who had returned in time to hear the last of this, lifted his son to his knee. "Hartley, this is very important now, son. I want you to look me in the eye and tell me the truth. Did you take Ms. Donahue's purse off the table?"

Hartley smeared away a tear. "I *am* telling the truth. I'll show you where I found it."

Several of us followed as Hartley led us to his little "cave" behind the bushes around the side of the house. "It was right here," he said, stomping on a pile of leaves. "I saw part of it sticking out."

Darby and Jon, followed by Josie and some of the other children, raced up just then tugging an embarrassed Amos by the collar. "Wait till you see this!" Jon called out, laughing. "Amos has been to the beauty parlor."

Pink lipstick had been smeared all around the dog's mouth and the sight of it brought a welcome laugh.

"I really don't think that's his color," Grady said as the dog tried to slink away. "Poor Amos! I think I can get most of that off with soap and water, but you might have a rosy smile for a while."

"I guess I'll be buying Belinda a new lipstick," Marge said, smiling for the first time in a while.

"Do you think Hartley's telling the truth?" I whispered as we walked back to the house together.

My cousin nodded solemnly. "Hartley might try to get away with fibbing to me," she said, "but he would never lie to his daddy."

"I can't believe somebody would deliberately take that purse and hide it, knowing Belinda was allergic to bee stings. How would they know she was going to wade into a nest of yellow jackets?"

"Beats me," Marge admitted, "but as I said before, it didn't get there by itself."

CHAPTER THIRTEEN

Deedee, who had turned up her nose at the vases Ma Maggie and Belinda had provided, arranged wildflowers in a fruit jar and tied a red-checked bow at the top. I had to admit it looked kind of pretty.

Now she set the jar in the middle of the serving table and stepped back to admire her handiwork. "I think Marge and Burdette need to keep an eye on that little Hartley," she said, looking around to see if they were nearby. "First he took Belinda's purse, and then told an out-and-out lie. They should be grateful the woman didn't die."

"We're all grateful for that," I said. "The child is three years old, Deedee. I seem to remember your throwing a green apple at me when you were a lot older than that. It gave me a black eye."

"You nearly ruined my favorite doll," my cousin said. "I saw you dunk her in the birdbath. Her hair never looked the same."

"I was baptizing her," I said. Actually, it had been Marge's idea but I didn't say so. Marge was already on Deedee's black list, it seemed.

Deedee adjusted the bow and gave it a fluff, as if dismissing the subject. "Still, they need to take that child in hand. I think they actually *believed* him."

"I believe him, too," I said.

This was met with silence that weighed a ton. I put plastic dinnerware in a napkin-covered basket and waved a fly from a bowl of watermelon rind preserves. Josie and Darby, along with some of their cousins, tried to snitch cookies from the dessert table and I chased them off, as well. "We'll eat in about ten minutes. You don't want to ruin your dinner!"

Of course, they did. A meal of desserts would suit them fine, but I had to say it anyway, as my mother had, and her mother before her.

Behind us, cousins, aunts and uncles sipped drinks and chatted in lawn chairs in the shade of oak trees that had been there so long even the oldest could remember playing beneath them. Our uncle's neighbor, Judge Kidd (I was almost a teenager before I learned his real name *wasn't* Goat), offered fifty dollars to anyone who would ride Shortcake—an obvious dig at Uncle Ernest, who ignored him. Belinda, ensconced in a lounge chair, was being tended by Uncle Ernest on one side and Ma Maggie and Aunt Leona on the other. Burdette, Parker and some of the others had made themselves comfortable on the porch while Uncle Lum wandered through the crowd taking pictures with the new camera Aunt Leona said cost entirely too much.

Now Deedee moved up to stand beside me. "You're joking,

of course." She spoke in a low voice, as if someone might be listening over her shoulder.

"No, I'm not."

"I can't believe you're saying that. There's no way that handbag could've been accidently dropped behind those bushes. How else could it have gotten there?" My cousin let out a sigh heavy as a rain cloud and reached past me to begin uncovering the dishes. "Surely you don't believe somebody took that bag on purpose? Just which of our relatives do you think would do a thing like that?"

I didn't answer but I had one in mind.

"Did you happen to notice who was conspicuously absent during all that panic about Belinda?" I asked Marge as we helped ourselves to Cousin Emma's sweet potato bread and Great-aunt Gertrude's bread and butter pickles.

We carried our plates to a spot of shade a little away from the rest and sat on the grass. Long shadows scalloped the lawn and there was just enough breeze to keep it from being hot.

She nodded. "I assume you mean Violet. Says she was in the kitchen the whole time and didn't realize what was going on." Marge bit into a drumstick and licked her fingers.

"I know she's always been a little dipsy, but she wouldn't deliberately hurt anyone. I know she wouldn't . . . would she?"

"Is this a private party or can anybody join in?" Grady stood beside us with a plate heaped with more food than anybody had a right to eat.

"Pull up a patch of grass and sit down," I told him. "We were just talking about Violet."

Grady started in on his potato salad. "What about her?"

I reminded him about Violet's catty little incident earlier. "She was just plain nasty to Belinda. I've never seen her behave like that."

"Cousin Violet's clannish, Kate," Grady said. "She's never cottoned to outsiders. Haven't you noticed that?"

"Not being an 'outsider,' I guess I've never paid much attention to it," I told him.

"Maybe she thinks Uncle Ernest is going to marry Belinda," Marge suggested.

"So?" I shrugged.

"I'm not supposed to know this," Marge said, "but I overheard Ma Maggie and Uncle Ernest talking about it one day. Violet's parents died when she was fairly young and our great-grandparents helped raise her. I think there's some kind of provision for her—financially, I mean. Uncle Ernest takes care of it, sees that she has enough to get by on."

"And she thinks Belinda would put an end to that?" I took a swig of iced tea and made a face. Aunt Leona must've made it.

Grady frowned. "You know what I think? I think you two have blown this all out of proportion. Our Violet wouldn't do that. I doubt if she even knew Belinda was allergic to bee stings."

"Our Violet knows more than you think," Marge told him, casting threatening looks at her son. "Darby Cranford! Don't you dare eat another cookie until you've finished your dinner!"

"Mean ol' Marge!" Grady elbowed her and she threatened

him with the ice from her glass of tea. I laughed, watching them. It reminded me of the good times we had when we were growing up together, and for a little while, I was feeling better about things until Grady said he'd seen a policeman back again talking to Uncle Ernest that afternoon.

"I saw them when I got back from the store just after noon," I said. "You mean they've been here since then?"

He nodded. "Two of them, actually. They were talking over by that scuppernong arbor near the toolshed. Didn't stay long. It was right before everybody started to get here."

We finished our lunch in silence. Uncle Ernest, currently engaged in finishing off a piece of lemon chess pie, seemed to have relaxed a little. Now and then he leaned over to say something to Belinda, and later I saw him making the rounds to speak with some of the visiting relatives. Everyone laughed when Judge Kidd, a longtime widower, teased Belinda about keeping company with Uncle Ernest when she could have him for the taking. "When that old fool breaks his neck on that crazy hoss, just remember I'm only a couple of miles down the road," he said.

"Coming from somebody who couldn't stay on a mule, those are mighty powerful words," Uncle Ernest said, referring to an incident during their boyhood. And chuckling, the two men went off together for another drink of bourbon.

Cousin Violet had made herself in charge of refreshing everyone's drink and now made her way through the crowd with a pitcher of lemonade in one hand and iced tea in the other, although I knew some of the guests were drinking something stronger. I watched her stop at Belinda's chair and say something to her. Belinda smiled and offered her glass for Violet to refill.

Grady was eyeing her, too. "I see Belinda's chicken bog has made a big hit," he said. "Dad had two helpings."

I wondered if Violet had noticed.

Ma Maggie and I were getting ready to serve the peach ice cream when Burdette called to me from the porch. "Kate! Somebody wants you on the phone."

Uncle Ernest had never gotten around to accepting cordless phones—said he couldn't hear as well on them—so I had to run all the way to the house to answer.

"This is Lieutenant Vickers. Our dispatcher said you asked me to call."

"Yes, I just learned they're investigating the death of Beverly Briscoe, who was killed in Pensylvania last winter, and I remembered something that might be important enough to pass along." I told him what Beverly had said to me last December about the "weird" neighbor who made her uncomfortable. "It could be nothing," I said, "but if there is something to it, I wouldn't want them to overlook the possibility he might have been involved."

"You were right to report that, ma'am, but the victim's mother had mentioned earlier that her daughter felt uneasy about this neighbor. When the investigators there looked into it, though, they discovered the man had been away on a business trip for several days at the time Ms. Briscoe was killed."

I thanked him and hung up, wondering, if not that man, then who would have a reason to take the life of a seemingly harmless person like Beverly.

It wasn't until after I got off the phone that I wondered if I should have told him about the anklet we found in that old trunk.

While I was inside, I decided I might as well drag out the croquet set, and was disappointed to find that Augusta and Penelope were no longer in the attic. From the window there I could see some of the adults and older children choosing sides for softball. Josie and Jon, I noticed, were picked to play on Burdette's team, while Darby and Cynthia were chosen by Grady. A teenage cousin from South Carolina had lined up the smaller children for a relay race, and far down in the meadow where Belinda had been stung by yellow jackets, a young girl sat alone in tall daisies and Queen Anne's lace.

Why had no one warned her? The last thing we needed was another accident. I shouted from the window for someone to hurry and bring her back, but of course, no one could hear me. Then on closer look, I recognized the girl. It was Penelope, and she seemed to be making a necklace of daisies for the large brown rabbit in her lap. Ears laid back, the rabbit nestled snugly while two smaller ones played about her feet. Again, I was reminded of my wedding day and the yellow-clad bridesmaids with their frothy bouquets, and the image of it mocked me.

I wondered if Augusta was nearby and hoped she hadn't gone very far.

"Did anybody remember to take Casey some supper?" I asked my grandmother later as she helped me set up the wickets for croquet. "I feel awful about the way Uncle Ernest talked to him."

With a worn mallet she pounded in a stake to mark the end

of the court. "Marge and Leona went down there with a plate a while ago but he wasn't there—or else he didn't come to the door. I'm afraid Ernest's not himself lately, which isn't surprising, what with Ella's falling and that skeleton turning up right next door."

"How is Ella?"

"Ernest said she was about the same when he went over early this morning," she told me.

"I just hope he doesn't learn about Violet's little fit in the kitchen today," I said, "but I'm afraid Belinda's bound to tell him."

"Maybe not. Belinda's a pretty good sort, and we all know Violet can get on her high horse sometimes. I always felt Violet was always more resentful than she let on that she and Hodges never married, although she seemed satisfied at the time with the relationship they had. I just don't pay much attention to her when she acts like that, and I hope Belinda won't, either. Why, Violet's probably forgotten it already."

But I wondered if Belinda had.

"How do you think her purse ended up behind those bushes?" I asked.

"Why, that rascal Hartley took it, or one of the other children," she said, "although I'd put my money on Hartley. All he wanted was her makeup to smear on poor old Amos. I just thank the good Lord we found it in time!"

I knew from experience not to argue. "Ma Maggie, has there ever been anyone in our family named Valerie?"

She frowned. "Valerie. No, not that I can recall. Why?"

I told her about finding the anklet in the trunk.

"My gracious, child, what were you doing up there on a hot day like this?"

"I went to get the croquet set and just got curious. Who do you think it might have belonged to?"

"Could have been left here by one of your mother's friends, or Jane's," she said, speaking of Marge's mother. "They used to bring friends out here to pick blackberries or eat watermelon—Ernest had a good patch of melons back beyond the orchard—but I honestly can't remember anyone named Valerie."

We chose our colors for a match against Deedee and Great-aunt Gertrude's daughter, Dorothy, a shy, rather plain woman who taught domestic science at the high school over in Dobson. Ma Maggie always had to have red and I chose blue—which is how I felt. Several people had asked about Ned and I was tired of making excuses. Not getting an answer at my parents' house, he had called, I learned, soon after we arrived to make sure we reached there safely. Aunt Leona, who had answered the phone, said my husband was late for a meeting and didn't have time to talk. We hadn't heard from him since, and even though I knew we had both agreed to this separation, the hurt of being ignored, and probably unloved, as well, gnawed at me so much I felt I should be bleeding inside.

"Have you heard if the police believe Ella was pushed?" I whispered to my grandmother as Deedee took her stroke.

"You know as much as I do about that, but they seemed to take it seriously about the cat being confined inside that box." Ma Maggie's face grew stormy. "I'd like to get my hands on whoever did it. What a mean, rotten trick to play!"

"You think it was meant to be a joke?"

"I doubt if whoever did it intended for Ella to fall down that embankment," she said, shaking her head. "No, I just can't bring myself to believe that!"

"But who—"

"I don't want to jump the gun and accuse anyone falsely, but the two Trotter boys live less than a mile from us and they've been in trouble with the law more than once. I know Ernest has run them off at least twice when they tried to take a shortcut to the river."

"Did you mention that to the police?" I asked.

"No, but I think Ernest did, and if they're guilty, I hope they put them under the jail!" And my grandmother studied her red ball and gave it a good whack with the mallet, sending Deedee's green one out of the field of play.

It was near dusk by the time we finished our fourth game (Ma Maggie and I won three of them), and crickets had begun to sing their evening song. The softball game was still going on in the meadow Casey had mowed earlier and Deedee and I wandered over to watch. Great-aunt Gertrude and her daughters and some of the South Carolina cousins left for home but most had stayed to either watch or take part in the game, now tied in the eighth inning.

Marge waved to me from her position as shortstop and I found an empty chair beside Uncle Ernest, who fanned mosquitoes away from Hartley, sleeping in his lap. Beside them, Judge Kidd rambled on about the cruddy job the town council was doing while my uncle either grunted in agreement or made a peculiar sucking sound, which I knew was a preamble to an argument.

The judge grinned when he saw me and I guessed what was coming.

"Had a chance to ride that new hoss yet, Kate?" He moved his unlit cigar to the other side of his mouth and winked at me from beneath frosty brows.

"You first!" I said, laughing, although I wished he'd shut up about the subject.

"Got a derby winner for sure!" he bellowed, eyeing his friend. "If they'll just forget that crazy rule they have about having to have a jockey."

"We'll just see who laughs last," my uncle said. "I'm not in the old folks' home yet."

"Huh! Be lucky if you live that long!" Goat told him.

Frogs cleared their throats in the woods behind us and I inhaled the watermelon smell of freshly cut grass—and something else. Strawberries. The scent was sweet but light, laced with the faint aroma of vanilla, and I knew Augusta was near. Naturally, I thought, she wouldn't want to miss a ball game. After all, hadn't she been taught by the great Connie Mack himself?

I smiled, knowing she was there, and watched Jon step up to bat and hit the ball into the outfield on the first pitch. Josie would be next.

Uncle Lum snapped pictures and team supporters cheered as Jon skidded safely into second, then Josie, flushed and determined-looking, tapped her bat on home base and waited for the pitch. She took a strike. And then another. I bit my lip, knowing how much it meant for her to succeed. But on the third pitch, she smacked the ball with a loud crack, sending it straight down the field past Cynthia, who was playing second base.

"Way to go, Josie!" I yelled, jumping to my feet as my daughter took off for first and Jon for third. By then Cynthia had retrieved the ball, and I drew in my breath as she pitched it wildly to the left, hitting Josie in the shoulder when she was about three feet from reaching first.

Doubling over, Josie grabbed her shoulder and I could see she was trying not to cry. It was all I could do to keep from running on the field and folding her in my arms, but I knew it might embarrass her, so I joined the others gathering around her and tried not to make a scene.

"Darby, you and Jon run to the house for ice!" Burdette shouted, leading Josie to the side of the field. "Now, let's take a look at that shoulder."

Josie's face was red and her hair stuck to her forehead in wet ringlets. Somebody put a cup of ice water in my hand and I took it to her while Marge retrieved the Atlanta Braves baseball cap Josie's dad had given her.

"You did that on purpose!" Josie yelled, glaring at Cynthia, who lingered in the background.

"I did not! I was trying to pitch to first." Cynthia stepped closer.

"Then you need to learn how to pitch! Your aim was a mile off base," Josie said, allowing me to sponge her face with a wet paper napkin.

"I'm sure Cynthia didn't hit you intentionally," I whispered. "Come on, let's go to the house where it's cooler."

"Cynthia, tell Josie you're sorry right now." Parker Driscoll spoke sternly to his daughter.

"I will not." Cynthia pulled away from Deedee, who had a hand on her shoulder. "And I know how to play softball as well as she does!"

"If you did, you would've thrown the ball to third so Jon wouldn't make a run," Josie told her.

"Here now, it's over and done with and nobody meant any harm," Burdette, the peacemaker, said calmly. "Now, let's get some ice on that shoulder."

Josie turned away from Cynthia and let Burdette administer the ice pack while she sipped her water.

"At least I don't act like a tomboy like you—and I don't care if I hit you or not!" Cynthia spouted, walking away.

"Cynthia!" Parker stood frozen, looking like he wished the earth would open up and swallow him.

"Oh, now, I'm sure she didn't mean that," Deedee said, starting after her daughter.

But Josie got there first. "Then I don't care if I hit you!" she said, and slapped her cousin smack in the face.

"Josie McBride, you come right back here and apologize!" I shouted as Josie stalked away. Cynthia screamed and ran sobbing to her mother.

"I'm really sorry, Cynthia," I said, and I picked up the ice pack and hurried after Josie, wishing awful things on my husband for not being there.

Marge caught up with me. "Kate, wait up a minute! Don't be too hard on her."

"I won't," I said. "I'm angrier about what happened to Josie than what she did to that crybaby Cynthia, but she still needs to apologize, and I want to get this ice on her shoulder."

"I'm afraid it's going to make a bruise." Marge frowned and looked around. "Now, where in the world did she go?"

"Back to the house probably." I walked faster.

But Darby raced to meet us before we got to the house. "Josie ran into the woods!" he called out to us. "I tried to stop her, but she wouldn't listen. I'm afraid she's run away!"

CHAPTER FOURTEEN

I broke into a run. "Hurry and get your dad . . . bring everybody you can find!" I called to Darby over my shoulder.

"And tell them to bring flashlights!" Marge yelled after him. I heard her close behind me as I raced around the house, past the rose garden, the scuppernong arbor, finally skirting the old apple orchard where hard, green fruit clung to the trees. And there we came to a stop.

"Which way do you think she went?" Marge asked, trying to see into the dense thicket ahead of us.

"I don't know, but surely she wouldn't go far! Josie's afraid of these woods. She's probably hiding behind a tree somewhere."

"Josie!" I cupped my hands and called to her. "Honey, it's okay! We'll work this out. Come on back, now!"

Wading a little farther into the trees, Marge did the same.

It seemed a year went by while we stood in silence waiting for an answer. None came.

"Josie, this has gone far enough. You're frightening me. Come out *right now!*" I didn't even try to disguise the fear in my voice.

"Why don't you go to the left and I'll take the other way," I suggested to Marge. "We can cover more ground like that, but watch your step. It's tricky down there."

"Just don't wander too far. We won't be able to see without lights for long," she said, and I soon heard her scrambling through the underbrush not too far from where Ella had taken her plunge.

I looked at the sky. Although twilight had settled upon us, it was still light enough to see in the open, but it was already dark in the tangle of underbrush and trees that seemed to have swallowed up my little girl.

I knew there used to be a path around here somewhere, but the entrance must have grown over. I tore aside a honeysuckle vine and stumbled over uneven ground shouting Josie's name. Briars snagged my shirt as I pushed past a straggling stand of cedars and through a forest of rhododendron to find what appeared to be a narrow path on the other side. The trail twisted around a tumble of moss-covered boulders, then hummocks, slick with pine needles, as it wound its way to the river below. Hikers and trespassers looking for a shortcut came this way now and then, although Uncle Ernest discouraged it, and in years past I had explored this same path with cousins and friends. If Josie had run blindly into the woods, she might eventually come upon it—or I hoped she would.

"Josie!" I stopped to call again. "It's getting dark. If you're here, answer me!"

Not too far away I could hear Marge doing the same. Close

149

by, startled birds flew up from a rotting tree trunk and a chipmunk darted under a root, but Josie didn't answer.

This was my fault. Josie was old enough to realize her father and I were having serious problems, and instead of trying to explain the situation so that she might understand, I had avoided dealing with it—and with her. And now look what had happened! My child was not only angry and confused, but wandering lost in a wilderness that stretched on for miles.

"Oh, Josie, please, please, *please*! Where are you?" Sobbing, I tripped over a root and went sprawling. A stick jabbed into the palm of my hand, bringing blood. Good! I deserved to hurt.

"Kate! Here, wait for me!" Grady's voice and crashing footsteps brought me to my feet, but I couldn't stop crying.

My cousin put an arm around me, urging me back the way I had come. "We're going to find her, Kate, but it isn't going to help Josie if you fall apart now. We're getting together a search party, but we have to get organized before we go wandering off helter-skelter." He gave me a gentle shove from behind. "Come on, now. Burdette and Parker are working out some kind of plan, and the sooner we get started, the better."

"You're right. I'm sorry, but, Grady, I'm just so scared!" I accepted his offer of a tissue and blew my nose.

"Hey, you're entitled. But put the tears on hold, okay? Makes it hard to see where you're going."

I struggled to keep from crying all over again when my grandmother, waiting at the top of the hill, wrapped me in her arms and smoothed my hair as she had when I was little. She smelled like mustardy potato salad and I guessed she had been in the kitchen putting away leftovers. "She can't have gone very far," she told me. "The police are on their way, but I expect we'll have her out of there before they even get here."

Uncle Ernest, looking as if he had aged ten years, held out a long-sleeved shirt. "Here, slip into this, Kate, my girl. You'll need something over those arms." The shirt was of faded blue cotton, thin from many washings, and the cuffs hung inches below my wrists. "What's this you've done to your hand?" he said, shining a light on my palm.

"Nothing. Scratched it, is all." I tried to pull away, but my uncle was surprisingly strong for his age.

"Nonsense. Goat, do you still have that first aid kit in your car? We'll need peroxide and a bandage. Can't have that getting infected."

Judge Kidd, silent for once, nodded grimly and sent Jon on the run for the kit. And so, while others were dividing into teams to look for my daughter, I stood pawing the ground while Uncle Ernest bandaged my wound.

Deedee, Belinda and Aunt Leona had rounded up every flashlight in the place, as well as bottled water for all the searchers, while Uncle Lum dispensed a variety of hats and bandannas.

"I don't need a hat," I said, waving him away. "All I want to do is find Josie."

Ignoring me, he tugged a bucket-shaped piece of canvas over my ears. "You'll be glad of this when you wade into that blasted thicket. Now, get over there and let Violet scoot you with insect repellent. It won't keep them off entirely, but it might help some."

And Josie was somewhere in that dark, threatening place with no water, no light and nothing to protect her from the mosquitoes. Earlier that day I had hastily anointed my daughter with the lotion repellent I carried in my purse, but that had certainly worn off by now, and I felt sick when I remembered she wore only shorts and a T-shirt.

I hurried to where Burdette and Parker were dividing searchers into teams. Marge was to go with her husband and a couple of our South Carolina kin, while Parker, Deedee and Uncle Lum made up another team. Darby cried to be included until his dad convinced him we needed him there to blow a whistle from time to time in case any of us got lost. And since Uncle Ernest knew the area better than any of us, we reminded him, he should be the one to wait behind for the police. That left Grady, Aunt Leona and me to make up the last group.

I had my doubts about taking my aunt along. Although Aunt Leona seemed agile enough, she wasn't the outdoorsy type, and I was afraid she would slow us down.

I was right. We hadn't gone very far when we encountered the first obstacle.

"Mom, you'll have to sit and slide down this bank on your fanny," Grady told her, shining the beam of our one flashlight on the sloping ground.

"Well, all right, if you say so," she answered, and did. But then we had to haul her up the opposite side.

Aunt Leona dusted off her pants and adjusted her pert, visored cap. "My goodness, it's dark as pitch out here! I can't see a foot in front of me."

I was just about to volunteer to go it alone when Grady gently turned his mother around. "Mom, I know you want to help, but I think you can do that better by giving Ma Maggie and Violet a hand with the kids. They'll all need baths and something to sleep in, and I'm sure they'd be glad of the extra help."

Below us a flashlight wavered and Uncle Lum called out Josie's name.

"Dad!" Grady waved his light and hollered. "Could you help Mom back to the house? We don't have but one light between us, and Kate and I want to cover as much ground as possible before it gets any darker."

"Be right there!" his dad answered, although he didn't sound too pleased about it. "I told you this would be too rough," he muttered under his breath as he helped Aunt Leona up the other side of the bank. "You would have to come, though, wouldn't you?

"You two go on, I'll catch up!" he yelled to Deedee and Parker, who had hesitated briefly before moving on.

I wondered if he would be able to find them again, but just then that wasn't my problem. Grady and I had been assigned an area to the right of the trail and I didn't want to waste any more time getting to it.

"I didn't see Casey back there," I said as we stumbled about, casting our light under bushes, behind rocks, any place where a child might be resting, sleeping, or—God forbid—lying hurt.

"Burdette said he went on ahead." Grady reached back to give me a hand over a particularly rough patch of ground. "Said he'd make better time and cover more ground alone."

"That makes sense. Do you know which direction he took?"

"Whichever one he wanted to, I guess," Grady said. "I don't think Casey Grindle likes to take orders from anybody, especially after the way Uncle Ernest treated him today."

I agreed, but the caretaker's feelings were the least of my worries. Every few steps we stopped to call to Josie, and now

153

and then, true to his promise, we could hear Darby blowing his whistle far above us in the distance. For a while we could still see the lights Uncle Ernest had rigged in the clearing, but as the woods became denser and the night blacker, we finally lost sight of that.

Below us I heard the rush of the river, and now and then caught a glint of light from the water. The sight and sound of it terrified me. Josie was a good swimmer, but the current was deep and swift, and in the darkness, she wouldn't be able to see where she was going. Fear was like a heavy, growing thing in my middle. *Oh, please don't let my little girl wander into that treacherous, black torrent!*

Grady must have read my mind. "Josie knows better than to go near that river, Kate. If we can hear it, so can she. She's probably curled up somewhere waiting for us to find her."

"Then why doesn't she answer? Why?"

But my cousin didn't answer because he didn't know.

And what had happened to my guardian angel? I looked over my shoulder, hoping for a glimpse of a flaming-haired vision with flowers in her hair. "Okay, Augusta, you can come out now!" I spoke loudly enough for Gabriel himself to hear. If I ever needed heavenly help, it was now.

Grady glanced back at me. "Augusta? Who's that?"

"A figment of my imagination, that's all," I told him, hoping she would hear.

I waved gnats from my face, glad of the hat Uncle Lum had forced me to wear, and balanced on one foot as I pried my shoe from the mud. "I wonder how far we've come." I couldn't see any of the other lights, and it had been some time since we last heard Darby's whistle. Surely the police had come by now.

Every few steps Grady, who walked ahead, stopped to flash the beam of his light in circles, and together we called Josie's name. I tried to think what I would do if I were ten and wanted to hide from my family. Ordinarily, Josie wouldn't venture into these woods alone, but she was upset, and at that time it was still light. She probably ran as far and as fast as she could until either her temper cooled or she ran out of steam. My daughter could be anywhere.

I had tied a water bottle to my belt loop with the bandanna and it sloshed against my side as I walked. Pausing, I unscrewed the cap and took a swallow. We were just above the river now, walking parallel to the banks below. "Where now?" I asked.

Grady untangled himself from a vine and held it aside for me to pass. "To the right, I think. Parker and Deedee are supposed to be searching over to the left—and Dad, too, if he caught up with them. Burdette's group's combing that area below Remeth churchyard."

"Seems the police should be here by now," I said.

"Right, and they'll have better equipment than we do. I don't think our batteries are going to last much longer." The beam was getting dimmer and Grady only switched it on now from time to time. "Do you want to start back?" he asked.

"NO! Not yet! She might be just over the next hill, on the other side of the next tree. We can't give up yet."

"We won't be giving up, Kate. I'm sure the sheriff will organize a larger party—might even bring in bloodhounds. We won't be much help in finding Josie if we can't see."

He was right, of course, but I kept on going. "Please, just a little farther. Didn't Uncle Ernest used to say there was a cave down here somewhere? Some kind of rock shelter? Josie might have stopped there to rest."

"That's just one of his tales, Kate. I've never seen a cave down here, and if there was one, I can't imagine Josie going in it."

"When's the last time either of us were this close to the river?" I asked. "I don't think I've been back since Bev and I found that dead man. Tobias King. Even his name gives me the creeps. Remember?"

My cousin didn't answer but stopped abruptly to stare into the dark void that was the river below.

"What is it? Do you see something?" I moved quickly up beside him.

"No, it was just that feeling . . . like a rabbit ran over my grave." Grady flicked the switch on the flashlight, then shook it. "Damn! The batteries are gone."

"Let me see . . ." I reached for it. "Maybe if we reverse them." It never worked, but I always tried it anyway.

"Forget it, I did that a while ago." Even in the dark, I could see the worried look on my cousin's face.

"Then I guess we should try to find our way back," I said. "If we can get close enough, we might be able to see the lights from Bramblewood. And we can always yell for help."

Grady brushed debris from a rock and sat, offering me a place beside him. "Let's rest a minute first." He held a hand at arm's length in front of him. "How good are your eyes, Kate? This is about as far as I can see. I don't think it's safe to start back in the dark."

"Josie is somewhere in this dark," I reminded him.

"And I would hope she has the good sense to stay where she is until somebody finds her."

"You mean you plan to stay here *all night?*" I said.

"Or until somebody comes looking for us. They know we're out here, Kate. If we try to walk out of here, there's no telling what we might stumble into."

A wind ruffled the leaves and I hugged my uncle's big shirt around me, but it wasn't the wind that chilled me. I must have shivered because Grady asked me if I was cold.

"I just wish those batteries had lasted a little longer. I don't like this place, Grady. We can't be too far from where Tobias King was killed," I told him. "Did they ever find out anything about him? I don't suppose we'll ever know who killed him."

For a minute my cousin sat beside me rattling the batteries in the flashlight—*click, click,* back and forth. "I'll tell you who killed him," he said finally. "It was me."

CHAPTER FIFTEEN

I don't think I said anything for a minute or two, but sat on that dirt-encrusted rock listening to the race of the river, inhaling its damp, dark smells. A bug crawled on my neck and I slapped it away. "That's not funny," I said. "I'm not in the mood for jokes, Grady."

"I wish it were a joke. I'd give anything if it were a joke." Grady sighed and I could just make out the outline of his face in the semidarkness. "Tobias King was my father," he said. "My natural father, I guess you'd call him, except he was about as unnatural as a father could be. And Tobias King wasn't even his real name. It just happened to be the one he was using at the time."

"What do you mean, you *killed him?*"

"It was an accident. I didn't mean to. Hell, Kate, I was eleven years old and I hated his guts. I did my best to stay as far away from him as I could." Grady picked up a stick and threw it into the water.

"So, what was he doing here?" *And why are you telling me this?*

"He planned to blackmail Mom and Dad. Said they'd have to pay good money or he'd take me back. That would've been a laugh! Like he ever cared about me to begin with."

"But they had already adopted you. How could he—"

"He wasn't around when my real mother died—hadn't been around for years. I guess everybody thought he was dead, too. At least they didn't expect him back, so technically, he might have had a case."

"But how . . ." Did I really want to know this? I took another swallow of water. It was warm and I wasn't sure I was going to keep it down.

"Remember how we used to explore down here? Uncle Ernest had told us that yarn about a cave somewhere, and I thought I might find the Confederate gold in there. Anyway, the old man must've known where to find me because he was waiting here one day—grabbed me just before I came out into the clearing." Grady fanned himself with the cap he'd bought at some golf course in Tennessee. "Liked to have scared the— Well, it shook me up pretty bad.

"He'd been drinking and stunk to high heaven. I'll never forget the feeling of his filthy hands on my arms. We struggled, with me pulling one way and him another. At that point, he wasn't too steady on his feet and I lit into him, butted him with my head and shoved him as hard as I could."

I could feel Grady looking at me, but I couldn't meet his gaze. "His head hit a rock when he fell," he said.

"And when Bev and I found him that day, you pretended you didn't know anything about it."

159

"It wasn't until the *next* day that you saw him. I was scared to go back there by myself, afraid he *wouldn't* be dead. He sure wasn't moving, breathing, either, but here he was reappearing after all those years. I thought he might be like one of those bad guys in the movies who just keep on coming back when you think they're dead."

I tried not to flinch when my cousin touched my arm. "I'm sorry, Kate. But I had to find out, and I couldn't tell anybody what I'd done."

"You've never told this to anybody? Not even Beverly?"

He shook his head. "Especially not Beverly. You know how softhearted she is. Was."

"But you said yourself it was an accident. Nobody in their right mind would've blamed you for what you did in self-defense."

"True, but a kid isn't rational about things like that. All I knew was that I had killed the old man . . . and I was glad. By the time I was old enough to realize what I *should* have done, it was too late to try and make things right. After all, what good would it have done? What good would it do now?"

"So, why are you telling me?"

"Being here in this place stirred things up, I guess. And frankly, it's been bothering me for a long time, like a wound that never healed. Can you imagine me sharing this with Mom, or even Dad? You're the closest to a sister I ever had, Kate."

I patted his arm but didn't speak. I suppose I should've been honored, but I wished my cousin had waited until it was daylight and I had Josie back again to unburden himself.

"Bev had a hard time that day you found him," Grady went on, "and I felt bad about that, but if I had told her what really happened, she would've felt a lot worse."

Dry leaves rustled nearby and I slipped from the rock, hoping it might be Josie or one of the others coming to look for us. "Josie! Josie!" I shouted. "Are you out there? Honey, it's Mom!"

"It's only an animal—raccoon, I think—heading for the riverbank," Grady said gently.

"Then let's yell anyway. Yell together! Maybe *somebody* will hear us. I just can't sit here doing nothing."

We spent the next few minutes screaming into the night, and between the two of us managed to find our way a few more feet alongside the river without falling in. I felt my way to a slender tree and leaned against it, waiting for an answer that never came.

"You know, Kate, Josie might already be back at Bramblewood. She's probably up there now pigging out on the last of the chocolate chip cookies," Grady said.

I almost smiled. He had said the right thing, even if I doubted it was true. My injured hand was throbbing, and next to having Josie back, I wanted a hot shower more than anything I could think of, but I would crawl all night on my hands and knees if I thought I might find her.

I heard Grady take out his water bottle and drink. "I wish things had been better between Bev and me before she died," he said, replacing the cap.

"But I thought they were. Wasn't she planning to come back to this area when she finished the requirements for her degree? Sounded to me like the two of you had sort of rekindled things." This was *not* a good time, I reminded myself, to tell him the police believed Beverly's death wasn't an accident.

"To some extent, yes, but things were more or less unsettled." He turned his head away when he spoke and I had difficulty hearing him over the sound of the water.

"It wasn't your fault, Grady. Beverly made her own choices—and in the end she had chosen to come home. Her mom told me Bev could hardly wait."

"It wouldn't have been any too soon. You should've seen that dinky place she lived in . . . way out in the middle of nowhere and so small you didn't have room to swing a cat!"

"But how . . ." I stopped myself before I said it. *Grady had said he'd never visited Beverly in Pennsylvania!*

". . . how long had she lived there?" I continued. "Probably not more than a couple of years. I mean, most people don't seem to mind an inconvenience like that if it's temporary. And I got the idea she really enjoyed her part-time job up there. Worked in a nursery or a garden shop—something like that—didn't she?"

I babbled on and on, trying to cover my tracks. I couldn't see Grady's face in the darkness, so I wasn't sure if he'd noticed my slipup or not.

Grady had admitted killing his own father. In self-defense, he'd said. But how could I be sure he was telling the truth? And then there was Ella's tragic tumble. Grady had been at Bramblewood that day long enough to have planned it, and he knew how much she cared about that cat. Maybe the housekeeper had learned something about Grady's encounter with Tobias King. Ella Stegall usually minced no words. She would have confronted him with it.

And Beverly. Dear God, I didn't even want to think about the possibility that my cousin had something to do with our old friend's death. Their breakup years before had had a traumatic effect on Grady. Had she rejected him again? Or maybe he had confided in her about what happened to his father, just as he had to me.

I could be next. Instinctively, I stepped back, putting the small tree between us. What was the matter with me? This was Grady! The same Grady who had helped me to build a treehouse, taught me to ride a bike. How could I think he would intentionally harm me—or anyone else?

Grady was quiet, and I wondered if he guessed what I was thinking. Finally he spoke. "It doesn't look like we're going to get out of here anytime soon. I think we should try to find a place where we can at least close our eyes and rest a little—maybe get a few minutes of sleep."

I wasn't about to close my eyes, and there was no way I was going to sleep with my child cowering and afraid somewhere in this wild, rugged place, but I let my cousin take my hand and lead me to a place where he said he thought the terrain leveled off a bit.

"I'm sure we passed a place just a little way up the hill where we might be able to stretch out—looked like a few small pines in sort of a clearing. There, when somebody comes looking, they'll be able to see us better."

Grady's words were comforting and he gave my shoulder a reassuring pat, just like the old Grady would—the one who could always think of something fun to do, and who never failed to make me laugh. Guilt overwhelmed me. What was I thinking? Just because my cousin knew Beverly had lived in a small apartment, didn't mean he had *been there*. Bev had probably told him about it.

Then my foot slipped as Grady helped me over a log, and when I reached out to steady myself, my hand brushed the front of his shirt. It was an old shirt of Uncle Lum's that Grady had put on for protection against brambles and insects, just as I wore one of Uncle Ernest's, and the pocket drooped low on his chest.

I recovered quickly, said something lame about being clumsy and tried to pretend I hadn't felt the flashlight battery in my cousin's shirt pocket. Had Grady removed a battery so we wouldn't be able to see?

I had to get away! Even if I stumbled about in the darkness, surely I could find a place to curl up in and hide until light. I *had* to!

"This should be okay, don't you think?" Grady shoved aside the branches of a sapling blocking our way, then stomped in a circle, kicking stones and limbs to the side. "It's not the Hilton, but at least we don't have to worry about falling into the river—ouch! Watch out for that limb—almost took off the top of my head!"

Then why don't you put that damn battery back in the flashlight so we can see?

"It's fine," I said instead, "but first I have to have a little privacy. Guess I drank too much water."

"You mean you have to pee? My God, Kate, I'm not going to look. Couldn't see even if I wanted to."

"But you could hear. Come on, Grady, I'm modest. Give me a break!"

He snorted. "Since when? I remember when we used to go skinny dipping out at Periwinkle Springs."

"Yeah, back when we were kids." I waited. "Just go a few steps away and turn around. Is that too much to ask?"

"Oh, I guess not," he said finally. "But you're going to be sorry if I fall and break my neck."

He turned and went back the way we had come, and I listened, counting his steps: twelve . . . thirteen . . . fourteen . . . then waited until I couldn't hear him anymore. I had no idea where to go, which way to turn, but I had to do something fast.

Then, on the other side of what looked like a huge rhododendron bush, something moved, pale and ghostlike in the darkness. It seemed almost filmy, flitting among the branches, and I was about one breath away from a scream when I caught the fragrance, subtle and sweet.

Strawberries.

"This way. Hurry!" Augusta reached out and took my hand, and at her touch I wasn't afraid anymore.

"It's about time!" I said as I followed her, dipping under overhanging limbs, skirting stumps and stones. "Where have you been?"

"Never far away, Kathryn. You should know that by now."

"And where's Josie? Is she all right?"

But Augusta didn't answer.

Behind us, I could hear Grady calling my name.

CHAPTER SIXTEEN

Augusta moved so quickly I almost walked headlong into a tree while trying to keep up.

"Slow down a minute, will you?" I whispered. "I can't see where I'm going."

She paused to look back at me and her halo of bright hair was a light unto itself. "I thought you were in a hurry," she said.

"I am. Of course I am, but some of us don't have angel vision. Where are you taking me?"

"You'll see." She waited for me to catch up and we walked close together, her necklace making a glittering arc of gold and green with every step. "And I don't have 'angel vision' as you say. It's simply instinct and experience. This isn't the first time I've explored unknown territory, Kate McBride."

"Uh-huh," I said, pausing to listen. I couldn't hear Grady calling anymore but the sounds of the river seemed closer, louder, somehow swifter.

Together we sailed over a shallow ditch, then, weaving in and out among trees, followed the line of the hill.

"Why, if it weren't for my help, Lewis and Clark might never have found that overland route to the Pacific Ocean," Augusta informed me.

"Really? I thought Sacagawea showed them the way," I said.

"Who do you think guided Sacagawea?" Augusta's eyes held a teasing glint but I didn't think she was joking.

"Is Josie all right?" I asked. "Where is she?"

"I'm taking you there, and other than an injured ankle, she seems to have survived her impromptu adventure very well." Augusta put up a hand to warn me as a snake—or I think it was a snake—slithered inches from our feet. Too terrified to move, I latched onto the angel's arm until she assured me we were in no danger. And I learned she wasn't above giving me an urgent little poke when I didn't move fast enough to suit her.

"Tell me why you're suddenly so afraid of your cousin?" Augusta asked. "I sensed you were frantic to put distance between you. How did this come about?"

"You don't know?"

"I dislike to eavesdrop. Was it something he did . . . or said?"

"Both." I told her about Grady's confession and my suspicions about his being involved with Beverly's death. "And what's more, I think he took a battery out of the flashlight so we couldn't find our way back," I said.

"Now, why would he do that? Are you sure about these things?" Her voice had just a tinge of angelic judgment in it, I thought.

"The part about Grady killing his father—yes. I don't know about the rest." I held my injured hand close to me as I walked.

I wanted to stop for water, but was afraid it would slow us down. The sound of the river had intensified into something like a roar.

"Please tell me we're getting close," I said. "Seems we've been walking for miles—and I don't understand why some of the searchers haven't found her yet. They should've had time to cover every inch of this place by now."

"It's a big mountain, and as you know, it's not easy to see in terrain like this—especially in the dark," Augusta said.

"But shouldn't we have at least heard them?" I said. We were climbing again and the slope was slippery with leaves and pine needles.

"It's difficult to hear over the sound of the waterfall," Augusta said.

"Waterfall?" I could tell we were getting even closer to the rumble of its thunder. "Did Josie—"

"No, Josie's all right. Now, watch for a large expanse of rock just ahead." Augusta reached back to guide me around it. "From what Penelope tells me, Josie didn't enter the woods where everyone thought she did, but wandered along beside it for almost a mile before she came to what she thought was a path."

"Penelope?"

"Penelope was the one who found her, Kate."

The ground seemed to be leveling out now and Augusta paused to part the branches of a huge tree, dark and feathery, with a fresh green scent. "Watch your head," she said, stooping under the canopy.

I followed, and even in the darkness I could make out two figures sleeping there, nestled close together with some kind of animal between them. On closer look, I saw it was a fawn. One of the figures was Josie; the other, the apprentice angel Penelope, who slept with one arm over my little girl's shoulders, and I knew I would never, *never* criticize the young angel's awkwardness again.

If Augusta hadn't stopped me, I would have run to Josie at once. I could hardly wait to throw my arms around her, hold her safe against my heart—and I didn't plan to let her go any time soon, either.

The angel lightly finger-touched my arm. "Shh! Don't wake them! It's been a long night and they're both worn out."

I sat as close as I could to my daughter's side without nudging her awake. The fawn twitched an ear but neither girl moved. "Where did Penelope find her?" I asked.

"About halfway to the river. She'd wandered onto that trail in the woods—to get out of the heat, I suppose, as it was still light then. Penelope was playing leapfrog, she said, with some young foxes in the meadow and followed, hoping Josie would turn around and start for home."

"I wonder why she didn't," I said.

"I think something or someone must have startled her," Augusta said. "Penelope says that's when Josie fell."

"Fell?" Once again I reached for my daughter, and once again, I was stopped by Augusta's touch. "Fell where?"

"The hill gave way to an abrupt drop—it wasn't far, mind you, but Josie took a tumble of sorts." Augusta's smile reassured me. "I think she might've twisted her ankle in the process, and the fall probably stunned her, as well. The child was already disoriented and by now it was getting too dark to see."

"So how did she get here?" I took off my outer shirt and

tucked it around my sleeping child. The sound of the swift, cascading water seemed almost soothing now.

Augusta smiled. "I imagine Penelope managed that some-how—probably with the help of her friends."

"Her friends?" If there was another around like Penelope, surely I would have *heard* her.

"You must have noticed, Penelope has a way with animals. The little fawn's mother can't be too far away."

Surely I must be dreaming! My eyes felt heavy. If I closed them for a minute, I would wake up in bed back at Bramblewood.

I blinked. The umbrellalike branches of the great hemlock tree spread over us like a spring-scented tent where my daughter lay curled in sleep with a baby deer and an adolescent angel. My own angel offered me a bed of leaves and pine straw. "You need to sleep," she said. "You'll be able to find your way out when it's light."

"You're not leaving?"

"I'll be here as long as you need me." Augusta, sitting beside me, reached elegant arms over her head, leaned from side to side and executed an angelic little shimmy-stretch. "Ah, that's better!" She sighed. "This is a delightful little nook, don't you think? Our Penelope did well for us."

"She most certainly did," I said, noticing the pride in her voice. "But Augusta, I'm afraid. What if Grady finds us here?"

"Ponyfeathers!" Augusta wiggled a pink-tipped toe. "You let me worry about that."

"What?" I laughed, then tried to cover it with a yawn. "But how are we going to find our way home?"

"Just follow the flowers," she said.

The pine straw bed looked more and more inviting. "Follow what flowers?"

"You'll see," Augusta said. I could tell she was sort of peeved with me for laughing, but I had my Josie back and nothing else mattered just then. Besides, she'd get over it in time.

Just before I dropped off to sleep, I watched the fawn nuzzle Penelope's cheek and give her a lick of a kiss.

The next morning the angels were gone.

Dark green branches filtered pale yellow sunlight when Josie stirred next to me and I drew her into my arms and held her close.

My daughter clung to me and cried and we sat swaying, saying nothing for a while until Josie finally spoke.

"Mom! I thought I'd never see you again . . . but how did you find me?" she asked.

"I had some help from a couple of angels," I whispered, stroking the fine hair from her face. She had a bruise on her forehead, I noticed, and an angry-looking scrape on her cheek. "How's your ankle, honey?"

She made a face. "It hurts. And I'm thirsty—haven't had anything to drink since—How long have I been here?"

"Since late yesterday." Thank goodness I had saved almost half my bottle of water and I gave Josie what was left. Her ankle was swollen, but she still wore her socks and sneakers, so I made a figure eight with my bandanna and tied it around her injured foot, shoe and all. "Do you think you can walk?" I asked.

"I'll try. Mom, I'm so glad to see you! I just want to go home!"

I peered through a limb of the tree that had sheltered us. Although the woods were spotted with sunlight, fog clung to the earth in patches, making it difficult to see the ground. The waterfall that had lulled us the night before seemed threatening in its nearness. What if we wandered too near the edge?

But Augusta would never had left us if she'd thought we wouldn't be able to find our way out. *Follow the flowers*, she had said. Well and good, I thought, if only we were able to see them.

"Josie, I know you're eager to get back, and believe me, so am I, but we're going to have to wait a while until this fog lifts a little," I told her.

While we waited, I found a Y-shaped stick and padded it with the bottom half of Uncle Ernest's shirt to make a crude crutch for Josie.

"I had the funniest dream last night," she said, resting against my shoulder.

"Funny peculiar or funny ha-ha?"

"Funny peculiar." She raised up on an elbow to look at me. "A girl was with me . . . she looked like that girl I saw in the ocean, and she had a fawn—the sweetest little deer."

"Really? What did she do?"

"Mostly she was just *there*, and I think she sang—hummed, really—songs without words. She brought me here in my dream, and Mom, she was so real! I remember her beside

172

me when I went to sleep, and I wasn't scared or anything." Josie reached up to pluck a piece of hemlock from my hair. "Do you really think there are such things as angels?" she asked.

"I wouldn't be surprised," I said.

When the fog had cleared enough, Josie and I crept carefully from beneath the branches of the hemlock tree and looked about. Somewhere in front of us the river plummeted from what sounded like a great height, then roared along its way. Instinctively, I stepped backward. "Do you see any flowers?" I asked with a protective hand on Josie's shoulder.

"What kind of flowers?"

"I'm not sure." I put one arm around her waist and we made our way to the other side of the hemlock where the trees thinned into a small grassy meadow.

"I see them!" Josie pointed to a winding pathway of pastel flowers in pink, yellow and blue. "How did you know they'd be here?"

"Guess I must've dreamed it," I said, but I don't think she believed me.

The going was slow and tedious even over the more-or-less level ground, and when the pathway wound into rougher, steeper terrain, I carried Josie on my back, using the crutch as a walking stick. I rested, panting, at the top of each hill and tried not to think of water. The flowery trail, although beautiful, seemed to go on forever.

"Mom, we'll never get there at this rate. I'm too heavy! You can't carry me forever." Josie sat beside me on a rock and stretched her legs in front of her.

"Oh, yes I can, and I will. It just might take a little longer. Look, the hill slopes downward in front of us, and it looks like the path winds around it. You should be able to walk for a while."

Half rolling, half sliding, we made it to the bottom of the hill, and with my help, Josie hobbled along for probably another hour until we came to a stream. It was a clear, shallow brook and even the sound of it refreshed us, but we knew better than to drink. Kneeling, we dashed water on our arms and faces, and I filled the water bottle to cool us later.

We seemed to be in the bottom of a ravine, and from there the path zigzagged up the side of a hill with what seemed an impossible height. I took a deep breath and bent to help Josie on my back. We would just have to take it in stages.

What had started as steps became crawls as we made our way over rocks and between saplings, and I was terrified that I might put my hand on a snake—or even worse, slip with Josie on my back and injure both of us. And where, I wondered, were Augusta and Penelope? Probably back in my parents' kitchen stuffing themselves with pastries and coffee! *The flowers are a nice touch, but would it have broken some heavenly law to lead us back an easier way?* I thought.

"Mom, wait! I hear something." Josie rolled from my back and crouched beside me.

"What?" *A bear? A snake?* I stiffened, ready to throw myself on top of her.

Somewhere in the distance a dog barked, and minutes later,

Amos bounded out of the underbrush and threw himself upon us in a frenzy of licking.

"Amos, wait!" Someone called from the top of the hill. A man. Grady. "Thank God!" he said. "I thought we'd never find you!"

CHAPTER SEVENTEEN

Tousled and dirty, my cousin didn't look any better than I felt. Had he really been searching all this time? I put my arms around Josie and drew her to me, putting the dog between the two of us and Grady as he approached at a run.

"Josie, am I glad to see you!" he shouted. "Are you all right?

"Kate, why did you wander away like that? Where have you been? I was worried sick! Thought you'd fallen into the river."

My daughter and I were alone with Grady Roundtree in the middle of a wilderness with no one but a dog to protect us, and from the way Amos was carrying on, he seemed to take to Grady as much as he did to Josie and me. This was not the time to make accusations.

"Got turned around," I told him. "Couldn't see to find my way back."

"I called and called." I couldn't tell if Grady believed me or not. "Couldn't you hear me? Why didn't you answer?"

"The waterfall . . . all I could hear was the waterfall," I said. "Sorry. I didn't get lost just to worry you, Grady."

My cousin grinned. "That's okay. You found Josie, and that's what matters. Where was she?"

"Asleep under a tree," Josie told him. "An angel took me there."

Grady winked at me and laughed. "Well, thank heavens for that!"

"How did you find us?" I asked my cousin as Josie pulled beggar's lice from Amos's matted fur.

"Darndest thing! I started back this morning as soon as it was light enough to see, when who should come running to meet me but Amos here!" Grady took off his hat to wipe his forehead. "Amos was the one who led me to you. Every time I tried to go in a different direction, he'd bark and run back and forth like a maniac until I followed him. Seemed to know where he was going—and since I didn't, I let him have the lead."

Grady frowned. "Josie, what happened to your foot?"

"I think I must've sprained it," she said. "Mom's been carrying me when we have to climb a hill."

"My Lord! No wonder you look like you've been jerked through a knothole backward, Cuz!" My cousin began to take off his outer shirt. "No offense, Kate, but you do seem a bit worse for the wear."

"I'm fine," I said. "Just tired."

"Your arms look like road maps with all those bites and scratches. Here, put this on. It doesn't smell too good, but then, neither do we."

Grady gave his shirt a little flip to put it over my shoulders, and when he did, something rolled to the ground.

Dear God, was it the battery? How could I pretend I didn't see it when it was lying at my feet?

But it wasn't a flashlight battery half-buried in the grass between us, it was a roll of film.

Grady reached down and retrieved it. "I've been carrying that blasted film all night. Dad loaned me his shirt when we started out and he forgot to take the film out of the pocket."

I stared at the small container of film that was about the same size as a flashlight battery, feeling as if I'd been slapped in the face, then turned away so Grady couldn't see my expression. *Please, God, give me a break, and don't let Grady ever find out what I had thought of him!*

"How far do you think we are from Bramblewood?" I asked when I could compose myself.

My cousin scooped Josie up in his arms for the trek uphill and I followed gratefully. "Can't be too far now, but we must've wandered off a long way out of the search area last night, Kate. Aside from Amos, I haven't seen or heard a soul." He glanced back over his shoulder. "How long have you been walking?"

"Forever!" My stomach growled. "Probably about two hours."

"How did you know where you were going?" Grady asked.

"We followed the flowers," Josie told him.

Grady set her down at the top of the hill and looked back at the way we had come. "What flowers?"

"Why, there was a path of them," Josie said. "Blue and pink and yellow—so pretty! Mom, we should've picked some."

I nodded in agreement. We should have, of course, because the trail of flowers wasn't visible anymore.

With Amos running ahead, we walked for probably less than an hour before we heard someone shouting, and Burdette, and a man I learned later was from the sheriff's department, ran out of the thicket to meet us.

"Thank God! I don't think I've ever been as happy to see anybody in my life!" Burdette, who didn't even try to hide his tears, wrapped me in his big arms, then took Josie from Grady to carry the rest of the way. I was glad to let the young policeman help me over the rough spots until we were in sight of Bramblewood.

The two of them had made good use of their whistles when they found us, so a group that must have been made up of just about everybody in the county was waiting to greet us, with Marge and Uncle Lum running ahead. Uncle Ernest, shirttail out and glasses askew, hurried along behind. Marge went right to Josie, Uncle Lum grabbed Grady and Uncle Ernest held out his arms to me. "I don't want to ever, *ever* go through a night like that again!" he said at last.

"Neither do I," I told him, trying not to cry as I was being passed from one relative to another. Even Deedee seemed glad to see us back. I managed to do okay until the crowd parted and Ma Maggie reached out to me. My grandmother held me until I had cried myself dry.

I scanned the crowd as we walked to the house arm in arm,

hoping he would be here. Ma Maggie told me Uncle Ernest had shooed the media away earlier, but I was certain news of Josie's disappearance had leaked to the press. If Ned knew Josie was lost, why wasn't he here tearing the woods apart stick by stick to try and find her? But Marge and Burdette had arrived at the house ahead of us with Josie, and I didn't see my husband anywhere.

But of course, he wouldn't have had time. I had been in the woods so long, I had lost track of the hours, but surely he had telephoned, I thought. Ned must be on the way.

Naturally, Ma Maggie guessed what I was thinking. "Kate, we didn't know how to get in touch with him, honey. Marge and I both tried to remember the name of that company he went with, but all we knew was that he was somewhere in California. You know we would've called him if we knew how."

"It's not your fault," I told her. "I should've taken care of that earlier, but I had no idea she'd wandered off so far—or that we would get lost trying to find her." Except for her swollen ankle and a multitude of scrapes and scratches, my daughter was fine, so there was no urgency in locating her father, but Josie would be eager to talk with him, and I knew he needed to be informed. I tried to phone Ned as soon as I got to the house, but the hotel lines were tied up and I couldn't get through. He would just have to wait.

Water had never tasted as good, and I'm sure Josie, Grady and I must have consumed at least a gallon while Marge and my grandmother, with Violet's help, put together a late, late breakfast of eggs, grits and ham with a huge bowl of fresh peaches and cantaloupe.

"I thought we had wandered off the ends of the earth," I

said over breakfast. "It was too dark to see and we couldn't hear a soul. Didn't seem like anybody was ever going to find us."

"We would've searched over there today if you hadn't turned up," Uncle Lum said. "I think Casey looked some in that area yesterday until the sheriff told him to cover the woods below Remeth. Nobody had any idea you and Josie had gone so far!"

I helped myself to another piece of ham. "Neither did we," I said.

Grady complained that Josie and I used up most of the hot water before he got his turn in the shower and I knew he wasn't exaggerating. If my hand hadn't been hurting where I had jabbed it earlier with a stick, I probably would have showered even longer. And fortunately for us, one of the rescue workers had medical training and was kind enough to stick around long enough to see to Josie's ankle and bandage my hand. By five o'clock that afternoon, Josie was so tired she could hardly hold up her head, so we set up a cot for her in the far corner of the living room where I could keep an eye on her. I wasn't ready to let my daughter out of my sight. Grady had fallen asleep on the wicker settee on the porch, and I knew I should try to rest, as well, but too much had happened to allow me to settle down just yet.

Things began to quiet down after the rest of the searchers left, and Uncle Ernest drove off to see about Ella at the hospital while Uncle Lum and Aunt Leona escaped to front porch rockers where now and then they spoke softly. Marge and family had left earlier, promising to check back with us the next day, and only Violet, Ma Maggie and I remained in the house.

The old house seemed to echo after all the activity of the

day before and the frenzied flurry on our return that afternoon, and the big room looked even grayer than usual with its frayed rugs and worn furniture where the faint smell of Uncle Ernest's pipe tobacco blended with Aunt Leona's Misty Glade cologne. But gray and quiet were fine with me. I was content to be just where I was, and stretched out in the squishy old armchair where I could keep an eye on my sleeping child. Ma Maggie and Violet sat across from me on the sofa, and from the expression on their faces, I think they expected me to disintegrate at any moment.

"What?" I said.

My grantmother lifted an eyebrow. "What do you mean, *what?*"

"You keep staring at me like I'm going to break or something. I'm fine."

"Good," Ma Maggie said. "That's fine," and kept on staring.

"You don't have to watch over me or anything. Nothing's going to happen, so just relax, okay? Why don't you two go home and get some sleep?" I was sure neither of them had closed their eyes the night before.

"I think I'll stay until Ernest gets back," my grandmother said. "I'm concerned about him. Something's not right."

"It won't do any good if you get sick, too," Violet said. "Your blood pressure's probably through the ceiling already." She made a face. "Let Belinda worry about Ernest."

"Belinda's not here," Ma Maggie told her.

"I know she's not *here*," my cousin Violet said. "Left for home soon as Kate and the others turned up, but she doesn't live that far away. Let her hold Ernest's hand."

My grandmother shook her head. "No, I mean Belinda's not

in town. I think she went to a daughter's or something." She lowered her voice. "I heard Ernest tell her to go away."

"What do you mean?" Violet leaned forward with the beginning of a smile on her face. "I thought they were a couple now."

"Oh, not like that!" Ma Maggie waved her hand. "He told her he'd feel a lot better if she went away for a few days. After what happened yesterday with the yellow jackets and all, Ernest said he thought she'd be safer somewhere else."

For once Cousin Violet was speechless. But not for long. "For heaven's sakes, surely Ernest doesn't think that attack was planned. You can't train a bunch of bees to go after a person!"

"No, but it looks like somebody deliberately hid her purse, and I'm beginning to think it wasn't Hartley." My grandmother peered over the sofa to see if Josie was listening, but I could have assured her my daughter was sleeping too soundly to hear anything we said. "In fact," she went on, "if it weren't for Hartley playing with Belinda's purse, we might not have found that antidote in time."

"Still, Violet has a point," I told them. "It isn't going to do Uncle Ernest or Belinda or anybody else any good for you two to stick around any longer. I'm going to sleep down here on the sofa tonight, and I doubt if Uncle Lum and Aunt Leona— or Grady, either—will be going anywhere until tomorrow at least."

"Won't be going then unless we get some of this mess cleared up," Violet said, raising a brow—or trying to. "That nice young policeman—the one who's been talking to Ernest so much lately—well, he told everybody not to go anywhere for a while."

"What? When did this happen?" I glanced at my grandmother. Sometimes Violet gets things all mixed up.

But Ma Maggie didn't dispute it. "Well, not everybody," she said, nodding. "Just those of us who were here when that happened to Ella. It was while you all were gone, Kate. That fellow from the sheriff's department was here most of the day while everybody was out looking for you and Josie—Grady, too. He said he thought it best if we didn't stray far from Bishop's Bridge for a few days. Just until they can get to the bottom of all this."

"I reckon he must think one of us pushed poor old Ella into that gully," Violet said. "Although for the life of me, I can't imagine why." She shook her head at me. "I hope you have a good alibi, Kate."

"It's not funny, Violet!" My grandmother stood and gathered her things. "None of this is funny. Somebody gave poor Ella a shove, and somebody took Belinda's purse and hid it where they didn't think we'd find it—not in time, anyway."

Cousin Violet folded plump arms across her ample bosom. "Well, I can assure you, it wasn't me! Why, my dear Hodges used to say I didn't have a mean bone in my body."

Ma Maggie said it wasn't her, either, and that she wasn't going to worry about it any more tonight, but was going home to bed, and if we had any sense at all we'd do the same.

My cousin Violet had her eccentricities but I never considered her capable of murder any more than I had my own grandmother. For a while, I had even suspected my cousin Grady, but now I wasn't even sure about that. Then who? I wondered. And more importantly, why?

Before she left for home, Ma Maggie patted my shoulder,

planted a light kiss on my forehead and told me to go to sleep. I could see her darting obvious glances at Violet, urging her to do the same, but as usual, her cousin ignored her. From the way Violet was acting, I guessed she had something to tell me she didn't want my grandmother to hear. And I was right.

Violet waited until we heard Ma Maggie say good-bye to Uncle Lum and Aunt Leona, cross the porch and start down the steps before she shoved Uncle Ernest's old hassock next to my chair and plopped down beside me. "Now, I don't want to alarm your grandmother," she said under her breath. "You know how worked up she gets sometimes over the least little thing . . ."

"Uh-huh," I said, trying not to smile.

"Look, I know you all think I'm just a crazy old woman, and maybe I am," she said, "but Maggie's right about one thing. Something's mighty wrong here, and I think I know who's at the bottom of it."

I looked at Violet. The woman was completely serious. "I couldn't stand it if anything happened to one of you," my cousin went on. "But I'll need you to help me, Kate."

When she reached for my hand, I couldn't ignore the chipped purple nail polish and a bracelet that looked as if it came from a box of Cracker Jack, but for some reason I wanted to believe her—at least long enough to listen to whatever she had to tell me.

But before Violet had a chance to speak, Uncle Ernest phoned to tell us that Ella had died.

CHAPTER EIGHTEEN

here's nothing you or anyone can do," Uncle Ernest told Aunt Leona when she and Uncle Lum offered to meet him at the hospital.

"He's on his way home," my aunt said, hanging up the phone. "Said he'd make arrangements in the morning. Poor man must be exhausted."

We all were, and since I would be sleeping on the living room sofa, I offered Violet my bed so she wouldn't have to drive home so late at night.

"I don't suppose Ella mentioned anything else about who might have attacked her," Violet said.

"Uncle Ernest said she slipped away peacefully without regaining consciousness," my aunt told her.

"I doubt if she knew," Uncle Lum said. "And even if she did, we'll never find out now."

Cousin Violet squeezed my hand as she left to go upstairs. "Talk to you in the morning," she whispered.

Grady stumbled past me sleepily, mumbled good night, then followed his parents upstairs, and I found an extra pillow and a light blanket for the sofa and checked to see if Josie was still asleep. My daughter hadn't moved from the position she'd been in earlier and I risked a light kiss on her cheek as I adjusted her covers. I decided to try calling Ned before I went to bed, and braced myself for his response. My husband was going to be angry that I hadn't gotten in touch with him sooner.

But I reached the hotel desk only to be told that Ned McBride had checked out earlier. And no, he said, Mr. McBride had left no word as to where he might be reached.

I thought I would drop off to sleep the minute my head hit the pillow. Wrong! I listened to every breath my daughter took, then heard Uncle Ernest drive up, come through the back way and go quietly to his room, wondering the whole time why Ned had left the seminar in California before it was due to be over. Had they rescheduled his speech? And wasn't he supposed to have been on some sort of panel, as well, I thought. If my husband had heard about Josie's being lost, he would certainly have telephoned somebody at Bramblewood, but no one here had heard from him. So where was he?

I was turning over my pillow for the third time when I caught a whiff of a most delightful aroma coming from the kitchen and knew Augusta must be there.

"Tea or coffee?" she asked, lifting dark, moist brownies onto a leaf-patterned plate. "I thought we might take these out on the porch. It's cooler there now and everyone else seems to have gone to bed."

Penelope, in a daisy-sprigged shift of simple design with eyelet trim at the neck, pinched off the corner of a steaming cake and popped it into her mouth.

"Why, Penelope!" Augusta pretended to be shocked, but she smiled when she said it. We loaded a tray with the brownies, plus milk for Penelope, peppermint tea for me and dark, rich coffee for Augusta, and made our way to the porch, quietly skirting Amos sleeping by Josie's cot.

"Thank you, Penelope, for looking after Josie last night," I said as soon as we were settled. "I'm so glad you were with her. You probably saved her life."

"You're welcome," she said, and I could see the young angel's smile even in the dark.

The brownies were as good as they looked and smelled, and tasted of dark chocolate and strawberry jam. I ate two of them and licked my fingers after every bite. I waited until Penelope had fallen asleep on the settee before I spoke.

"Violet thinks she knows who's behind all this," I told Augusta. "I don't know whether to take her seriously or not. She's as flaky as a bowl of cereal, but I'm so confused, I'm ready to grasp at anything."

Augusta sat in the rocking chair next to mine slowly sipping her coffee. "What does she say?"

"Only that she's worried about us and has an idea who might be responsible."

I let peppermint steam waft into my face. "Augusta, you

know I even suspected Grady, and I'm still not sure he's not mixed up in what happened to Beverly. He was there, you know. He as good as admitted it."

"He was there when she died?"

"Oh, I don't know about that, but he's been there. He told me about her apartment, and earlier Grady said he hadn't seen Beverly in years." I sipped my tea and felt its warmth relax me. "Do you think there might be a connection between Beverly's death and Ella's?"

Augusta swung one gold-sandaled foot and trailed amethyst and sapphire stones through her long fingers. "I think it might have begun with the young couple who came through here on a raft," she said. "Back when Ella first arrived. There has to be a connection somehow."

"You mean because of the anklet we found in the attic? Valerie was one of the names that girl used."

She nodded. "Possibly. That's one reason, but not enough." Augusta sighed. "I'm afraid your cousin Violet is right. We do need to get to the bottom of this before someone else gets hurt."

"Grady admitted to accidently killing his father, and he may or may not have had anything to do with the way Beverly died—although I don't even want to think about that—but he wasn't even born when those two came through here on the raft," I said. "And that skeleton they dug up in Remeth churchyard is older than he is."

"But not older than your uncle Ernest," Augusta said.

"You don't think Uncle Ernest had anything to do with it, do you?"

The steam from Augusta's coffee curled around her face. "I

think he might have an idea who did." She looked at me over her cup. "I'm afraid your uncle's life might be in danger, Kate."

"I still can't see how Beverly's death could have anything to do with something that happened almost forty years ago," I said.

"If we only knew what your uncle was digging for in that rose garden." Augusta stopped rocking for a minute and held out her arms as Ella's cat Dagwood jumped into her lap. "Ah, there you are, my sweet! Poor kitty's probably wondering what happened to Ella."

"I'm afraid we've ignored him with all that's been going on," I said, reaching over to scratch between Dagwood's ears.

Augusta laughed as she snuggled the cat under her chin. "Cats don't mind being ignored," she said. "They'll let us know when they want attention—and right now, Dagwood wants attention."

"Augusta, you don't suppose Ella and Valerie are the *same?*"

"Somehow I thought Ella was here first . . . your grandmother would know."

"I know it was a long time ago, but I just can't see Ella ever being a wild hippie child." I smiled, picturing the dour elderly woman in headband and love beads.

Augusta spoke over the cat's loud purring. "If I remember right, it didn't seem as if your uncle actually *found* anything in that rose garden the other night."

"The storm came up and drove us all inside. If he found something, he didn't have a chance to hide it—unless it's in the toolshed. Of course, he could've put it somewhere else since."

I took the last sip of my tea and felt myself sliding lower in my chair. I hoped I could stay awake long enough to make it to the sofa, but I must have drifted off because I felt Augusta's hand on my arm and heard her gently calling my name.

"Tomorrow I want you to find out what seemed to startle Josie when she wandered into the woods," she said. "Then take her to your cousin Marge's where she'll be safe."

Not wanting to let my daughter out of my sight until she was at least thirty-five, I started to protest, but Augusta held up a slender hand.

"Don't worry, Kathryn, she'll be fine. Now, I'm afraid we're going to have to take Violet up on her offer. It's all we have right now, and the fact that everyone thinks she's . . . well . . . a little odd should be a definite advantage. Meanwhile, I'll look in that toolshed tonight to see if your uncle hid something there, but frankly, I don't expect to find it." She moved behind my rocking chair and gave it a little tip so that I had to grab the arms to keep from falling out. "Now, go on inside and get some sleep. We have a busy day ahead of us tomorrow."

Josie woke with a suspicious rash and a tremendous appetite. The rash looked like poison ivy and her appetite was for French toast with sourwood honey. I doctored the former with calamine lotion and served up the latter with bacon and a big glass of orange juice. The swelling on her ankle seemed to have gone down some but it was still sore, she said.

"Josie," I began as she finished her second piece of French

toast, "do you remember what made you go so far into the woods when you ran away the other day? Did something frighten you?"

Josie put down her fork. "I was mad. Mad at that hateful Cynthia! Every time I think about her it makes me even madder. Wish I'd slapped her twice!"

"I had an idea you might've been a tiny bit upset," I said, meaning to get back to that matter later. "But did you really mean to run so far?"

"I heard somebody."

"In the woods, you mean?"

Josie nodded. "There's a trail over there—way on the other side of that field where Uncle Ernest used to plant corn. There was somebody in there."

"Are you sure it was a person? It might have been a deer or a squirrel or something."

"No, I heard them talking. Sounded like there were two of them," she said.

"Could you hear what they said? Was it men or women speaking?"

Josie shrugged. "They were too far away. Just sounded like mumbling. I thought it might be those mean boys down the road and I didn't want them to see me."

"I don't blame you," I said. "I just wish you'd run the other way."

Uncle Lum followed his nose into the kitchen. "I don't think there's anything that smells any better than bacon cooking. You wouldn't have a few extra pieces of that lying about, would you?"

"Sure do, and I can fry up more. How about some French toast to go with it?"

"Oh, yes, please! But could you make it fast before Leona gets up?" My uncle helped himself to a mug of coffee and set himself a place at the table.

While bacon sizzled in the pan, I settled my daughter on the living room sofa with a Nancy Drew book that had probably belonged to my mother and left her happily turning pages.

"Uncle Lum," I said, setting French toast, golden brown and crusty, in front of him. "Do you remember when Ella first came?"

I had to repeat my question because my uncle was too happy to reply for a minute or two. I waited until he had washed down his first piece of toast with coffee and asked him again.

"Been close to forty years," he said. "Poor Ella, she hasn't had much of a life, I'm afraid. Didn't seem to bother her, though."

"Do you remember if it was before or after that hippie couple disappeared on the river?"

He stopped eating long enough to look up at me. "Now, why would you want to know that?"

I smiled. "Just curious."

Uncle Lum reared back in his chair and laughed. "I get it! You're thinking Ella might be that missing hippie girl who was wanted by the law. Well, you can forget it. Ella was already here when that happened. Uncle Ernest had fixed up that little guesthouse for her—the one Casey's in now." He frowned. "Don't reckon we'll ever find out what happened to those two."

"Do you remember anybody around here named Valerie?" I asked, sliding two more pieces of bacon onto his plate.

They didn't last long. "Can't say that I do. Doesn't ring a bell." My uncle finished his breakfast and rinsed away the evidence in the sink, smiling all the while.

Uncle Ernest declined my offer of a more robust breakfast in favor of his usual soft-boiled egg. Somber and silent, he seemed to want to be alone, so I left him while I folded away Josie's cot and took our pillows and blankets upstairs. I was just getting ready to come down when Violet stuck her head out of my bedroom where she'd spent the night. "Has Ernest left yet?" she wanted to know.

I looked over the railing to see my uncle leaving by the front door and knew he was going to take care of Ella's funeral plans. "He has now," I said.

"Good," she whispered. "We need to talk."

I allowed my cousin to pull me into the room and close the door behind us, while all the time she spoke in hushed, conspiratorial tones. I could tell she was enjoying it. "Now, this has to be between just the two of us," she said, sitting me firmly on the side of the bed. "I think I know who's behind all this, but I can't be sure—not yet, anyway. I do know one thing, though: We have to get your uncle Ernest out of this house or his life won't be worth a plugged nickel."

I frowned. Augusta had said almost the same thing. "How do we do that?" I asked.

"I'm working on that," Violet said, and told me her plan.

"Who do you think it is?" It wouldn't surprise me at all if she suspected the ghost of the long-dead Yankee soldier or the spirit of that skeleton they dug up in Remeth cemetery, but my cousin wasn't ready to reveal the identity of who she thought the murderer might be.

I sat there for a few minutes thinking about what Violet had said. Her plan to reveal the guilty party scared me half to death, but it frightened me even more that most of it made sense.

CHAPTER NINETEEN

hat's going on?" Marge wanted to know when I dropped off Josie that morning.

"What do you mean?" I asked.

"You know very well what I mean. Something's going on. You know I'm always glad to have Josie here, but yesterday nobody could pry her away from you with a crowbar, now you're willing to leave her with me. Why?"

"Just take care of her, please," I said. "I can't explain, but she's better off here."

Marge folded her arms and stepped closer. "This doesn't have anything to do with her running away, does it?"

I shook my head. "No, really."

"Or with Ned. He hasn't called, has he?"

I told her about phoning the hotel to learn my husband had checked out. "You're sure he didn't call while we were gone?" I asked.

My cousin looked like she wanted to cry. "Kate, if he had,

we would've told you." She put an arm around me. "He must not have heard about Josie, or you know he'd be frantic. Uncle Ernest did a pretty good job of keeping the news mongers out—although it did make the local news.

"I'm sure you'll hear from him today," she said as we walked to my car together. But Ned McBride wasn't my main concern just then. If I could just make it safely through the next twenty-four hours, maybe I could begin to put my own life back in order. But right now, he would have to get in line.

Still, I couldn't help but wonder why we hadn't heard from Ned. Had he taken sick? Been fired from his job? All kinds of scary notions went through my head—except the scariest one: He just didn't care enough to call. But surely that couldn't be true!

When I got back to Bramblewood, Ma Maggie was there to greet me with happy news. My mom was on the phone to tell us Sara had delivered a healthy baby boy in London a few hours before. They had named him Andrew Joseph after our dad and his dad, and we all crowded around the telephone taking time about congratulating the new parents and grandparents. Much to my relief, kin on this side of the ocean silently agreed not to mention the scare of Josie's overnight adventure.

After I phoned Josie to tell her about her new little cousin, I escaped from Violet's watchful eye long enough to wander into the rose garden. Uncle Ernest had not yet returned from town, but Lum and Leona were still here and my grandmother seemed to have settled in for the day. Deedee, I was told, would be along later.

The day had turned cloudy and there was a heaviness in the air. I felt vulnerable in the garden, as if I were being watched, and I didn't like it. In spite of my guardian angel, whom I knew must be somewhere near, I sensed an inert danger. Trouble was simmering, and Violet and I had the stick to stir it.

I had received no sign from Augusta that day, so I assumed she hadn't turned up anything interesting in the toolshed. And at first the garden seemed as it had before, except that someone had filled in the hole Uncle Ernest dug earlier. In earlier years, my uncle had taken excellent care of the roses, and even though he had neglected the garden somewhat recently, the bushes were in full bloom. There were several varieties ranging in color from white to deepest red and they smelled the way I'd want to smell if I could only bottle the scent. I inhaled the aroma of sweet summer and thought of how much Uncle Ernest must have loved his young wife to have kept up her garden in this way.

Now and then I saw evidence of an earlier digging, probably done the same night the rainstorm drove us inside, but at the far end of the garden I noticed an excision almost surgical in its neatness. No wonder we hadn't noticed it before! The line was so fine, I almost passed it by, and if it weren't for a small clod of raw red dirt, I don't think I would have looked at it twice. On closer inspection, I found the rose bush there, a deep pink specimen, a little droopier than the others, and I soon knew why. Someone had excavated beneath it with a straight-sided shovel, removed whatever was in there and filled the cavity with clumps of rock and clay.

"Find anything interesting?"

I hadn't heard footsteps behind me so I must have jumped when Grady spoke because he threw up his hands and stepped back. "Hey, Cuz, it's just me! Didn't mean to scare you."

"Didn't hear you coming. After the last few days, I'm getting downright neurotic." I plucked a rose and sniffed it, trying to appear normal.

"So what's with the bush here?" Grady knelt to examine the thin line in the dirt.

Obviously he had been watching when I found what was underneath, so I showed him how the hole had been filled with little regard for the rose's root system.

My cousin frowned. "Wonder what was under here? Reckon Uncle Ernest knows? You said he was out here digging the other night."

"I'm not sure. It could've been done since, but whoever did it knew what he was doing, I almost didn't notice it."

"What about Casey?" he said.

"Casey's a gardener. He'd know better than to shock the root system like that . . . look what it's done to the bush. Besides, I heard Uncle Ernest tell him to stay away from the rose garden."

"How's Josie?" Grady asked. "Her foot any better?"

"Swelling's down some, thanks. She has poison ivy, though." I started walking back. We were only a few yards from the house; nothing could happen to me here, yet that feeling of unease persisted.

Walking along beside me, Grady must have sensed it. He put out a hand to stop me. "Wait a minute, Kate. Something's wrong. What is it?"

I tried to laugh. "You mean other than we all spent the night roaming around the mountain and somebody pushed Ella into a ravine? Not to mention the skeleton they dug up next door and the yellow jackets that attacked Belinda."

199

"I thought you said you weren't going to mention that."

When Grady grinned, he looked and sounded so much like his old self I had to laugh. But now he turned serious. "You're afraid of me, aren't you, Kate?"

"What? Don't be silly! Of course not. What a thing to say!"

"Yes, you are. I can tell. What's the matter? You think I did in poor Ella?"

We walked to a bench beneath the scuppernong arbor and he sat and put his head in his hands. "Just tell me what it is, will you? *Please?*"

I sat beside him and pulled his hands away. "It's just that . . . well, you said something the other day that made me wonder, that's all."

"When? Said what? You mean when I told you about my . . . father?"

"No, not that, although that did come as kind of a shock. You described Beverly's apartment, Grady, when you said you'd never been there." I glanced at the back porch. No one was there. And Augusta? She was probably somewhere shepherding Penelope.

"I see." My cousin linked his fingers together and stared at the earth between his feet. He didn't speak again for a while.

My mind went crazy. This is where the murderer says, *And now no one need ever know* . . . as he chokes the victim. I hoped my wandering husband would turn up sometime soon to take care of Josie in case Grady took a notion to do away with me. The idea was so ridiculous, I almost laughed.

"You're right, I *was* there," Grady said finally. "I wasn't going to tell anyone. There didn't seem to be any reason . . ."

"You were there when Beverly died?"

"No! No, I drove up there a few weeks before. Didn't mention it to anybody—it was a spur of the moment thing, but Bev and I hadn't seen each other in . . . well, years really. We'd talked over the phone for hours, and everything seemed to click between us—almost like it used to. I just needed to see her, to be with her, and Bev felt the same." Grady pulled a leaf from the scuppernong vine and rolled it between his fingers.

"So, how did it go?" I asked.

He took a deep breath and dropped the leaf to the ground. "Okay, I guess. It was good to see her again. We went out to dinner, had some wine. She told me about her work and what she planned to do when she got her degree. We talked about old times . . ."

"And?" I waited.

"And . . . nothing."

"What do you mean, nothing?" I asked.

"Just that. We had a pleasant time together, but that was all. There wasn't any chemistry between us. It was gone—zilch!"

"Do you think she felt the same way?"

Grady shook his head. "Don't know. It's hard to say. Bev seemed eager to be back in North Carolina, closer to her family and all that, and I'm sure she was glad to see me. To tell the truth, I was so disappointed after building this all up in my mind, I didn't pay much attention to how Beverly reacted. I was disgusted with myself for dragging it out like that, for wasting all those years hoping someday Bev would change her mind."

"And when she did, you didn't want her?"

"Something like that. Frankly, I was hoping Bev felt the same so it would save me the embarrassment of going through all that. Kate, you must think I'm a real jerk."

"You can't help how you feel," I said. "So that's how you knew about her apartment, how small it was and where it was located."

He nodded. "Right. That place was out in the boonies."

"Grady, while you and Bev were talking, did she mention having a quarrel with anyone?"

"Not that I can think of. Why?"

"She didn't seem afraid or suspicious of anybody at the university or maybe somebody she worked with?"

Grady got to his feet. "Why are you asking me this, Kate? Is there something I don't know?"

I was explaining that the police there thought Beverly's death wasn't an accident when Uncle Ernest drove up. Once he'd gotten out of the car, he barely nodded to us as he approached; his pace was slower than usual and his hair looked as if he'd stuck his finger in a light socket. My uncle seemed to have aged five years in the last few days.

I knew it probably wasn't the proper time to ask him, but I had to know. "Uncle Ernest, it looks like somebody dug up something under one of the rose bushes. Did you know about that?"

He looked at me as if he didn't understand. "What, Kate?"

"The rose bush—the pink one in the back. Somebody's been digging under there. Looks like they tried to put it back so nobody would know."

He took a crisp white handkerchief from his pocket and

wiped his face, and it occurred to me that Ella must have ironed that handkerchief. "Let's don't worry about that right now, Kate, and I'd just as soon you stay away from the garden for now."

I nodded. I felt like a little girl with her hand in the cookie jar. "I'm sorry about Ella, Uncle Ernest. Is there anything I can do to help?"

"It's all taken care of. Service is tomorrow at three—Presbyterian church, of course." It surprised me when my uncle smiled. "Ella left instructions, you know—had everything written out. And guess what hymn she wants? 'Shall We Gather at the River'! And her terrified of water!"

I left Grady to mull over what I had told him about Beverly and followed my uncle inside where Violet waited in the kitchen. She had a tall glass of sweet tea ready with lemon and mint, just the way Uncle Ernest liked it, and before the man had a chance to do otherwise, Violet had him seated at the table. She pulled out a chair and plopped down across from him, then indicated that I was to do the same.

"Kate and I are concerned about Maggie, Ernest," she began in a confidential whisper. "She's uneasy, you know, living alone with all that's been going on."

My uncle glanced at me and I repeated what Violet had said.

He drained his glass and waited while Violet refilled it. "I never knew Maggie to be the nervous type," he said.

Violet smoothed her purple hair and patted his hand. "Well, of course, she won't let on, but I know she's been awake half the night."

I almost laughed. My grandmother usually slept like a rock.

"We were thinking, since she's alone over there it might help her to get a good night's rest if you were to stay with her—for tonight at least. We have Lum and Grady here with us and I'll be sleeping on the cot—just until this passes over."

Uncle Ernest took off his glasses and polished them. I doubt if he'd been out of his own bed more than two or three times in the last forty years. He was not a happy man. "You want me to stay tonight at Maggie's?" He sighed. "Well, Violet, if you really think it would help—"

"Oh, I do, I do!" For a minute I thought she might hug him, but Violet restrained herself. "But don't let on to anybody about this, please. It would embarrass Maggie for anybody to know she's having these problems. You know how independent she pretends to be."

My uncle nodded numbly. I wanted to jump up and run. Surely lightning would strike us at any moment! If my grandmother ever found out what we had done, Violet and I would really have something to worry about!

A few minutes later I heard Violet telling Ma Maggie that Ernest was concerned about her staying alone and insisted on being with her that night.

"Why, I'm perfectly all right by myself. Ernest knows that." My grandmother spoke a little too loudly and Violet made even more noise trying to shush her.

"He wants to do this, Maggie. He's your brother, he worries

about you. One night isn't going to kill you, so just humor the man, will you?" I could tell Violet was losing her patience.

"Oh, all right, but I'll have to make up the bed in my guest room. I just hope I can find the sheets!" Ma Maggie grumbled. "And for the last three nights some idiot woman has been calling me at four in the morning asking to speak to somebody named Homer Earl. I keep telling her there's no Homer Earl there, but she can't seem to get it through her thick skull! Hope Ernest doesn't mind losing out on his sleep."

"And please don't say anything to him or anybody else about this, Maggie," Violet said. "He'd hate for everybody to know he's such an old worrywart. Promise it will be our secret."

"Oh, for heaven's sakes, all right!" My grandmother waved her away. "But I think you're both about three pickles shy of a quart."

She doesn't know the half of it, I thought.

CHAPTER TWENTY

If there had been a way to hide from Deedee, I would have done it, but neighbors bearing food had already started to pour in and I had to mingle and be polite. Uncle Lum and Casey rummaged around to find extra tables to hold all the cakes and pies, and Ma Maggie was trying her best to keep a record of who brought what. Uncle Ernest's neighbor Goat had just brought over a huge basket of fruit and I was trying to find a place to put it when Deedee appeared from behind an arrangement of red gladiolus and whisked it out of my hand.

"Here, let's put it in the middle of the table," she said, shoving aside a graceful centerpiece of hydrangeas, roses and Queen Anne's lace the florist had delivered earlier.

"Let's not," I said, and setting things the way they were, I moved the basket to the buffet. A vase of pink carnations sat on the table by the door and a billowy multicolored arrangement from Ella's circle at the Presbyterian church cascaded from the mantel. The house was beginning to smell like a funeral parlor and I tried to avoid even looking at the spray of purple artificial flowers with a toy telephone in the center bearing the message *Jesus called!*

Deedee fiddled with a dish of cookies, turning it this way and that. "So . . . how's the runaway this morning? Feeling better?"

"*Josie's* all right," I said. "I think she came through just fine after spending a night alone in the woods. She's a brave little girl and I'm proud of her."

"I noticed you and Grady were alone all night, too!" My cousin snickered—she actually *snickered!*—I don't know any other way to describe it. "That must have been interesting. Wonder what Ned will think about that."

"In the first place we weren't alone together, although if we had been it wouldn't have made any difference. And I'm sure Ned will just be relieved that we all found our way back home."

"You mean he doesn't know?" Her eyes narrowed. "Where is Ned, Kate?"

Thank heavens Aunt Leona came between us just then on her way to the kitchen with a dish in her hands. "Gracious, look at all these sweets! And here we have another lemon meringue pie. I don't know what we'll do with it all."

I had a good notion of what to do with that pie but it would've been a terrible waste and then I'd have to clean the floor. Deedee must have guessed what I was thinking because she stepped back and put a Boston fern between us.

"What do you suppose is going on with Uncle Ernest?" she whispered.

"What do you mean?"

"He *says* he sent Belinda away for her safety but nobody knows where she is. It's just peculiar, that's all."

"I think that's the point—that nobody knows where she is," I said, looking around for a way out.

"Yes, well, there was that incident with the bees, you know, and then all of a sudden, she's *gone*." Deedee glanced behind her and leaned closer. "The police have been asking questions, too, since they found that skeleton over there in the cemetery." She shrugged. "Haven't you ever wondered what really happened to Rose?"

Cousin Violet took that opportunity to announce to one and all that she thought she *knew* who was behind all the things going on around here.

The room became as quiet as if she'd asked for organ donors. Judge Kidd, who had been dribbling salted nuts into his mouth, stopped with his hand in midair; Ma Maggie's glasses slid down her nose and Grady and Casey, who had been shifting furniture about to make room for everybody, dropped a heavy armchair somewhere near my foot.

Deedee looked at me and rolled her eyes, and Uncle Lum and Aunt Leona just tried to laugh it away.

Uncle Ernest wandered in about then with the guest book he'd brought from the funeral home and wanted to know why everybody was so quiet.

"Cousin Violet says she knows who killed Ella and hid Belinda's purse!" Deedee told him, not even trying to supress her giggles.

"What about that skeleton, Violet?" Goat spoke up. "Reckon you know who put that there, too."

"I didn't say I *knew* who did it! I said I *thought* I knew who did it," Violet said. "And I have evidence, too."

"Oh, this is ridiculous!" Ma Maggie stood stiff as a starch-dried shirt. "Violet, you've gone too far. This is no time to be silly."

"Murder isn't silly, Maggie Brown!" Violet glanced quickly at me and I knew I had to jump in soon.

"I think we'll let the police take care of that, Vi," Uncle Ernest said. "Now, why don't we all help ourselves to some of this wonderful food? I'm tempted to start with dessert myself."

"Where's your evidence, Cousin Violet?" I asked, grinning. "Bet I know where you've hidden it."

"That's for me to know and you *not* to find out," my cousin said, drawing her pudgy self up as straight as possible.

"I saw you out there in the toolshed. What have you got in there? You've locked it away in that shed somewhere, haven't you?"

"Certainly not!" Violet marched off in a well-rehearsed huff and the rest of my relatives lit into me at once.

"Kate! What in the world were you thinking of teasing Violet like that?" My grandmother gave me a look that would freeze a sunbeam.

"Kathryn, I'm surprised at you," Uncle Lum said.

Uncle Ernest just looked sad and shook his head. I was glad when Aunt Leona grabbed my hand and led me away to help in the kitchen.

As soon as I could get away, I crept to the telephone in the hall and called my friend at the Bishop's Bridge *Bulletin* to ask if he'd heard anything more about the skeleton they'd dug up next door.

"Why, Kate, sure is good to hear your voice after that scare you gave us the other night!" Charles Hollingsworth's voice sounded kind of rusty but nice. "As a matter of fact, I did hear something about that—sort of secondhand, you might say." He lowered his voice. "If you repeat this, please don't give the source, as I'm not supposed to know. The policemen who were talking weren't aware I was around—if you know what I mean."

"In other words, you were eavesdropping?"

"Guilty." He paused. "Kate, the skeleton wasn't that of a woman as we suspected. It was a man. Been there close to forty years, they think."

"A man? Are you sure?"

He laughed. "Well, I didn't examine it or anything, and wouldn't have known the difference if I had, but that's the latest word. I think the sheriff was kind of surprised, too."

I thanked him and went back to see if I could find Violet after her shocking announcement and abrupt departure, and discovered her on the back porch with a plate of peach cobbler in one hand and a slab of pound cake in the other.

"What are you doing out here all by yourself?" I asked. "People will be wondering where you are."

She dabbed her plum-colored lips with a paper napkin. "Then let 'em. I'm keeping an eye on the toolshed . . . and for heaven's sakes, keep your voice down, Kate! I don't want anybody to know I'm out here."

If a person could bellow in a whisper, my cousin Violet did, and if anybody had been within twenty yards of the toolshed, they would've heard every word she said.

"After what we said in there, I don't think anybody will come close to that place in broad open daylight," I told her.

Violet laughed and nudged me with a hefty elbow. "But just wait until tonight! Fooled 'em good, didn't we?"

"We'll see," I said.

I went inside to give Ma Maggie and Aunt Leona a break with hostess duties and was grateful that some of the neighbors had taken over in the kitchen. Uncle Ernest, his friend Goat and Uncle Lum, along with several other men, had made themselves comfortable on the front porch with glasses of something that looked like iced tea, but I knew darn well it wasn't. I was glad when Marge came by with Jon and Hartley a little later to see if she could help. A friend had taken Darby and Josie, along with her own children, to an afternoon movie, she told me.

"You can keep me company and tell me who some of these people are," I said. "They seem to expect me to remember that their sister went to school with my mother in the third grade, or that Aunt Somebody-or-Other was a bridesmaid in my grandmother's wedding." I wanted to tell my cousin about Violet's far-fetched plan, but if it didn't work out, I knew I'd never hear the last of it. I did tell her what I'd found out about the skeleton belonging to a male.

Marge directed a new arrival to the kitchen with a plate of sliced ham before replying. "Really?" she said. "Well, that's kind of a relief, isn't it? I mean—we thought it might've been—you know."

"I know," I told her. "So where do we go from here?"

"*We* don't go anywhere, Kate McBride, so don't even think about it." My cousin stepped back and frowned at me, turning her head to the side so that a strand of bright hair fell across one eye. "You aren't cooking up some crazy scheme, are you?"

"Don't worry, I've had enough excitement," I said, feeling that surely nothing would come of Violet's wild plan. Still, I was relieved to see Burdette bouncing up the steps so I could change the subject. "Here comes your hubby," I said. "Uncle Ernest says he's to take part in the service tomorrow."

Marge nodded. "Ella earmarked several Bible verses for him. Thought a lot of Burdette, she said—even though he is a 'heathen' Baptist!" My cousin shook her head and smiled. "Poor Ella," we said together.

By late afternoon visitors had thinned and we were running out of places to put all the food. Deedee had left earlier to collect Cynthia from pageant rehearsal and Marge and Burdette followed soon after. I managed to entice Cousin Violet from her back-porch sentry duty long enough to join us for an early supper as Ma Maggie and Uncle Ernest planned to stop by the funeral home before going to my grandmother's for the night. Formal visitation was scheduled at Bramblewood after the service the next afternoon.

"Maggie and I have some things to discuss and I'll be late getting home, so please don't wait up for me," Uncle Ernest told us at supper. My grandmother looked at him kind of funny but didn't say anything, and I think I was the only one who noticed that he carried a small overnight bag with him when he left.

Thank heavens Violet stayed out of sight until Lum and Leona, tired after a long day, went upstairs early, and Grady had taken off to visit a friend he'd known in high school. I didn't blame him for not wanting to hang around Bramble-wood. I wouldn't be here myself if I hadn't been fool enough to go along with Violet's crazy scheme.

"Lord, I never realized it took so blasted long to get dark this time of year!" Violet said as she paced back and forth in the dusky kitchen. I had finally convinced her we could keep an eye on the toolshed just as well from inside.

It was after nine and, so far, nobody had approached the shed. I hadn't seen Augusta or Penelope all day, but I had a feeling they weren't very far away—or I hoped they weren't.

"What makes you think Uncle Ernest is in some kind of danger?" I asked. "If you think you know who's behind all this, I wish you'd share it with me."

Violet rattled the ice in her glass of lemonade. "When I'm sure, Kate, when I'm sure. I just have a nasty feeling, is all."

"You better have more than a feeling to make me miss another night of sleep," I told her. I didn't add that I had an uneasy sense that something was going to happen tonight, too.

My cousin finished her lemonade and poured herself another glass. "Are there any more of those cheese straws Cecilia But-terfield brought over? All this waiting's making me hungry."

I sat by the window and listened to Violet munch. Tonight she had worn dark purple so she wouldn't be easily seen in the dark. Earlier I had telephoned Josie to tell her good night and she had asked if her dad had called. It broke my heart to admit I hadn't heard. "I imagine we'll hear something tomorrow," I said, trying to sound optimistic. But I was beginning to grow as worried as I was angry. If Ned had left the hotel the day before, he should have been in touch by now. And in spite of my resentment, I found myself praying that nothing had happened to my husband.

I wasn't surprised when after less than an hour, Violet dozed off sitting at the table with her head on her chest, and I took advantage of the situation to dig a penlight from my purse so that I could read a paperback mystery, one of Tamar Myers's funny Magdelina Yoder series, under the cover of the kitchen table. I needed something light to help me pass the time. Magdelina was having an hilarious confrontation with her sister's rotten little mutt when I thought I noticed movement out of the corner of my eye and, for a fraction of a second, a beam of light cut across the lawn.

Turning off my penlight, I moved closer to the window. It was difficult to see in the darkness and for a moment everything was still. Maybe I had imagined it. Then a dark figure stepped from behind the arbor and dashed across the lawn to the shed behind the house.

CHAPTER TWENTY-ONE

"Violet, wake up! Somebody's out there!" My cousin's head had dropped lower, and what had been light snoring sounds were now close to the dish-rattling stage. I gripped her shoulder. "Shh! You've got to stay with me. It looks like somebody was curious enough to take the bait."

"You don't have to shake me, Kate. I was only resting my eyes a minute." Violet adjusted her glasses and looked where I was pointing. "Are you sure it wasn't a shadow or something? I can't see a thing."

"That's because whoever's out there has gone into the tool-shed. I thought you said it was locked."

"*You* said it was locked. There's no way you can lock that old door." And my cousin Violet began to chuckle.

"What's so funny? Don't you dare go bananas on me now!" I really wanted to shake her this time. "Didn't you say some kind of evidence is hidden in there?"

"Just because I *said* it doesn't mean you can take it to the bank, Kate."

"Then where is it? What did you do in there?"

Violet crept close behind me as I slowly opened the door to the back porch. Of course, it squeaked. "Nothing," she said. "I just did a little painting, is all."

I was almost afraid to ask. "What kind of painting?"

"I guess you could call it fuschia or maybe hot pink," she said. "It's that kind that glows."

"You mean fluorescent? What did you paint?"

"Oh, just a couple of feet of the floor inside the door, but I didn't do it until this afternoon and it's supposed to take about twenty-four hours to dry." Violet's shoulders were shaking with laughter, and I was scared to death that whoever was out there could hear her.

"Keep your voice down . . . think of something sad," I whispered. "Think of poor Ella." *And think of what might happen to us if whoever that is comes this way!*

With our backs to the wall, we inched our way to the other end of the porch where wisteria vines concealed us from view. Parting the tendrils, I found my eyes had adjusted to the darkness enough to see the outline of the toolshed to the right of the muscadine arbor. A few seconds later, someone came out.

I motioned to Violet, then stepped aside so she could see, and she grabbed my wrist in a tourniquet grip. "Can you tell who it is?" she asked.

"Looks like a man." I almost laughed. "Seems to be having trouble with sticky feet." The person crossing the lawn stopped every few steps to wipe his shoes on the grass. Even from where we stood, I could see the cotton candy glow of his footprints until finally, having had enough, I suppose, the figure bent and pulled off his shoes.

Violet drew her purple shawl about her as if she meant to follow but I put up an arm to bar her way. "Oh, no you don't!" I said. "I'll trail him at a distance and see where he goes. Wait here until I get back!"

She snatched at my shirt. "But what if you don't?"

"Then holler like hell! Now, *please*, Violet! He's getting away!"

I had to hope she stayed where I told her as I didn't have time to look back. Thank heaven the person running ahead of me didn't look back, either. I don't believe he knew he was being followed, but he had to have known he had wandered into Violet's trap and was probably being watched. As I passed the garden, the smell of roses drifted out to meet me and I wondered again what my uncle had been searching for in there. Farther on, mounds of honeysuckle on what used to be a pasture fence filled the air with its sweet, heady scent. A chorus of frogs had started rehearsals nearby, and somewhere in the distance a lone dog bayed. The night was warm, and now and then a breeze ruffled leaves in the ash tree at the edge of the field with a soothing, oceanlike sound. But I wasn't soothed.

I waited in the big tree's shadow while the dark figure in front ducked behind a row of cedars and came out on the other side. Then, slipping into his shoes, he crossed the gravel farm road and seemed to pick up speed as he darted behind the shed where Casey kept his car. I had to run to keep up.

A mosquito kept buzzing around my ear, I had a pain in my side and somehow a pebble had worked its way into my shoe, but I didn't dare take time to stop and dump it out. Using the cedars for cover, I tried to keep up without being seen but there was no way to cross the narrow road without taking a chance in the open. Should I keep low and creep, praying I wouldn't be noticed, or hope for the best and run?

I ran. My heart did a bongo-beat solo I was sure you could hear a mile away, and I felt so light-headed I clung to the first object I came to, which happened to be a pine sapling, sticky with resin. A skunk had wandered through the area not too long before, so I was kind of glad of the strong pine smell. But the man I had been following seemed to have disappeared, and if I was going to find out where he went, I couldn't stand there forever—no matter how scared I was. *What if he's waiting for me up ahead*, I thought. Or even worse, maybe he had crept up behind me.

"Sure seems like a good time for a guardian angel to appear if one's on duty!" I muttered under my breath, glancing around for any sign of Augusta. But the only movement I saw was a bat fluttering over the top of the shed. She must be around somewhere, I thought, since, if I remembered correctly, the angel had given her consent to Violet's plan, but she was taking her own sweet time making her presence known!

I was about halfway between the tree and the shed when I heard the unmistakable sound of a screen door shutting. Dear God, was the man in Casey's house? I had overheard the caretaker mention to Grady on the porch right after supper that he planned to go to bed early in case Uncle Ernest needed him to help get ready for the visitation tomorrow.

A light came on in the hallway of the house and I hurried to the cover of a billowing forsythia bush underneath the window just in time to see the figure pass by the open door of the kitchen and enter the bedroom behind it. I looked for a place to hide near the bedroom window, but the area was bare of shrubbery, so I edged along the side of the house, hoping to crouch beneath it before he turned on a light. I was too late.

A dull yellow light filled the window square, but there was a brighter strip at the bottom. Whoever was in there had pulled down a shade leaving an inch or so uncovered just above the sill. *Thank you, God*, I thought. Or was Augusta responsible for my good fortune? Maybe she hadn't deserted me after all! I was feeling a little more confident about my chances when I walked smack into a spiderweb big enough for a tarantula and let out a sound that was something between a gargle and a groan. Immediately I hit the ground, brushing what felt like a convention of tickly spiders from my face and hair while waiting for the worst. There was no way he couldn't have heard that yell!

Well, actually there was one, I noted, as a toilet flushed somewhere inside.

Unless he had flushed the toilet to make me think he hadn't heard me! In which case he would be slipping around the side of the house to confront me . . . just about now.

I looked up to see a figure pass by the window in the bedroom and held my breath, waiting for him to raise the shade and find me there. Since I hadn't heard any yelling or sounds of a struggle inside, it seemed a safe bet the figure I had been following was Casey Grindle himself, but I wanted to be sure—that is, if I lived that long.

All right, Kate McBride, it's now or never! I felt like a voyeur looking in a strange man's bedroom window, but it was for a good cause, I told myself. Standing on tiptoe, I could just see over the sill to watch Casey staring in apparent dismay at the pink-spotted soles of the shoes he held in his hand. He had shed the dark gray cap he had been wearing and I suddenly realized I had never seen the man without something on his head. I soon understood why.

When Casey began to unbutton his shirt, I started to turn away. Now I knew who had been looking for Violet's "hidden evidence" in the toolshed, although the reason wasn't clear, and I certainly didn't need to stay long enough to watch the caretaker disrobe. But what was I to tell them when I reached the house—that Casey was looking for something in the toolshed? He was the caretaker, wasn't he? Maybe he needed a tool.

Oh, wake up, Kate! Not in the middle of the night! The man's up to something.

Another door opened, and I risked one more glance. Casey, whose back was to me now, took a suitcase from the closet shelf, and when he turned, I almost toppled backward onto the lawn. *Casey Grindle had breasts!*

I blinked. There was no mistaking it. The shirt hung open in front revealing a lace-trimmed bra, and unless Casey was into cross-dressing, *he* was a *she*. I watched brazenly as the caretaker peeled off the dark pants and shirt, tossed her ruined shoes in the trash can and slipped into a neat navy pantsuit and matching flats. She looked to be in her late fifties or early sixties, and although on closer observation I was able to notice her more feminine characteristics, the woman was of hefty build, and from where I stood, seemed to have enormous feet.

I stood there in something close to a trancelike state while

Casey (if this *was* her name) pulled items from closet shelves and dresser drawers and dumped them into her suitcase. She didn't mean to hang around long.

Did her rush to leave have anything to do with Ella's death or Belinda's encounter with yellow jackets, I wondered. And Violet had seemed to think Uncle Ernest was in some kind of danger. At least he would be staying the night at Ma Maggie's, I thought, although I couldn't imagine why Casey Grindle—or whoever she was—would be interested in harming my uncle.

A persistent mosquito stirred me into action. I had to get back to the house, and to Violet, who was probably frantic by now—if she hadn't dozed off again. I left the caretaker rummaging through boxes under her bed and backed away from the window, skirting the shed that housed Casey's car, then made my way carefully across the gravel road and climbed up the slope on the other side. So far, so good! Once I reached the stand of cedars, I would be out of the line of vision and could run without having to worry about being seen. I didn't understand the reason for Casey Grindle's abrupt leaving, but I knew we had to stop her.

The night air was cool on my face as I ran, and if I hadn't been on a crucial mission, I would have relished the experience. Or most of it.

Inhaling the Christmassy smell of cedar, I took a deep breath, emerged at full speed on the other side of the small grove of trees and skidded at least a couple of feet on the dew-wet grass. Then, feeling like Brer Rabbit, I rolled through a nasty patch of briars and bumped to rest against a tree stump.

"Oh, dear! I hope you haven't broken anything. . . . But I'm afraid you're going to have to hurry." Augusta, in a whispering dress of lilac chiffon, leaned over me with an expression of concerned impatience.

With difficulty, I pulled myself to my knees and began to pluck briars from my hands. "Well, fancy meeting you here," I told her. "A little late, aren't you?" I rubbed my aching shoulder.

She stood, plainly indicating I was to do the same. "Preventing minor accidents is not in my job description, Kathryn. Can you imagine how much *time* that would take? I should think you'd know better than to run on wet grass in the dark like this—besides, I was busy elsewhere."

"Doing what?" I struggled to my feet and trotted obediently beside her. The angel's brilliant necklace winked at me in orchid and indigo.

"I'm not sure where this Casey is going, but I thought it best to delay her," she said, pausing to look at me. "You *are* all right, aren't you?"

"Oh, I'm just fine," I said. I frowned. "Delay her how?"

"I never learned much about vehicles," Augusta said, "but I do know one can't get past a large obstacle. There was a dead sweet gum tree beside the drive, just before you reach the main road. It needed only a little encouragement to fall."

"How clever of you, Augusta! That should buy us time."

My companion was silent for a minute and began to walk faster. "However," she said, "I'm afraid I underestimated the woman's strength. Lifted that tree right off the road and tossed it aside. Amazing! Not as amazing as Sampson, of course, but I believe he had more hair."

I wasn't about to get into all that. "How long has she been gone?" I started to run—regardless of the wet grass.

"Not long. Just a few minutes, but I think we should hurry, Kate."

"Augusta, just who is Casey? You know something, don't you?"

"I have an idea. . . . And I'm a bit concerned about your uncle."

"Not to worry. He's staying with my grandmother tonight," I said.

For an angel, Augusta didn't look so calm anymore. "Then I think you should telephone him as soon as you reach home."

I was out of breath when we reached Bramblewood, and it seemed every light was burning. Grady ran across the lawn to meet me. "What in hell's going on? Violet had us scared to death. What's this wild tale anyway? Are you all right?"

I followed him into the kitchen where his mom and dad tried to comfort Violet who, between sobs, was blaming herself for my likely demise.

"Oh, why, why did I let her go?" she wailed. "Out chasing around in the dark of night after that . . . that wicked person! Who knows what will become of her!"

"Probably nothing good," I said, giving her a reassuring hug, "but don't write me off just yet."

"Kate!" Cousin Violet almost smothered me in her embrace. "You're *here*! Did you find out who it was? Where is he?"

"Will somebody please tell us what this is all about?" Uncle Lum glanced at his wrist to discover he wasn't wearing a watch. "It must be after three!"

Aunt Leona tried to cover a yawn. "We were about to send for the police."

"If you'll let me catch my breath and get a drink of water, I'll tell you," I said. And did.

When I finished, Violet nodded, purple curls bobbing. "Casey. Just as I thought."

"Casey's a *what?*" Grady shook his head at me. "Come on, Kate, you're making this up!"

Violet's face was solemn. "No! No, she's not. I've suspected it for some time."

"Suspected what?" Uncle Lum asked. "We can't have somebody arrested for pretending to be the opposite sex. Casey seems harmless enough to me."

"Maybe. Maybe not, but we need to call Uncle Ernest right now," I said, heading for the phone.

"At this time of night?" My aunt gathered her robe together. "Can't it wait until morning?"

I didn't answer. And neither did Uncle Ernest.

"Nobody's answering," I said, dialing again. "Even if Uncle Ernest can't hear it ringing, Ma Maggie would. They have to be there! Where else could they be?"

"I expect they've turned off the ringer," Aunt Leona said. "Your grandmother says some woman has been calling in the wee hours wanting to speak to somebody named Homer Earl?"

Uncle Lum nodded. "That's what they've done, all right. Uncle Ernest wouldn't put up with that."

"Whatever it is will keep, though, won't it?" Grady said. "Casey's leaving in the middle of the night is strange, I'll admit, and an inconvenience to Uncle Ernest, but I can't see that it's earth-shattering." He shrugged. "Obviously the man—woman—whoever it is—has an identity problem."

Cousin Violet snorted. "That's where you're wrong. She knows very well who she is, and so do I. She's Rose. She's your uncle Ernest's wife."

CHAPTER TWENTY-TWO

*V*iolet twisted her shawl so tightly I almost expected it to bleed drops of purple dye. "Thank God that woman doesn't know where Ernest is tonight or I honestly think she wouldn't hesitate to—"

"Oh, come now, Violet," Uncle Lum said. "Even if she is who you say she is, why would she want to harm Uncle Ernest?"

"He—I mean, *she*—was right here in the house practically all afternoon today," Aunt Leona said. "If Casey meant to do anything, she had a perfect chance. I know she was upstairs helping to bring down chairs, and she was in and out of the kitchen the whole time."

We had gradually filtered into the living room, and now Grady, obviously torn between rushing to rescue Uncle Ernest or going back to bed, paced in front of the sofa. "What do you mean Casey doesn't know where he is?" he asked, coming to an abrupt stop.

"We—that is, Kate and I—sort of arranged it between us," Violet said. "We asked both Ernest and Maggie not to mention to anyone that Ernest would be staying there." She shrugged. "I'm afraid we had to tell a few fibs."

Grady frowned. "But—Well, damn, I wish you'd said something to me! When Casey was here earlier, I might've said something I shouldn't. You don't really think there's a chance—"

"Like what?" I said. "What did you say?"

"I overheard Uncle Ernest asking Ma Maggie if she had any of that chocolate powder he mixes with milk when he can't sleep—you know, that yucky stuff he orders from a catalog—and she said she didn't, so he went in the kitchen—I guess to get that can he keeps in there. Later I saw him on his way out with an overnight bag, so I just assumed that's where he was going."

"And you told *Casey* this?" I'm afraid I grabbed his arm a little harder than I meant to.

He didn't seem to notice. "Just before I left to go out tonight, Casey came by to ask Uncle Ernest what time he needed him—her—whatever—tomorrow and I told him he was spending the night at Ma Maggie's." Grady's face was almost as pale as the Annabelle hydrangeas on the table behind him. "Dear God, I had no idea—"

"Of course, you didn't," Aunt Leona said, putting a motherly arm around him.

I just couldn't help it—I covered my eyes with my hands, wishing, I guess, that the gesture would make this rotten predicament go away. Even though I hadn't been to bed that night, I knew I wouldn't be able to sleep until we were sure

Uncle Ernest was safe, but I felt what Ma Maggie calls "bone weary." Weary of a husband who apparently had deleted me from his life, weary of people getting killed, or almost killed, and of having almost lost my child in a wilderness—not to mention old bones coming to light and the elusive Rose turning up.

Then I felt a light touch on my shoulder and knew Augusta was nearby. The air, heavy with the scent of funeral flowers, suddenly seemed summer-morning fresh with just a hint of the angel's delicate strawberry scent. And then it was gone—and so, I sensed, was she. But where?

"Leona, are you sure Casey was in the kitchen today?" Violet asked. She looked so wobbly, I eased her into a chair. Augusta was trying to assure me that everything was going to be all right, but I couldn't tell my cousin that. I wasn't sure I even believed it myself.

Aunt Leona thought for a minute. "Why, yes. In and out . . . with all that food and people coming and going, it was like a circus in there. Don't you remember, Violet?"

My cousin Violet chewed her lip. "Did you notice if he ever went into the pantry?"

"I hate to interrupt," I said, "but shouldn't we—"

"I'm sure he did." Grady looked at his mother. "Said you asked him to bring out some watermelon pickles . . . you did, didn't you?"

My aunt's silence gave us the answer.

Uncle Lum stood at the foot of the stairs twisting the loose knob carved like an acorn on top of the newel post. Now he gave it a final spin. "That's where Ernest keeps that can of Chocolate Comfort. If it's there, it should be in the far left corner on the top shelf," he said, hurrying toward the kitchen. "I just hope we're not too late!"

But our uncle's Chocolate Comfort was gone.

"I knew he must've taken it!" Grady said, trailing after his father. "You don't really think Casey might have—"

"Look, we don't have time to argue about this!" I stomped my foot for attention.

It didn't do any good. "Not Casey, Grady," Violet said. "*Rose.* Ernest has been drinking that stuff since we were children. It's almost a ritual with him, and when they stopped carrying it in the stores several years ago, he began ordering it from a specialty catalog." She turned to Lum. "You know what a creature of habit he is—always has been. And Rose knows it, too. He's been keeping Chocolate Comfort in the same place since before he and Rose were even married."

"But the woman's been gone almost forty years, hasn't she?" Grady backed out of the kitchen, followed by the rest of us. "Why would she come back now? And what reason does she have to do away with Uncle Ernest?"

But nobody took time to answer because all of us except Aunt Leona, who stayed behind to call the police, were racing to crowd into the car.

I didn't hear the horse until we were speeding down the driveway. At first I thought it was part of the nightmare I was living and I must be imagining it, but the others heard it, as well.

Grady, who was driving, threw on the brakes. "Will you look at that? Shortcake's out! Look at her—must be breaking the speed limit. Something must've spooked her."

"There's nothing we can do about it now," his father said. "Guess she jumped the fence back there, and wild as she is, she'll be the very dickens to catch."

Violet leaned over me to look out the window. "Funny, though, she's keeping to the shoulder. But look at her run! Acts like the devil himself is on her back!"

I laughed. *Not a devil, an angel!* Penelope, long skirt flowing behind her, leaned low over the horse's neck as Shortcake galloped over the top of the hill and out of sight.

"Maybe we'll catch up with her a few miles down the road," Grady said as we turned in the same direction. But there was no sign of the horse or her rider on the other side of the hill— only a trail of gossamer mist and the sound of fading hoofbeats.

Small, shy Penelope, so gawky and klutzy I wouldn't trust her in the same room with my few pieces of fine crystal, rode like a jockey and looked like the Sugar Plum Fairy. It was a shame, I thought, that the others couldn't see her.

Cousin Violet tapped her foot as if she could make the car go faster. "Ernest might as well kiss that horse good-bye. I doubt he'll see Shortcake again."

But I was just as certain he would, because I thought I knew where Penelope was headed.

Ma Maggie's two-story brick sat a few yards from the road behind a scattering of sycamore trees, but even through the dark foliage I could see a light in the kitchen window.

"Somebody's up!" Violet pointed out as we careened into the driveway and came to a gravel-scattering halt by the front steps. Grady and I vaulted onto the porch and hammered on the door, leaving Uncle Lum to cope with hauling Violet out of the backseat.

A light came on in the hall and another on the upstairs landing, and at the same time, I heard again the sound of galloping hooves, this time rounding the corner of the house.

"Good Lord, it's Shortcake!" Uncle Lum shouted from behind us. "Has that horse gone completely crazy?"

I stood and watched as Penelope, with a blissful look on her face, flew past us and sailed over the clump of holly bushes in my grandmother's yard in a perfect jump. Then, settling for a more sedate pace, horse and rider trotted out of sight.

"Did you see that?" My cousin Violet gasped. "Looks like she's headed back home."

Grady pounded again on the door and leaned closer to look in the glass panel at the side. "Here comes somebody," he said. "It looks like—it's Uncle Ernest!"

My uncle's hair looked even scruffier than usual and his face was bare without his glasses, but he was still alive.

"What on God's green earth is going on here?" he asked, jerking open the door. "First some girl rides a horse right under the kitchen window, and now here you are making all this racket in the middle of the night! Would somebody mind telling me what this is all about?"

"You can count me in on that, too," my grandmother echoed behind him. With her hair covered in what we called her pink "sleeping bonnet," and modest lace-trimmed robe, she looked like an illustration from Dickens. "Is somebody sick? What's wrong?"

"No, no, we're fine," Uncle Lum assured her. "But we were afraid something might have happened to Ernest and couldn't reach you by phone."

We followed her through the dining room with the familiar bird-print wallpaper where we usually congregated for family dinners, and into the kitchen where a coffee mug sat on the blue Formica counter.

"Oh, that! We turned off the ringer so that fool woman wouldn't keep us awake," she said. "And what's the matter with Ernest? He looks fine to me."

"You didn't drink any of that Chocolate Comfort, did you?" Violet asked Uncle Ernest, snatching up the empty mug.

My uncle grabbed the mug right back. "I was about to—if everybody would just leave me alone." Uncle Ernest reached for the can of Chocolate Comfort sitting on the counter, but I slid it out of his reach and zipped it to Grady, who clamped it to his chest with both arms.

"It seems a hell of a time of night to be playing keep away!" My uncle banged his empty mug on the table. "First, that girl who's been hanging around makes enough racket to wake the dead just under the window—and on a horse that looks an awful lot like Shortcake—and now this." He frowned. "I wonder—does that child's parents even know where she is?"

232

Uncle Ernest pulled out a chair and sat, looking up at us with his stern professor glare. "And just what do you have against my having some warm milk with chocolate so I can finally get some sleep?"

I saw Grady and his dad exchange puzzled glances at the mention of the girl on horseback, but the comment seemed to go right past Violet.

Lum sat next to his uncle and drummed his fingers on the table. "We think someone might have put something in there that doesn't belong," he said finally.

"For the love of God, who?" Uncle Ernest looked from one to the other of us as if he thought Lum was joking.

I told him how Casey had come looking for something in the toolshed that night, and how I had followed the caretaker back to the cottage, but I could tell my uncle was getting more and more impatient.

"Kathryn, my goodness, child, is that all? Don't tell me you've all come over here in the wee hours just to tell me that?" he said.

I glanced at Violet, who nodded. "There's more," I told him. "Casey's gone—packed and gone."

"Gone?" Uncle Ernest frowned and shook his head. "Not surprised. Strange fellow, that one."

I took a breath and plunged in. "Not fellow, Uncle Ernest. Casey's a woman."

I thought he was going to laugh until Violet put a hand on his arm, and I'm sure he could tell by the look on her face that this was no laughing matter.

"Ernest, it was Rose," she said. "The man we knew as Casey is Rose."

"Rose!" My grandmother grabbed the back of a chair, and I grabbed her—with one eye on Uncle Ernest.

My great-uncle is getting up in years and I was afraid he might keel over with a heart attack or something. I mean, think of the shock of having one's spouse return after an absence of forty years—and with evil intent, at that! Uncle Ernest, however, surprised us all.

"I suspected she must be around here somewhere," he said, speaking in a low voice, "but *Casey!* Casey Grindle. I'll swear I never would've thought it." He looked at me. "What makes you think Rose might have put something in my chocolate mix?"

"We're not sure, but we didn't want to take any chances," Grady said, and told him about Casey's going into the pantry on a fabricated mission.

"We'll have to have the ingredients tested, of course," Uncle Lum said.

Uncle Ernest sighed. "I think you'll probably find you're right." He looked at the mug, still in his hands, and came as close to crying as I think I've ever seen him. "And to think she's come to this." He shoved the mug aside, then quickly stood and shook his head as if he meant to shake away the past. "I think we'd better phone the police," he said.

"Aunt Leona's already taken care of that," I told him, and at the same time we heard a car drive up out front. I could see the swirling blue light from the window.

The two young officers who stood in the doorway looked as tired and perplexed as I felt. "Somebody at your place called and said they thought you might be having some kind of trouble," the taller of the two said to Uncle Ernest.

"That could very well have been the case if I hadn't had a jolt of the truth," my uncle said. "I have good reason to believe my caretaker—who seems to be on the run, by the way—might be responsible for the death of Ella Stegall, and God only knows who else before her!"

CHAPTER TWENTY-THREE

My grandmother marched immediately to the kitchen and put on a pot of coffee. "What makes you think that Casey . . . Rose . . . would want to kill poor Ella?" she asked Uncle Ernest.

Violet answered for him. "Ella recognized her voice—I'm sure of it. You know how blind she'd become, and they say people tend to make up for that with other senses. And remember what she said to me about a voice or voices? We thought she must've been talking about hearing somebody in the woods back there, but I think she was beginning to remember where she'd heard Casey's voice before."

"I don't know how," Uncle Lum said. "I never heard Casey say much of anything."

"And since I don't hear too well, she must've known she was safe with me," Uncle Ernest said. "But people tend— tended to ignore Ella. Poor thing, she was always just there in the background. I expect Rose forgot about her and let her guard down. We've had repairmen from time to time, and that crew came to spray the orchard not too long ago. Casey usually dealt with them and Ella might have overheard."

"Or she might have heard her speaking to the cat," Violet said. "Casey didn't like Dagwood. He dug in her flowerbed, got in her way, all those things cats do. Once I heard her tell him to stay away from the mower or he'd be mincemeat, and Casey sounded like he . . . she wouldn't be all that upset about it, either."

Ma Maggie frowned. "What did you do? Did you say anything?"

"I told Ella I thought she'd better keep a closer watch on Dagwood," Violet said.

"Knowing how outspoken Ella was, I wouldn't be surprised if she didn't confront Casey about her identity," Uncle Ernest said. "And that signed her death warrant."

"But we can't arrest someone on supposition," the younger policeman said, reaching for his radio. "I'm afraid we'll need more than that."

"I'll show you more than that—a lot more than that. Meanwhile I suggest you run a background check on Casey Grindle and see if it matches up with Rose Dutton—who, by the way, is probably over the county line by now." Uncle Ernest spoke with authority, and when he stood and looked at the two, I understood why his students had called him "Emperor Ernie."

"I believe if I were you, I would get in touch with the powers that be right now, and put out an APB before she gets any farther," he told them.

I wasn't surprised when they did.

237

I was surprised a little later, however, when the sheriff himself showed up at Bramblewood, leaving the two deputies in charge of seeing that my uncle's can of Chocolate Comfort got to the lab. It was barely daylight and Violet had gone to bed as soon as we got to the house, but I had downed two mugs of my grandmother's "stand-alone" coffee and was good for another hour or so at least. Besides, I wanted to know just what Uncle Ernest had in mind when he told the police he had something more to show them.

"If this is as important as you seem to think it is, I want to have a look at it myself," Sheriff Yeager told my uncle. He was a stocky, balding man who looked to be in his fifties. I had seen him the day after Ella's fall and again with the searchers when Burdette and the others led us out of the woods. This morning his khaki uniform was neatly pressed, his black shoes gleamed and he smelled of woodsy aftershave. I marveled at how quickly he had managed to look regulation spiffy at such short notice.

Aunt Leona was still asleep, and I doubted if we'd see Violet all day, but Grady, Ma Maggie, Uncle Lum and I followed the two men outside where Uncle Ernest unlocked the trunk of his ten-year-old Chevrolet that looked every bit as new as the day he bought it. Expecting to be shooed away at any minute, I stayed in the background as he carried a large cardboard box to the porch and set it down.

"What in the world is that?" my grandmother asked as her brother opened the box.

The sheriff carefully lifted out something wrapped in shredded black plastic that fell apart in minute tatters to reveal what looked to have once been a canvas backpack, black with dirt and decay. "Where'd you find this?" he said.

"Under a rose bush in the garden," my uncle said.

"You mean somebody buried it there?" Sheriff Yeager peered closer. "Do you know who it belonged to?" he said, speaking in my uncle's ear.

Uncle Ernest looked at the rest of us like he wished we'd go away, but it was too late. Unless threatened with dire punishment—like having to iron while watching table tennis—I was there for the duration. "Do you remember reading about the hippie couple who disappeared on the river back in the sixties?" he asked the sheriff. "I believe this belonged to the man—Shamrock, I think he called himself—and I'd be very much surprised if that skeleton they found in Remeth-churchyard wasn't his, too."

"Have you looked inside the pack?" the sheriff wanted to know, but my uncle shook his head. "Thought it best to wait, I was afraid I might destroy something."

The rest of us stood restlessly while the sheriff went to his car for gloves. "You couldn't pay me to touch that nasty thing," Ma Maggie said. I felt the same.

From the expression on his face, I don't think Sheriff Yeager relished the idea, either, but he lifted the flap after the buckle fell away in his hands, and reached inside.

I don't know what I expected him to find, but I found myself backing away as if something grisly might jump out at me. Instead he drew out what was left of a pair of moccasins, rotted remnants of what could have been clothing, a rusty key chain with a shamrock enclosed in plastic and a tarnished, water-stained wristwatch with the crystal miraculously unbroken.

The sheriff held the watch to the light and squinted at something on the back. "Still a little too dark to see out here," he said. "Let's take it inside. Looks like some kind of engraving."

Uncle Ernest switched on a lamp in the living room and the sheriff held the watch under the light. "Q.E.P., 1962," Grady read aloud, since he obviously had the best vision in the bunch.

Uncle Ernest ran his fingers over the engraving. "Quincy Puckett—don't know what his middle name was, but I'll bet this watch was a high school graduation gift."

Sheriff Yeager looked up. "If all this is true, who do you suppose put him over there in Remeth Cemetery?"

My uncle's face was solemn—more than solemn—his expression made me want to throw my arms around him and protect him from all this. Uncle Ernest was such a good man, and innocent in so many ways. How could this be happening to him?

"I don't *suppose*," he said. "Quincy Puckett was buried over there by Rose Dutton, otherwise known as Casey Grindle." He paused and looked at Ma Maggie. "And earlier, Waning Crescent."

Valerie Rose Dutton had been eighteen and beautiful when Uncle Ernest discovered her bathing in the river behind Bramblewood early one September morning in the mid-1960s.

"She told me she had been abducted and abused by a man who called himself Shamrock, and that he had held her prisoner and forced her into going along while he robbed merchants and committed numerous other crimes," my uncle related. "They had spent the night ashore, and when she awoke that morning, Rose said Shamrock had taken their raft and left her there. She'd been begging him to change, she told me, to give up the way they were living. She was afraid to leave him, she said. Afraid of what he might do."

We had moved to the kitchen where Uncle Lum fried bacon while I whipped up a dozen eggs for scrambling—holding out one, of course, to soft boil for my uncle. Uncle Ernest nursed a cup of coffee and looked out the window at what had been his young wife's garden. "She was so young, so very lovely, and I was in my midthirties and had never had a lasting relationship with a woman before—never felt that strongly about anyone."

"That's because he'd never seen one bathing naked in the river," Grady whispered behind me. I gave him my "shut up" look.

"I believed her, of course," our uncle continued. "I was a fool, but I didn't care. Even when the news came out about the raft being found and the girl, Waning Crescent, was named in the newspapers as an accomplice, I never doubted her story. Shamrock had purposely sunk the raft and continued on foot to throw off the police, she said, and I wanted it to make sense so badly, it did.

"She cried; Rose was good at crying, and begged me not to give her away. She had no family, she said. I was all she had in the world, and so we were married."

For somebody who had been awake since before dawn, my grandmother's eyes were wide. "You told us you met Rose during summer session at the college, said she'd just completed her sophmore year and was taking some time off to decide on her major."

Uncle Ernest almost smiled. "I was her major," he said. "For a little while, at least. I was happy, she was happy—or I thought she was, and nobody was the wiser. She left me only a few months before our second anniversary, said she'd made a big mistake." He rubbed gnarled hands over his face. "My God, how could I have been so stupid?"

"You said you weren't surprised that Rose had turned up," Grady said as he dealt plates around the kitchen table. "What made you think she was close by?"

Uncle Ernest put a pitcher of orange juice on the counter and searched the cabinet for enough glasses. "When they found that skeleton over in Remeth and the police told me it was that of a man who died about the same time Rose came," he said. "And we knew somebody had used Ella's cat to lure her to the edge of that drop-off. For the life of me, though, I couldn't figure out why Rose would do that until Violet said something about Ella's recognizing the voice.

"But it was that thing with the yellow jackets that convinced me. Somebody didn't want Belinda to find that epinephrine in time."

"Where is Belinda?" Ma Maggie wanted to know.

"In Atlanta with her daughter for a week or so," Uncle Ernest said. "After what happened at the reunion, I felt uneasy about her being here."

Grady just couldn't resist. "Are you two gonna get—"

242

"Married?" Our uncle poured juice all around. "Well, Grady, I haven't asked her yet, but when and if I do, you'll be the first to know—if she accepts, that is."

Sheriff Yeager, after an obligatory, "Oh, no—I couldn't!" not only joined us for breakfast, but insisted on making the toast. "I can't understand, though, why Rose has waited this long to turn up. Why now? And where's she been all this time?"

My uncle reached for the strawberry jam. "For one thing, she wanted me out of the way, and probably Belinda, as well. Guess we'll have to wait to find out why when they catch up with her—*if* they catch up with her."

My grandmother excused herself from the table and folded her paper napkin as if it had been fine linen. "Well, I'm going to have to wait a while to find that out, because I'm going home and take a nap—and you should, too, Ernest. Ella's service is at three and we'll have all those people dropping by afterward."

"I'll drive you home," I said, taking my plate to the sink. The idea of sleeping the morning away was sounding better and better to me—Rose, or no Rose.

Outside, Ma Maggie stood on the front steps staring across the road at the pasture. "Will you look at that, Kate? It's Shortcake! Now how do you suppose she managed to get back inside the fence?"

"Somebody must have found her," I said. But of course, I knew otherwise.

We were getting into my car when I saw a blue Toyota approaching the house at breakneck speed.

"Who in the world is that?" Ma Maggie said. "They're driving like a maniac!"

"I can't imagine," I said. "I don't recognize the car, do you?" Maybe it was somebody coming to tell us they'd arrested Rose, I thought, but if that were the case, wouldn't they have already contacted the sheriff? Whatever they wanted, it must be urgent.

I got out to greet the driver as the car slammed to a stop about four inches from Uncle Ernest's cherished Chevrolet, then stood watching mutely as my husband jumped out and ran across the lawn to meet me.

"Kate, is everything all right? You had me worried sick! I didn't know where you were! And what's that police car doing here?" He stood about a foot away from me and looked as if he didn't know what to do with his arms. Finally, he put them around me.

"What do you mean, you didn't know where to find me?" I said, reluctantly pushing him away.

"Nobody answered at your parents' house this morning, which is where you said you were staying, so I called Ma Maggie's and there was no answer there, either. Then I finally phoned Marge, who said you were here at Bramblewood. What's going on?"

"How much time do you have?" I asked.

Ned shoved back the lick of straw-colored hair that refused to stay out of his face. "I'm sorry about poor Ella. What happened? When I phoned yesterday, somebody told me she'd fallen or something."

"Phoned where?" Out of the corner of my eye, I saw my grandmother creeping discreetly into the house.

"Why, here. Didn't you get the message?" Ned started to put

his arm around me again, then thought better of it. "Can we go somewhere and sit down? I had to go practically around the world to get here, and frankly, I'm beat."

Oh, please, tell me about it! I directed him to the porch. "What message?" I said again.

"I called here yesterday and got some woman named Mabel. She's the one who told me about Ella dying." My husband collapsed in a rocking chair and closed his eyes. "Poor soul, what a way to go! Must have been a terrible fall." He yawned. "Anyway, she said she'd tell you I was on the way."

"Mabel Causby." I pictured a slight woman in her seventies with dentures that didn't fit. "She's in Ella's church circle."

"Said she'd write it down." Ned yawned.

"Don't go to sleep yet," I told him, "I'll be back," and I went inside to look at the note pad on the telephone table. I found a potted chrysanthemum on top of it. Underneath, on a scrap of paper, someone had scribbled: *Kate, your husband called. His flight's been canceled twice, but he says to tell you he's on his way and should be here by tomorrow.*

"Tell me about those canceled flights," I said, jarring my husband awake. "I thought you weren't coming back for another week."

"One of the speakers couldn't come at the last minute, and I had an opportunity to rearrange the schedule and get home earlier than I expected."

I noticed he used the word *home*. Ned stood and took both my hands in his. "Kate, I was miserable. Too much time to think, I guess. You and Josie—nothing else is important to me. Tell me I'm not losing you."

I wanted to fall into his arms, for everything to be the way it was before, but there was too much left unsaid. I turned away. "You hurt me, Ned. I needed you, and you shut me out. Why?"

"Kate, I'm so sorry. I wish I could explain." He put a hand on my shoulder and I felt his closeness behind me. "I don't understand it myself—except that I felt useless when I was out of work, had to depend on you to take care of us, and then when we lost the baby, I felt somehow that was my fault, as well."

"Ned, I explained to you what the doctor said. No one was to blame. I begged you to see a counselor."

"But I was the one causing all the stress—dumping added responsibility on you at a time when you should have been able to relax and take care of yourself." Ned's voice was hoarse with emotion. "I suppose I thought . . . well . . . that you and Josie would be better off without me."

I didn't know what to say to that, so I said nothing, but stepped over to the sturdy stone pillar by the front steps and placed my hands upon it, seeking its strength.

"I do love you, Kate," Ned said, speaking from behind me. "And I know I need help. Won't you give me another chance, please?"

Earlier I had attributed my husband's bleary eyes to lack of sleep, but when I opened my arms, I learned there was more as we cried quietly together.

I waited until both of us were composed before I told Ned how we had almost lost Josie.

"Why didn't you call me?" he said. "You know I would've turned the world upside down to get here!"

"Unfortunately, I was just as lost as she was, and neither

Marge nor Ma Maggie knew how to reach you," I said. "When we finally got back, I tried to call you at the hotel but they said you'd checked out."

Ned took my hand and led me to the porch glider where I sat with my head on his chest. "I tried to get an early flight back," he said, "but the first was delayed for several hours, the next was canceled and at least two were rerouted." He counted on his fingers. "During the last few days, I've slept around, Kate. I've slept in the Houston airport, the Chicago airport, the Atlanta airport—and probably some I can't even remember in between! Then this morning I finally made it to Charlotte, and here I am!"

I unbuttoned his shirt and slipped my hand inside. "And here I am," I said, and closed my eyes.

When I opened them, I moved apart from Ned as if someone had driven a wedge between us. Augusta sat on the bottom step with a silly smile on her face and a bunch of daisies in her hand.

"What is it?" Ned reached for me again. "What's wrong?"

I shook my head at Augusta and mouthed the words *go away!*

"Have you spoken to Josie?" I asked my husband. "Does she know you're here? She misses you so much, Ned. This has been hard on our daughter. We can't do this to her."

"Or to us." He kissed the top of my head. "She was still asleep when I called—and I missed her, too—missed both of you. But, Kate, we'll work things out. I know I've been making things difficult—seems I couldn't help myself, but a friend at work gave me the name of a good counselor . . . we're going to make a go of this. I promise." Ned grinned. "How long do you think Josie will sleep?"

I twirled my car keys in my hand. "An hour or two at least, and there's nobody at my parents' house."

I scooped up the bouquet of daisies Augusta had left on the steps and hurried to the car. I finally got to bed. But I didn't get much sleep.

CHAPTER TWENTY-FOUR

It began to rain as we left the cemetery after Ella's funeral. "It's almost as if God was crying because she had such a sad end to her life," Burdette said as we drove back to the house. Neighbors were kind enough to look after their children and Josie so that the four of us could help Uncle Ernest greet friends who came to pay their respects at Bramblewood, and there was a steady procession throughout the afternoon.

The last caller had just left when Sheriff Yeager drove up, and I knew when I saw his face he had something important on his mind.

Uncle Ernest hurried to meet him. "Have they found her?"

The sheriff took off his hat and looked around for a place to put it. "Not yet, but we found out where she'd been before she came here." He passed the dripping hat to Grady, who stuck it on the bust of Darwin the college had given my uncle upon his retirement. "It's that same town in Pennsylvania where Beverly Briscoe was living."

"I knew it, I just knew it!" Cousin Violet said. Her hunch about Casey had been right and she was reluctant to relinquish the limelight, but this time everybody ignored her, including me.

"Do you think they knew each other?" Grady asked.

"I'm sure they did." The sheriff accepted a seat on the sofa and a cup of punch from Ma Maggie. "When we did a background check, we learned they'd worked at the same place—the Sow and Grow—some kind of gardening store, I think."

Uncle Ernest started to sit, then changed his mind. "So . . . you think Rose had something to do with Beverly's death?"

Sheriff Yeager nodded. "It certainly seems likely. The police up there spoke with some of the employees and they told them Beverly talked about Bishop's Bridge a lot—you know, the people here and all. Couldn't wait to get back here, they said."

"I spoke with one of Beverly's coworkers at her funeral," Ma Maggie said. "Nice young woman—Debbie, I think her name was. She said they used to tease Bev about being from the South, but Bev just laughed and told them she was going to write a book some day about some of the more interesting people she knew."

"Meaning me, I suppose." Uncle Ernest finally decided to sit. "Only the word is *eccentric*, I believe."

I could tell the sheriff was trying not to smile. "Actually, she *had* told some of them about you, but I—"

"And how I still kept up my wife's garden even though she'd been gone almost forty years?" My uncle's eyes were bleak.

Ma Maggie put a hand on his arm. "Ernest, it was no secret that you never got over loving Rose—not for a long time, anyway. Beverly knew that as well as anybody."

"But why kill Beverly?" My husband stood behind me, his hand on my shoulder.

"Rose knew you had some valuable property that had become even more valuable over the years," the sheriff said to my uncle. "And from what we've been able to piece together, once she learned you hadn't remarried, that you obviously still cared about her, she must have thought she would inherit."

"Imagine the conceit!" Violet, who was collecting empty cups, almost dropped the tray. "To think you'd leave anything to *her*!"

I don't think I imagined this, but Uncle Ernest actually *blushed*! "To tell the truth, I never did get around to changing my will," he said. "Guess I'd better make an appointment with Goat."

"The sooner, the better!" my grandmother told him.

"But when Rose learned you'd started seeing Belinda, she knew she had to act fast," Burdette pointed out.

"Right." Sheriff Yeager finished his punch and gave the cup to Violet. "We're speculating here, but I think it's a given that Beverly told her you were interested in someone."

Grady nodded. "She would. It made a good story, and Bev loved telling stories." He smiled. "She really should've written a book."

"But that meant Beverly had to go," I said. "Rose knew Bev planned to come home, and would know immediately who she was."

"Casey arrived here soon after Beverly was killed." Uncle Ernest spoke softly. "My God! What kind of deranged person has she become?"

"A greedy one, I'm afraid," the sheriff said.

He was getting ready to leave when he got a call on his cell phone informing him police had apprehended Rose Dutton at a rest stop near Wilmington, North Carolina.

"Has she admitted anything?" Uncle Lum asked.

"Not yet, but they haven't had time to interrogate her," the sheriff said. "They did say, though, she didn't act surprised when they caught up with her."

While Ned and Burdette went to collect the children, Marge and I helped Leona in the kitchen.

"Can you believe Rose was posing as a caretaker to take care of her own garden?" Aunt Leona splashed detergent in the sink and turned the faucets on full force.

"Except Uncle Ernest wouldn't let her in there," Marge said. "But Rose knew about taking care of lawns and liked being outside, and Uncle Ernest says she was always good with flowers, so I guess it was a natural idea for a cover-up."

I snatched a dishtowel from the drawer and started on the punch cups. "Sounds like she kept her distance from Uncle Ernest as much as possible. I think Ella was the one she dealt with mostly."

"Yeah, she dealt with her all right!" Marge scraped food scraps into a trash can—no garbage disposal here. "I guess she thought Ella wouldn't recognize her or had forgotten all about her by now."

"I don't think Ella forgot much of anything," Leona said. "She could still quote some of those long epic poems she memorized in high school." She smiled. "You didn't want to encourage her."

"Ella must have said something to make Rose suspect that she knew who she was, and—oh, my Lord, it makes my blood run cold!" Marge shivered. "I guess Rose felt she had to get Ella out of the way before everyone got here for the reunion and she confided in somebody.

"Thank God Hartley found Belinda's purse before she ended up the same way! And to think I scolded him for playing with it." Marge took a broom to the kitchen floor as if she were walloping Rose herself.

"And I felt sorry for Casey when Uncle Ernest tore into him for not getting rid of those yellow jackets," I said. "But that was when Violet says she first began to suspect."

Aunt Leona passed me a dripping plate. "Well . . . Violet says a lot of things. Of course, she was right this time, but did she *really* think it was Casey?"

"Says she did, and that's why she came up with the idea to throw that out about evidence being hidden in the toolshed," I said. I stacked the plate with the rest and tackled the silverware. "I had no idea Casey was a woman, but for a while I thought he might be the hippie, Shamrock, come back to look for valuables—money or something—he hid here years ago."

Marge hesitated with her broom in midsweep. "It just

occurred to me we're not suspects anymore! We can go any-where we like."

"Oh, bosh, Marjorie! We never were suspects," Aunt Leona told her. "I don't think the police even seriously considered Ernest. How could anyone think he'd have a hand in killing somebody?"

I didn't want to admit the thought had crossed my mind.

For the first time in weeks, my husband, daughter and myself spent the night alone together as a family. The next day we planned to leave for home, and home had a different meaning now. A sweet word. Somebody should write a song about it.

The three of us grilled hamburgers in my parents' backyard while Josie and I caught Ned up on the events of the last few days, including the birth of my nephew. I watched his face when I told him about the new baby and saw a flicker of some-thing akin to regret, but it didn't linger. "We'll probably all fight over holding him when they come for Christmas," he said, laughing.

The mosquitoes soon drove us inside, and after Josie went to bed, Ned and I sat quietly together with a glass of wine in the family room. "We can try again, you know," I told him, touch-ing my glass to his.

"Try? Oh, you mean—" My husband laughed. "How about tonight?" He drew me to him. "Kate, I won't pretend that hav-ing another child wouldn't be wonderful, but if it doesn't ever happen, I'll still be happy. You and Josie are the most impor-tant people in the world to me."

"You're different." I pulled away to look at him. "What changed you? Why did you decide to come home?"

"I told you. We rearranged the schedule, and—"

I stroked his hand. "And what else?"

My husband sighed. "I really don't know how to describe it," he said, "but I had the strangest experience—almost surreal, I guess you could say."

Ned sat up to face me. "I was on the elevator hurrying to some meeting or other, and not in the best of moods because I'd spilled coffee on my shirt at breakfast and had to rush back to the room and change. There was no one on the elevator but me until this woman got on. She didn't say anything—just smiled—and I honestly don't remember much of anything else except that I thought about you and Josie—the home we had together, and it dawned on me that I was about to make the biggest mistake of my life!"

"What did she look like?" I asked.

"The woman on the elevator?" He frowned. "Fair—not plump by any means, but not skinny, either, and she had the most beautiful hair! It almost glowed. Must've been going to some kind of costume affair because she wore this floaty thing—all purple and gold—and a necklace that reached almost to her waist."

"And that's when you decided to come home?"

"Right. And the funniest thing, Kate—she smelled like strawberries."

CHAPTER TWENTY-FIVE

"Uncle Ernest says he's going to make this place into nature preserves," Josie announced the next day. We had returned to Bramblewood for a late breakfast and to tell everyone good-bye, and those of us who remained gathered on the shady front porch, Lum and Leona having left earlier.

"Nature *what?* Is he gonna make strawberry or peach?" her cousin Darby teased.

"I think she means *reserve*," Burdette said, "but preserve should apply, as well, as I believe he intends to keep it as it is."

"Sounds okay to me," I said. "But how did this come about?"

"Told me he wanted to have a place for people—especially young people, he said—to not only observe, but to be at home with nature." Burdette shrugged and shook his head. "Kate, have you noticed a young girl around here lately? About twelve or thirteen, Uncle Ernest thinks. He says she always has some kind of wild animal with her, like a rabbit or a fawn, and that she was the one riding Shortcake the other night. Uncle Ernest swears she came to warn him."

"I'm glad she did—whoever she was," Ma Maggie said. "The lab found a lethal amount of a barbiturate in Ernest's Chocolate Comfort. The sheriff said it was a sedative called Nembutal, and if he had gotten enough of it, it would have killed him."

"What if we hadn't reached him in time?" Grady, who was carrying luggage to his car, stopped on the top step to listen.

"But, Burdette, there wasn't anyone riding Shortcake." Violet looked at Grady and me to back her up. "Are my old eyes finally giving out on me, or is Ernest caving in under the strain? Did either of you see a rider?"

"After all, it was the middle of the night, and dark as pitch." I spoke up before Grady could answer. "I can see why he might have thought there was somebody on the horse."

Violet wasn't buying it. "But the girl—now, how do you reckon he came up with that idea? A young girl who plays with wild animals! Huh! Most of 'em play with things they have no business playing with, if you ask me!"

But nobody had, of course.

"Said he thought it was one of Josie's friends, or somebody visiting a neighbor," Burdette said, beginning to look concerned. "And you say none of you have seen her?"

"I've seen her!" Josie said. "She was with me when I was lost in the woods. I think she's an angel."

At that, Ned, who was standing near Josie, scooped our daughter up in his arms and kissed her. Josie, I noticed, didn't even protest. "She sounds heaven-sent to me," he said.

"Whoever she is, Uncle Ernest thinks she'd be perfect to help with the children when he carries out his plans for the nature reserve," Burdette said.

"Then I believe he'd better find someone else," I told him. "I think she's from out of town."

"Where is Uncle Ernest?" Marge looked about. "I haven't seen him since breakfast."

"Said he was going to ride Shortcake," Darby told us. "I wanted to come, too, but he said he wanted to surprise everybody."

"It will surprise me if he doesn't kill himself!" my grandmother said. "What in the world is he thinking of—a man his age? Somebody should go and stop him."

"I'm afraid we're too late." Ned called our attention to the figure approaching in the distance.

"By golly, it *is* Uncle Ernest!" Marge said. She nudged Ma Maggie. "Still alive and seems to be doing fine."

We all stood and applauded as Uncle Ernest trotted past, waving his hat like Teddy Roosevelt charging up San Juan Hill. I expected him to dismount and join us, but he kept on riding.

"Where are you going?" Darby shouted.

Our uncle waved his hat again. "Be back in a while—got to see a man about a will!" And with that he circled the orchard, picked up speed and galloped back the way he had come.

"Where's that old fool going now?" Violet said, staring after him.

"Why, to prove himself to Goat, of course," Ma Maggie told her. "They had a bet, you know."

Burdette looked out at the giant oaks, the daisy-flecked

meadow beyond. "All this beauty—it's a good thing he's doing, a mighty good thing." He shook his head. "And to think that Rose Dutton took at least two lives—and tried to take more—because she wanted it all for herself. I wonder what she would have done with it."

"Sheriff Yeager thinks a couple of developers were in the wings," Ma Maggie said. "One of them has admitted Rose had been in touch with him: of course, he didn't know all the circumstances, but it seems she had big things in mind—a resort, hotels, you name it."

"That could've been who you heard talking the day Ella was injured," Grady said to Violet. "Remember? You said you heard a man talking somewhere down in the woods."

"And Josie heard someone, too." I turned to my daughter. "The day you got lost."

Josie nodded. "I was afraid of them. I didn't know who it was so I was trying to get away."

"You probably had good reason," Marge said. "Sounds as if it might have been Casey and some potential developer looking over the property." My cousin made a face. "It's a good thing Casey didn't see you."

I didn't even like to think of what might have happened if Rose thought Josie had overheard her plans to develop Bramblewood.

"I should have told the police about that anklet I found," I said to my grandmother. "Remember? I asked if you knew anyone named Valerie?"

She nodded. "It must have belonged to Rose . . . but how would you have known?"

"Where did you find it?" Ned asked.

"In a trunk in the attic. I was looking for something else and it was wrapped in a scarf or something. I'm sure Rose hid it there. The police knew one of Waning Crescent's names was Valerie and it wouldn't do to have anyone find it."

Marge pulled Hartley into her lap, kissed him and let him go to play in the yard with the others. "But Uncle Ernest knew!" she said. "All this time he's known who she was."

"But he didn't know what happened to Shamrock," I said.

"The man had been struck with a heavy object," Burdette told us. "Bo Crane, who works for *The Bulletin*, said it would come out in this week's paper. They think he was hit from behind."

"By our charming Waning Crescent Rose!" Marge cuddled Dagwood in her lap.

"That's what they think," Burdette said. "They don't have a confession yet, but it certainly seems likely."

"Just think, if the garden club hadn't cleaned off Remeth churchyard, he'd still be buried there," Grady said. "Wonder what happened between those two."

"Maybe he wanted to turn himself in, or maybe they just had an argument," I said. "We'll probably never know."

"Rose knows," Ma Maggie said. "She buried that poor boy's body, but she didn't have a chance to get rid of his backpack until later. When Ernest found her bathing in the river that morning, she was probably washing off the blood!"

"Ma Maggie!" Marge and I shouted together.

She didn't even blink. "Well, it's true. And I imagine she had that boy's possessions hidden in the woods somewhere until she could plant them under a rose bush."

Cousin Violet made a rumbling noise low in her throat.

"*Rose's* garden! That place was almost sacred to Ernest. Wonder what will become of it now?"

"I guess that will be up to Belinda," Burdette said.

"You'll have to fill me in on that," Grady said. "Right now, I have to be on the road so I can make it to work early tomorrow." He grinned. "Selfish people, my bosses—they expect me to actually *earn* that paycheck."

I could tell by the look he gave me that Grady wanted me to walk with him, so I followed him to his car. "What do you think I should do?" he asked, when we were away from the others.

"About what?"

"About what happened to my father. Should I tell the police?"

"It isn't going to help your father," I said. "It all depends on you. How would it make *you* feel?"

"You're no help." He kissed my cheek and got behind the wheel.

"I can't tell you that, Grady. The only person who can decide that is you."

A part of me wanted to run after him as I watched my cousin drive away. "It's over now. It wasn't your fault. Forget it and be happy!" I wanted to tell him. But it was Grady's nightmare to conquer.

We had stayed much longer than we meant to and Ned had my car loaded and ready to go. He would follow me to the rental agency in the next town to turn in his Toyota, then join Josie and me for the drive home.

Marge and Burdette had left with their boys soon after Grady, but my grandmother and Violet remained to see us off.

"Tell Uncle Ernest we'll see him Christmas," I said, kissing the two of them for about the third time.

"If he lives that long!" My grandmother kept an eye on the road. "If you happen to come across a horse without a rider, let us know."

"He'll be fine," I told her. "Shortcake just needed some TLC." *And who was better to give it than an angel?*

Still waving, I started down the long drive, then, signaling to Ned behind me, came to an abrupt stop.

"Mom, what are you doing?" Josie wanted to know. "Did you forget something?"

"Yes," I said, getting out of the car.

"Hold on a minute. I'll be right back!" I shouted to my puzzled husband.

Kicking off my shoes, I ran across the lawn, beneath the pecan trees, the gnarled oaks and through the apple orchard to where I knew they would be.

"I couldn't leave without seeing you," I said, taking Augusta's hands.

She smiled. "I didn't think you would."

Penelope smiled, too. "Look what Augusta taught me," she said, and showed me how she could whistle through a blade of grass.

"That's terrific," I told her. "But you've taught us all a lot more than that. Thank you, Penelope." And I kissed her cheek. "Thank you both for everything."

Augusta sat in a carpet of flowers, the colors of which I had never seen before.

"It is good-bye, isn't it?" I asked, hoping she would deny it.

"I have something for you," she said, draping a garland of flowers around my neck. I noticed the colors were the same as the necklace she wore.

"Is this a parting gift?" I asked.

"You'll always be a part of me," she said.

I sat beside her in the meadow grass. "I don't want you to leave. Stay. Please stay."

Augusta Goodnight touched my face with a gentle hand. "Kathryn McBride, you already have everything you need."

And she was right.